Trouble on the Thames

Trouble on the Thames

Victor Bridges

With an Introduction
by Martin Edwards

Poisoned Pen Press

Published by Poisoned Pen Press in association with the British Library

First Edition 2015 First US Trade Paperback Edition

10 9 8 7 6 5 4 3 2 1

Library of Congress Catalog Card Number: 2015938527

ISBN: 9781464204937   Trade Paperback

Poisoned Pen Press
6962 E. First Ave., Ste. 103
Scottsdale, AZ 85251
www.poisonedpenpress.com
info@poisonedpenpress.com

Printed in the United States of America

Contents

Introduction

Trouble on the Thames is a short, fast-moving spy thriller written during the Second World War, but set shortly before the outbreak of hostilities. The hero, Owen Bradwell, is a courageous naval officer who fears that his career will be blighted because he has become colour-blind, but the threat from Hitler's Germany is such that the authorities are keen to deploy him on a special mission.

A former acquaintance of Bradwell's, called Medlicot, has shot himself, shortly before he was due to be arrested for treason. Medlicot had been trapped into betraying his country's secrets by Mark Craig, an American night club owner in the pay of the Nazis. Bradwell is sent to spy on the spy, but things take an unexpected turn when he is coshed, and wakes up to find himself in the company of a dead man, and a pretty young interior decorator called Sally. The plot is thickened with classic thrillerish elements: amnesia, black-mail, and a convict's escape from Dartmoor. Will Bradwell triumph over the villains, and will he and Sally fall in love? The answers to these questions are not hard to predict, but the journey to the story's resolution is lively and entertaining.

Today, the name of Victor Bridges is unfamiliar to most readers, but he enjoyed considerable success in his prime, and in 1980, his gifts as a writer were celebrated in an admiring essay in the encyclopaedic *Twentieth Century Crime and Mystery Writers*. Harald Curjel pointed out that Bridges's best stories often share common ingredients: "Always there is a thrilling chase down river after the villains or to escape from them...Bridges' plots are fairly and adroitly woven, and his prose is crisp and flowing in the John Buchan style." Curjel defined "Victor Bridges country" as lying "among the tidal estuaries and rivers of Kent, Essex and Suffolk...Here he created for us a 'Tir-Nan-Og.'"

High praise – yet Curjel's essay had been dropped by the time the third edition of the encyclopaedia appeared eleven years later. Like so many other once-popular wordsmiths, Bridges faded from view. The republication of this book by the British Library gives twenty-first-century readers an opportunity to make up their own minds about his abilities as a story-teller. For too long, apart from the work of Fleming, Le Carré, and Deighton, few pre-1980 espionage books have been readily available in print editions, and the Crime Classics series helps to redress the balance.

Victor George de Freyne Bridges (1878–1972) was born in Clifton, Bristol, and educated at Haileybury. A versatile writer, he was also so prolific that his bibliography is uncertain, details varying from source to source. In addition to novels, he turned out books of verse, short stories, and plays, as well as a book called *Camping Out for Boy Scouts and Others*, which appeared in 1910.

That interest in scouting and camping out hints at a boyish enthusiasm for adventure, and Bridges liked to describe his thrillers as "adventure stories." According to *The Times*, he started work on *The Man from Nowhere*, his first novel, in 1911 to beguile an illness. *Another Man's Shoes* appeared in 1913, and after that he was published for fifteen years by Mills and Boon, who were not at that time stereotyped as publishers of romantic fiction for women. *A*

Rogue by Compulsion, subtitled *An Affair of the Secret Service*, typifies an interest in stories about espionage which continued throughout his career.

Success came quite early, and the spy story *Mr Lyndon at Liberty* was made into a silent film in 1915. A year later, Bridges wrote the screenplay for a Dutch film, *Sparrows*. *Another Man's Shoes* was filmed twice within a decade of publication, as was *The Lady from Longacre*. His most popular book, *Greensea Island*, appeared in 1922, sold over 300,000 copies, and was filmed as *Through Fire and Water*, starring the renowned Clive Brook. *The Times* described it as "an exciting tale of love and buried treasure; but the excitement is never allowed to become strained or unnatural." Despite this success, Bridges' connection with the movie business does not seem to have survived the advent of the talkies.

Bridges co-wrote a comedy play, *The Backsliders*, with a fellow member of the Savage Club, Edgar Jepson, who was not only a prolific novelist (and co-author of the famous impossible crime short story "The Tea Leaf") but also founder of a literary dynasty whose members include his granddaughter, Fay Weldon. The play appears not to have been staged, but Jepson adapted it into a novel. Bridges developed into a reliable purveyor of action and adventure; of the splendidly titled *It Happened in Essex*, the *Sunday Times* reviewer enthused: "I read it with goggle eyes and bated breath."

Bridges enjoyed a lengthy literary career, and lived to the age of 94. When he died, his work was recalled by an obituarist in *The Times* as "graced by a pleasing sense of style…. Much that Bridges wrote was cast in a conventional mould and intended for unexacting eyes, but he always remained a literary craftsman, who could spring surprises with his humour and sense of suspense." It is not a bad epitaph.

Martin Edwards
www.martinedwardsbooks.com

Chapter I

The manservant who had been waiting in the hall opened the front door, and with a muttered word of thanks Lieutenant-Commander Owen Bradwell stepped out on to the sun-warmed pavement of Harley Street. Except for a slight tightening of the lips his clean-cut, deeply tanned face betrayed no sign of the desolating bitterness which was creeping through his heart. It was a moment when twelve years' naval training were not without their spiritual advantage.

A waiting taxi pulled up in front of him, and directing the man to drive to the New Century Club, he clambered in and sank back wearily against the cushion. His hand went to his pocket, and with a purely mechanical movement he pulled out a silver case and lighted a cigarette.

On that particularly fine September morning London was at the height of its form. The stream of traffic up and down Oxford Street appeared to be even more dense than usual, while both pavements were crowded with a throng of loitering pedestrians gaping into the shop windows and resolutely obstructing each other's progress. At frequent intervals a party of crutch-supported vocalists, shepherded by an importunate gentleman with a collecting-box, competed gallantly against the roar of the motor-buses.

Although it was over two years since he had last been in Town, Owen sat gazing out on the animated scene with a fixed, unseeing stare. He was far too occupied with his own thoughts to take in any impression from outside; and it was only when the taxi came to an abrupt halt that he suddenly realised he was already in St. James's Square. With an impatient shrug he pulled himself together, and tossing away the stump of his cigarette, jerked open the door.

He had barely set foot inside the big, sombre hall of the Club when he caught sight of Joe Anstey emerging from the library. The next moment his fingers were being crushed in a welcoming grip, and the cheery voice of his host was pouring out a flood of greetings and questions.

"Well, well, this is grand. How are you, and where the devil have you sprung from? Nearly threw a fit when I got your wire. Hadn't the remotest notion you were back in England, let alone up in Town. When did you get home, and why on earth didn't you let me know you were coming?"

"Give us a chance," pleaded Owen. "I'll answer everything as soon as I feel a trifle stronger. What I want at this moment is a large whisky."

"That's easy. Shove your hat up there and let's go into the bar. I've ordered lunch for one o'clock, so we'll just have time for a quick one."

He led the way into a very long, narrow room, equipped with a counter and a selection of easy chairs. A small group of members who were sipping cocktails and nibbling stuffed olives glanced round with a friendly air, but, disregarding the unspoken invitation to join their company, he piloted his guest towards an empty leather settee at the farther end of the apartment. A mournful-looking waiter who was lurking in the background shuffled forward to take their order.

"Double whisky and a dry sherry," he rapped out, and then, leaning back contentedly and crossing his legs, subjected Owen to a brief but critical scrutiny.

"You haven't altered the least, except that you're a shade thinner. I suppose that comes of living on puppy dogs and bird's-nest soup."

"To be quite honest, I've never tasted either." Owen laughed. "The Admiralty are desperately conservative. Even out in China we still got our roast beef and treacle tart. I did try one native joint in Hong Kong just out of curiosity, and as a result I spent most of the next two days in strict retirement." He paused as the waiter came back with the glasses. "Barbarous habit filling oneself up with whisky just before lunch, but the fact is I'm feeling a trifle dim. Just had what you might describe as 'a kick in the pants'."

"That so?" Joe raised his eyebrows. "Nothing really serious, I hope?"

"Tell you about it later." Owen drained off his tumbler and set it down on the shelf beside him. "First of all, I want to hear your news. How are things generally, and what about the punting championship? Manage to pull it off again this year?"

"Didn't even enter. Too infernally busy."

"You don't say so! Has there been a boom in motor tractors, or have you suddenly gone ambitious and taken to politics?"

"Neither." Joe glanced across in the direction of the bar and lowered his voice. "Don't want to broadcast the information, but as a matter of fact we're working for the Government. We've started a new factory up in the Midlands and we're turning out aeroplane parts. At least, we shall be in about six weeks' time."

"Good work. I imagine we can do with them, from what Churchill was saying in the House the other day. I heard some of his speech on the wireless."

"Do with them!" repeated Joe. "If you want my opinion, we can do with about ten times the number we're arranging for now. I don't mind betting a fiver we'll be at war with Germany inside the next eighteen months."

"I imagine you'd win." Owen's lips twisted into a mirthless smile. "At least, that seems to be the general opinion amongst our people. If anything, they're inclined to put it a shade sooner."

"They're probably right. Those thugs in Berlin mean business, and all the soft soap in the world isn't going to make the slightest difference." Joe raised his glass and gulped down the remainder of the contents. "However, we won't discuss it now or it will spoil my appetite. How do you feel about going in and making a start? I told them to put us on a grilled sole, and if they haven't forgotten it ought to be just about ready."

Without waiting for a reply he hoisted himself up, and making their way across the hall into the big dining-room opposite, they headed towards an empty table in the window that looked out into the Square. Some half-dozen members had drifted in before them, and a low buzz of conversation was already in full swing.

In spite of the haunting depression at the back of his mind, Owen himself was soon talking away as vigorously as anyone. During his absence abroad he had largely dropped out of touch with what was going on in London, and the wealth of interesting gossip which his host was in a position to supply made the time slip past with an agreeable and surprising rapidity. Inquiries and news about old friends and acquaintances seemed to follow each other continuously. The same process continued cheerfully all through the meal, and it was not until they had arrived at the stage of coffee and cigars that the grim subject which he had been only too willing to postpone forced itself inevitably into the foreground.

"Now," demanded Joe, with a sudden turn of seriousness, "what's this trouble of yours that you were hinting at in the bar? Not been making love to the Admiral's wife or anything stupid of that sort?"

"I haven't even tried." Owen paused. "No, it's something much less romantic, but just as unpleasant in its consequences." He dropped a lump of sugar into his cup and stirred it round slowly. "To put it into plain, unvarnished English, I've suddenly gone colour-blind."

"Colour-blind!" Joe sat up sharply. "My dear chap, I—I'm devilish sorry. That's a pretty rotten business for you, isn't it?"

"Not too good. Knocks out the chance of my ever becoming another Lord Nelson."

"But when did it happen? Quite recently?"

"Coming home from China. I went up on deck one night just as we were passing a tramp steamer, and the first thing I noticed was that there was something wrong with her port light. Instead of being red it was a kind of dirty yellow. I spoke to the look-out about it, and he thought I was joking—couldn't understand what I meant. Then—well, then I began to get the wind up. So I toddled down below again and routed out the Doc. He put me through one or two tests, and by the time he'd finished I knew what I was in for. Of course he did his best to cheer me up and tell me that I'd probably recover, but I could see by his face that it was only a lot of well-meaning bunk. He simply hadn't the heart to dish me out the truth."

"Are you absolutely sure? Isn't there the slightest chance—?"

"Not an earthly. As soon as we got to Plymouth I went before a Medical Board. The Head M.O. was a very decent bloke, and he said that before giving a final opinion he'd like me to run up to Town and consult a specialist called Mitchell-Carr in Harley Street. I felt at the time that he was merely letting me down as gently as possible."

"Have you seen this chap yet?"

"Had an appointment this morning and came straight on here afterwards. He tried me out with the whole bag of tricks. I needn't bore you with details, but I gather that unless I run into someone who can perform miracles I shall never be able to spot a red light again except when I'm practically right up against it. Won't make any difference to my sight otherwise, but so far as going to sea's concerned—well, it's just a case of sweet Fanny Adams." He shrugged. "They don't entrust expensive battleships to wash-outs like me."

There was a lengthy pause.

"It's a sickening piece of bad luck, and I'm more sorry than I can say." Joe was staring across at his companion with an obviously genuine sympathy. "Still, you mustn't talk as though things were utterly hopeless. If that's the only trouble, surely it doesn't mean your having to leave the Service? Won't they be able to find you something ashore? There must be heaps of jobs where colour-blindness doesn't matter a curse."

"Oh, I dare say they'll offer me a berth in what we call 'a stone frigate.' Sitting at a desk all day in some Godforsaken office, or piloting a party of M.P.s who've taken it into their heads that they want to look round a dockyard. What makes me so desperately mad is that it should have happened just now. As you said yourself, we're obviously heading for war, and if I could only have carried on for another three or four years—" He checked himself abruptly, and with the faintest possible shrug picked up the glass of brandy in front of him. "Well, there it is, and what's the use of talking about it? Better wait till to-morrow and see whether this bird Greystoke has anything to suggest."

"Who's Greystoke?" demanded Joe.

"Don't ask me. All I know about him is that he's a pal of my skipper, and that he used to be second in command at

Portsmouth. I believe he's something at the Admiralty now, but what his actual job is I haven't the remotest notion."

"How does he come into it, then?"

"I rather fancy that the old man must have written to him about me. Anyhow, I got a chit just before I left asking me to call at his place in Queen Anne's Gate. Probably turn out to be a complete frost, but I may as well push along there and 'mak siccar.'"

"How long are you staying in Town?"

"Haven't decided yet. Depends upon what Greystoke has to say. I've booked a room at the Paddington, and if it turns out that there's anything doing I shall probably hang around for a day or two. They've given me a fortnight's leave, so there's no particular point in bundling back to Plymouth."

"Why not come along to the flat? I'd love to put you up, and you'll be a whole heap more comfortable."

"That's rather a happy notion." Owen paused. "Quite sure I shouldn't be a nuisance? I'm not very good company just at the moment."

"My dear chap, if you feel that way you can lock yourself in your bedroom all day and Watkins will bring you your meals. It's quite likely I shan't even be there. Halsey's in charge of the new show, but I may get a wire from him any time saying that he wants me to come up, and if I do I'll have to paddle off at once. In any case, I shouldn't expect you to be bright and interesting. If I'd had a knock like that I should simply loathe the sight of everyone."

"You're an understanding bloke, Joe." Owen smiled gratefully. "I think I will plant myself on you if you're prepared to risk it. I'm certainly not looking forward to sitting in a hotel smoking-room making polite replies to some devastating bore." He paused. "I want to be somewhere quiet where I can chew things over. After I've seen Greystoke I'm not s---

that I won't ask you to lend me one of your punts and have a few days on my own up the river."

"Sound scheme, provided this weather holds. I've left a couple at old Martin's boat-house at Playford, so you can toddle down there and take your pick. If I could spare the time—"

"Excuse me, sir, but you're wanted on the phone."

A page-boy had suddenly appeared at Joe's elbow.

"Right you are." He pushed back his chair and rose to his feet. "I expect it's the office," he added, addressing Owen. "You won't mind my deserting you for a minute? Order yourself another brandy and have some more coffee."

There was an appreciable interval before he reappeared, and as he threaded his way back to the table it was obvious from his expression that something had occurred to upset his usual equanimity.

"Damned annoying," he announced, "but I'm afraid I'll have to break up the party. Those wretched Air people want me to go round there at once and hear about some new change they're making in their plans. Don't suppose it's the least urgent really, but we can't afford to be haughty with a Government Department."

"You're telling me." Owen laughed and hoisted himself up. "Don't worry, old man, just shove off and make yourself civil: I've tons to do this afternoon, anyhow. Got to look in at the tailor's for one thing, and then go along to the Stores and have my hair cut."

"Well, when you're through, collect your traps and bring them over to the flat. I'll give Watkins a ring and tell him to get your room ready."

"I expect he'll curse me for making a lot of extra work."

"Not a bit of it," Joe grinned. "You're a particular favourite of his, and he'll be as pleased as Punch. Shouldn't be surprised if he even polished up the door-knocker."

Chapter II

Ruth Barlow laid down her pen, and straightening up from the small desk at which she had been working, looked across at her partner. Sally was standing in the centre of the shop, her head tilted slightly to one side, her eyes riveted thoughtfully upon an open book of wall-papers. A ray of sunshine fell across her red-gold hair, lighting it up so that it glinted like burnished copper.

The shop itself, though not very large, had been cleverly and attractively arranged. Against the cream-coloured walls and peacock-blue hangings such furniture as was on view stood out with remarkable effectiveness. The place of honour was assigned to an old lacquered Chinese cabinet, supported by four gilt cupids with outstretched wings. Two magnificent bowls of yellow and red roses filled the air with their comforting fragrance, while above the mantel-piece hung a quaintly carved oak panel displaying the announcement:

BARLOW and DEANE
Interior Decorators

At the back an unobtrusive flight of steps led down to the basement below.

"Well, that's done, anyhow." Ruth stretched her arms and yawned contentedly.

"What's done?" inquired Sally.

"Balance-sheet for our first year. I've been grinding away at it the whole week."

"Oh, how exciting!" Moving quickly across to the desk, Sally bent down over the long page of foolscap paper, on which an array of figures, accompanied by explanatory statements, was neatly set out in a clear and business-like handwriting. "I think you're an absolute marvel," she continued. "When I see anything like that it always fills me with a kind of despairing envy. I could no more do it than jump over the moon."

"It's perfectly simple really."

"It may be to you. As far as I'm concerned, it's just so much double Dutch." Sally wrinkled her forehead. "What does it all tot up to, and how do we actually stand?"

"Not too bad." Ruth picked up the paper, and readjusted her spectacles. "Of course it will have to be checked by the accountants, but I don't think they'll find anything wrong. I make out that after paying expenses, deducting our salaries, and allowing two per cent for interest on capital, we wind up with the staggering profit of twenty-three pounds, fourteen shillings and sixpence halfpenny. What do you say to that? For a couple of lone females butting into a new business I call it pretty hot stuff."

"It's almost fantastic." Sally drew in a long breath. "Twenty-three pounds, fourteen shillings and sixpence halfpenny," she repeated. "Why, if we go on at this rate we shall end up by prancing around in mink coats."

"We mustn't lose our heads. All the same, I think we can afford to celebrate just for once. How about dining out to-night and doing a show afterwards? We shall each have twelve pounds to draw, and—"

"Rubbish, darling." Sally shook her head. "That money belongs to you, every blessed farthing of it. You put up the whole of the capital, and it's all wrong that you should only be getting two per cent on it."

"But that was the agreement."

"Agreement be blowed," retorted Sally. "I get my expenses and three pounds a week, and if there's anything over—"

"It's no use arguing about it," broke in Ruth calmly. "Two per cent is what we fixed, and two per cent is what I'm going to take. When the business really gets going we can make it a little more, if you like. At present it's halves, Partner, so just shut up and think about what you're going to have for dinner."

"But it seems so unfair," protested Sally. "If it wasn't for you there wouldn't be any profit. You sit here and do all the hard work—"

"Hard work my foot! Anyone can squat on their behind and just scribble down figures in a book." Ruth patted the hand that was resting on her shoulder. "Don't be so fatuously modest, my pet. Any success we've had has been due to the fact that you're not only a genius at your job, but you've a way of handling people which simply makes me gasp. How you put up with some of these ghastly females I can't imagine. If it were me I should lose my temper and tell them to go and boil their heads."

Sally laughed. "I'd like to see the water afterwards: it would be a funny colour in some cases."

"Talking of that, how about the Greig woman?" Ruth glanced at her watch. "Didn't she make an appointment for eleven-thirty?"

"She did, but she's sure to be half an hour late. If one's absolutely dripping with money—"

"Sh! Here is the creature! At least, that looks like her car."

A glittering limousine had come to a halt outside, and a moment or so later its owner, an expensively dressed, middle-aged lady, drifted vaguely into the shop. She was heavily made up and her hair looked as though it had been dyed in orange juice.

"Good morning, Mrs. Greig. How delightful to see you again!" With a dazzling smile Sally moved gracefully forward. "Until I got your note I thought you were still up in Scotland."

"We came back last week." The visitor sank languidly into a chair, and producing a slim platinum case, extracted a gold-tipped cigarette.

"Can you find me a match, my dear? Thanks terribly."

"Did you have a good time?"

"Positively loathsome." Mrs. Greig gave a faint shudder. "No one in the place seemed to be able to talk about anything except killing birds. My husband, of course, was enraptured. He adores shedding blood."

"Most men are like that." Sally nodded sympathetically. "It must have been very trying for you, though, with your artistic and sensitive temperament."

"Absolutely devastating. If I had stayed there another week I should have passed out from sheer boredom." The speaker shuddered again. "What I need is a spiritual tonic. I am thinking of redecorating the drawing-room."

"What an inspiration, and how typical of the true artist!" Sally clasped her hands admiringly.

"I thought that we might work out something in collaboration. I was very pleased with the room which you did for Lady Jocelyn. It struck me as having soul and imagination."

"That cheers me up tremendously. It's so encouraging to be appreciated by anyone who has real taste and understanding."

Ruth, who was seated behind the visitor's back, made a vulgar gesture with her fingers.

"Have you an idea for any particular colour-scheme?" pursued Sally hastily. "I always feel that one should start from that and then build up stage by stage until one gets a complete and harmonious picture."

"Yes, I know what I want." Mrs. Greig closed her eyes. "A warm, slightly golden effect—something that suggests sunshine and happiness."

"But how wonderful!" Sally paused as though overcome by the brilliance of the conception. "You know, if you had left it entirely to me, that's just what I should have chosen myself. I feel that for a personality like yours it would be the absolutely ideal background."

"It is the only atmosphere in which my soul can really expand." Mrs. Greig sighed delicately. "You have seen the room, of course, but you must come round to-morrow and we will go into the whole question together. Four o'clock would be a convenient time. I like to rest and meditate for an hour or so in the afternoon."

"That will be quite thrilling." Sally picked up a notebook from the desk and jotted down the appointment. "In the meantime I will see if I can make some sketches and bring them along with me. It will be so stimulating to work with you. I am certain that between us we shall be able to create something marvellous."

With a gracious smile Mrs. Greig consulted the diamond-studded watch which decorated her wrist. Then, dropping her still-lighted cigarette into the adjacent bowl of roses, she flicked aside a speck of dust and rose wearily to her feet.

"I shall have to be going now. I have promised the dear Princess faithfully that I will be at the Albert Hall to-night, and I must call in at the bank to collect my emeralds. Such a nuisance, but my husband will insist upon my leaving them there when we are out of Town. He has burglars on the brain—definitely."

Moving toward the door which Sally had politely opened, she stepped out into the busy world of the King's Road. A trail of exotic scent lingered behind her, and almost before she was safely out of earshot Ruth had risen from her chair with a disgusted sniff.

"Blast the scented pole-cat!" she exclaimed. "Like her confounded cheek, dropping her filthy cigarette into our roses." As she spoke she fished out the offending stub, and flinging it viciously into the fireplace, wiped her fingers on her skirt.

"Simmer down, darling." Sally smiled soothingly. "Think what a nice little packet we can make out of it. Why, if I can jolly her along properly we ought to pull in at least thirty or forty pounds."

"That's the only thing that stopped me from boxing her ears." Ruth gave a scornful shrug. "Rest and meditation indeed! What she means is that she stuffs herself full of lunch and then lies down to sleep it off. Snores like a grampus, too, I'll bet."

"Does a grampus snore?" inquired Sally. "I thought it only blew."

"Ordering you about, too, as if you were a skivvy! 'You must come round to-morrow—four o'clock will be a convenient time.' 'Pon my soul, some of these rich women ought to be taken out and ducked."

"Still, they *are* rich," commented Sally. "That's the only thing that really matters to us." With a deft touch she rearranged one or two of the roses which her partner's impulsive action had slightly displaced. "I think I'll go down and have a scout round the basement. We've quite a lot of odds and ends stuffed away, and with any luck I might be able to work some of them off. By the way, Sheila rang up while you were out and said she was going to blow in this morning. If she does, you can send her down."

"What does she want now?" inquired Ruth suspiciously.

"Haven't an idea. She only said that it was very urgent and would I make a point of being in."

"That means she is going to ask you to do something for her."

"Shouldn't be surprised."

"I don't see why she should always come bothering you when she's in a mess. You're too unselfish and good-natured, Sally, that's the truth. If she were my sister I'd soon tell her off."

"One can't be brutal to Sheila. It isn't her fault that she's constantly getting herself into jams: with a face like hers that's practically bound to happen. She'll be all right as soon as she's married Julian. He'll make her drop the whole of the crowd she knows at present, and she'll settle down in state as the wife of a future Prime Minister. Can't you picture her standing at the top of a marble staircase shaking hands with ambassadors?"

"Men are fools," declared Ruth contemptuously. "If Julian Raymond had any sense he'd have fallen for you instead of Sheila. You'd have made him a wonderful wife, while the only thing she'll do is to lounge around and spend his money."

"And a very nice way of passing the time." Sally's blue eyes twinkled mischievously. "No, my dear, you needn't waste your sympathy on me. I haven't the remotest ambition to be a political hostess, and as for living with a pompous prig like Julian—why, I should be so bored I should probably take to drink. Fancy having to lie in bed and listen to him rehearsing his speeches."

"Now you're getting crude." Ruth grinned and sauntered back leisurely to her desk. "Very well, I'll send her along if she turns up: only for Heaven's sake don't let her be too much of a nuisance. You've quite enough to do without setting up as a wet nurse."

"I will remember that my first duty is to the Firm."

Making a mock obeisance, Sally walked to the head of the staircase, and descending the short flight, unlocked a door in the narrow passage below. It led into a long, low-ceilinged room about the same size as the shop, the windows of which looked out into a small backyard.

Though at some former period in its existence it had apparently been a kitchen, it was now fitted up partly as a store-room and partly as a workshop. The big table in the centre was littered with a variety of objects, including scissors, paints, pencils, drawing-pins, and at least half a dozen rough, unfinished sketches. In one corner stood an ancient but comfortable-looking divan, while round the walls, still covered by an atrociously hideous Victorian paper, were ranged other pieces of contemporary furniture, interspaced with shelves and cupboards.

Taking down a dark blue overall from a peg behind the door, Sally slipped it on over her neat black frock. Then, with a purposeful air, she turned up her sleeves, and moving briskly across to the opposite end of the room, swung open the door of a big mahogany wardrobe. It was stacked full of what is inelegantly referred to as "junk."

◇ ◇ ◇

"Oh, good morning, Miss Barlow. Is Sally here?"

The visitor advanced towards the desk, and favouring her with an inhospitable glance, Ruth blotted the letter she had been writing and pushed back her chair. The superficial resemblance between the two sisters always had the effect of arousing her resentment: it was so obviously and annoyingly in favour of the younger. No one, of course, could deny Sally's attractiveness; but while she was merely pretty, Sheila possessed that starry, heart-arresting beauty that made men turn round and gape after her in the street. In Ruth's eyes this appeared to be a blunder on the part of Providence for which there was no conceivable excuse.

"Sally is in the basement looking through some stuff," was her grudging response. "We have just had a new commission, and she is pretty busy this morning."

"I'll go down, then: I must talk to her for a minute or two. If anyone else asks for her you might tell them that she's engaged."

Without waiting for an answer the speaker crossed over to the back of the shop, and making her way quickly down the staircase, pushed open the door of the store-room. There was a kind of nervous tension about all her actions which suggested that she was labouring under some strong emotional strain.

Sally, who was sitting on the floor surrounded by several rolls of artificial silk, scrambled up with a welcoming smile.

"Hullo, Sheila darling," she exclaimed. "Sorry the place is in such a mess, but I've been overhauling some of this truck to see whether I can palm anything off on one of our gilded clients." She tucked back a stray curl that had tumbled forward across her eyes. "What's up now?" she inquired. "Sounded on the phone as if you were in a bit of a spot."

"Oh, Sally, I'm nearly off my head." Closing the door behind her, Sheila moved towards the couch and collapsed weakly amongst a pile of cushions. "It's too ghastly," she faltered. "Unless you can help me it means the absolute end of everything—*everything.*"

"Bad as that, eh?" Raising her eyebrows, Sally walked slowly round the table, and seating herself alongside, patted her sister soothingly on the arm. "Come along, then," she continued in the sort of voice one uses to a small child. "Get it off your chest, and let's see what we can do about it."

With a stifled gulp Sheila glanced round apprehensively in the direction of the door. "I—I suppose it's quite safe to talk here? I don't want that Barlow girl to come bursting in. She hates me: I can see it in her face."

"Don't be a fathead. Ruth isn't exactly your cup of tea, but she's a grand sport, and the most generous-hearted soul I've ever known. Besides there isn't the faintest chance of her coming down here. If I'm wanted she'll just lean over the stairs and howl."

A longish pause followed, and then, lifting a pair of beautiful, woe-begone eyes, Sheila braced herself up for what appeared to be a supreme effort.

"It's that beast Granville Sutton," she whispered.

"Granville Sutton!" Sally frowned. "Why, six months ago you told me that you'd finished with him for good and all."

"So I had. At least, I thought so at the time."

"You haven't changed your mind, have you?"

"Of course not. I hate him. I loathe him. After the way he behaved."

"Then what on earth's the trouble?"

"It's—it's a letter of mine he's got." Sheila flushed and lowered her eyes.

"A letter?" Sally drew in a quick breath. "You mean the sort of letter that you wouldn't like anyone else to read?"

"I must have been mad. I can't imagine how I ever came to write it. I was so in love with him then I hardly realised what I was doing."

"Is he trying to blackmail you?"

The other nodded miserably. "He rang up last Friday and asked me to meet him in Kensington Gardens. He hinted what it was about, so I didn't dare to refuse. I hoped that perhaps I could persuade him to give it me back."

"How much did he ask?"

"He—he wants me to pay him a thousand pounds for it. He knows about my engagement, and he says that unless I am prepared to buy it for that amount he will put it in an envelope and post it to Julian." Sheila clenched her fists. "I could kill him. I would kill him if I only had the pluck."

"It's no good talking like that. What you really ought to do is to go to Julian and tell him the truth."

"Oh, Sally, I couldn't, I couldn't. You don't know him as well as I do. He loves me all right, he loves me frightfully, but if he thought there was any chance of a scandal, anything that might interfere with his public career—"

"He'd chuck you over at once—is that what you mean?"

"I'm sure he would. You see, he's so keen on getting into the Cabinet, and he takes everything so desperately seriously."

"Well, I wouldn't break my heart over a man like that. He isn't worth it."

"But I want to marry him. I'll never meet anyone else who'll suit me so well or give me such a good time. Besides, think of all the horrid things people would say if it was broken off now. Oh, I just couldn't face up to it. I—I'd rather go out and throw myself in the river."

"But a thousand pounds! Why, it's fantastic. How can you possibly get hold of it?"

"I can't. All I could raise would be five hundred. I could get that by selling Aunt Lucy's necklace."

"And you would, I suppose?"

"Why not? What's an ugly old necklace to me compared with the chance of marrying Julian?"

"Even then it would only be half what he's asking for."

"That's where I want you to help me. You're so clever, and you don't get frightened and rattled like I do. It wouldn't be the slightest use my trying, but if you were to go and see him and have a talk to him—"

"I!"

"Oh, you will, Sally, promise me you will." With an imploring gesture Sheila caught hold of her sister's hands. "It's so terribly important, and there's no one else I can trust. If you were to let me down—"

"Don't say any more about drowning yourself, darling, because I don't believe it." Sally smiled wryly. "Let's cut out the sob stuff and come to the point. What you're suggesting is that I should drop in on this beauty and do a spot of bargaining for you?"

Sheila wriggled uncomfortably and drew away her hands. "I feel it's an awful lot to ask," she murmured.

"Where does he hang out, and how could one get hold of him?"

"That's what makes it so difficult. He—he wants me to drive down to Playford on Sunday night and bring the money to his bungalow. He says he won't give me the letter otherwise."

"Playford? You mean that little place on the river?"

Sheila nodded.

"But what's the idea? Why can't you meet him in London?"

"I don't know. I expect he's afraid I might go to the police, and he thinks he'll be quite safe down there."

Sally remained silent for a moment.

"What time was this precious appointment for?" she demanded.

"Half-past ten, he said. You see how impossible it is? Suppose someone I know saw me going in there and went and told Julian."

"I imagine he'd be a trifle vexed."

"He'd never speak to me again. Besides, what would be the good of it, anyway? That beast Granville knows I'm frightened of him, and if I only brought five hundred he'd just say that there was nothing doing. Now if it were you—"

"What's the name of the bungalow?" asked Sally curtly.

"It's called Sunny Bank, and it's the last one you come to going towards Thames Ferry. It's some way from any of the others—a small, white place with a red roof and a green fence in front."

"Gosh!" said Sally. "It only wants pink curtains to make it the Ideal Home!"

Sheila stared blankly for a moment, and then a sudden gleam of hope leaped into her eyes.

"You mean you'll do it? You will really?"

"I suppose I'd better." Sally shrugged. "Can't say I feel wildly enthusiastic. I still think the right thing would be to tell Mr. Sutton to go to Hell, and then let Julian know all about it. If he had any decency he'd tear up the letter without reading it."

"He's not that sort." Sheila shook her head decisively.

"Well, you know him best. What I want to make quite clear, though, is that if I agree to tackle the job I'm going to do it in my own way."

"How do you mean?"

"I shall tell Sutton you'll pay five hundred and not a farthing more. He can either accept that and bring the letter here, or if he prefers to go without the money and gratify his spite he can hand it over to Julian as soon as he likes. I don't intend to haggle with the swine."

"Oh, but suppose—"

"No use supposing," continued Sally firmly. "It's the only way to deal with a blackmailer unless you're prepared to go to the police. From all I've heard about Mr. Granville Sutton, I'll bet you a shilling that he'll accept my offer."

" 'Pr'aps you're right: I hope you are." The other paused unhappily. "Anyhow, I'll take the necklace round to Hink's this afternoon and collect the cash. Would you like me to leave it here, or—"

"No, I don't want it at present. Pay it into your bank and wait till you hear what's happened."

"I will come round early on Monday morning." Opening her bag and producing a miniature compact, Sheila began to powder her nose. "Of course I'm fearfully grateful, darling. It's terribly decent of you to do all this, and I—"

"Don't start thanking me now: it will be time enough when you've got the letter." Sally rose from the couch and glanced at the various articles strewn about the floor. "I'm sorry I'm so busy, but I simply must finish this job before lunch. You go and fix up about the necklace and leave the rest to me. I'll talk to the beauty, and unless he's more of a fool than I take him for I'm pretty certain I'll manage to pull it off." She smiled encouragingly. "Anyway, I'll do my damnedest, so hope for the best and keep your chin up."

◇◇◇

"Well, what was it all about?" Leaning back and putting her hands behind her head, Ruth looked inquiringly at her partner.

"I don't think I ought to tell you." Sally came forward from the top of the staircase and perched herself on the arm of a chair alongside the desk.

"That means that she's landed herself into some fresh trouble and that you've promised to get her out of it."

"How did you guess?"

"My sweet child, I'm not halfwitted. When she came in I could see that she was worried stiff, and when she walked out she looked as sleek and pleased with herself as a cat that's just pinched the milk. I expect you've promised to do something desperately idiotic."

"That's what you'd call it, and I suppose you'd be right." Sally stroked her nose thoughtfully. "Perhaps I'd better 'come clean', as they say in the films. It's rather a sticky business, and in any case I shall want the loan of your car. You'll make a point of keeping the whole thing to yourself, won't you?"

"Have you ever heard me going round blabbing out other people's secrets?"

"Never," admitted Sally. "That's why I don't mind letting you in on it." She slid down into the chair, and leaning forward, helped herself to a cigarette from the box on the desk. "Sheila's being blackmailed," she announced bluntly, "blackmailed by that rotten twirp Granville Sutton."

There was a brief pause.

"What's she been up to?" demanded Ruth. "Having an affair with him?"

"Very much so, apparently. They were trailing about together a lot last autumn, and I told her at the time that I didn't think much of her taste. It was no use talking to her then: she was absolutely besotted about him. He's one of those plausible, good-looking crooks who can get round almost any girl if they choose to take the trouble."

"I know." Ruth nodded disgustedly. "The only thing that surprises me is that Sheila should be such an ass. I should have thought she was too keen on making a good marriage."

"It was a sort of obsession: didn't last very long. She had broken with him before she met Julian, and after that the only thing she wanted was to forget all about it."

"And now I suppose he's threatening to give her away?"

"He's got a letter of hers." Sally lit the cigarette which she had been holding in her hand and blew out a long trail of smoke. "I don't know exactly what's in it, but I gather that if it ever came into the wrong hands—" She shrugged expressively. "He's offering to sell it back to her for a thousand pounds."

"Is that all!"

"I told her she ought to go to the police, but of course she wouldn't listen to me. Her one idea is to marry Julian, and if she had the money she'd stump up like a shot. As it is, the most she can raise is five hundred."

"I see." Ruth's lips tightened. "And you're to do the bargaining, I take it?"

"I've promised to go down and see the skunk. He's got a bungalow at Playford, and the arrangement is that she's to meet him there on Sunday night. He's evidently afraid of a trap, and he's not taking any chances."

"So that's why you want the car?"

"I had to say I'd take the job on: what else could I do? Sheila's in a state of panic and she'd only make an unholy mess of it. I'm not the least frightened of the swine. I shall tell him that he can either bring the letter here next week and collect the five hundred or else he can hand it over to Julian and go to Hell. I'm absolutely certain it's the right line to take—don't you agree?"

"Speaking candidly, darling, I think you ought to be locked up." Ruth surveyed her companion with a sort of exasperated affection. "You're just about as hopeless as King Arthur and Don Quixote. Even if she is your sister, why the heck should you do all her dirty work for her? She's quite old enough to look after herself, and the sooner she starts the better. It may teach her to behave more sensibly."

"I'm only keeping a promise I made to Mummy." Sally paused. "She simply adored Sheila, but she was always terrified that something would happen to her when she grew up. I was sitting by her bed holding her hand the evening before she died, and she suddenly told me in a whisper that it was the only thing she was really worried and unhappy about. I swore faithfully that if Sheila was ever in any trouble I would do my very best to help her. I know it comforted her, because she gave a little smile and I felt her squeeze my fingers. I couldn't go back on that, Ruth—I couldn't possibly."

"My dear, I wouldn't ask you to." The elder girl nodded understandingly. "All the same, I'm not going to let you handle this job entirely by yourself. I'm coming with you."

"Oh, but you can't, Ruth! If Sheila knew that I'd given the show away—"

"Hst! Look out—here's a customer."

The shop door swung open, and stubbing out her cigarette, Sally jumped up hastily and stepped forward past the desk.

"We'll talk about it later," she whispered.

Chapter III

With that silent efficiency that characterised all his actions Watkins deposited a couple of silver dishes upon the sideboard and then cast a final glance round the neat and perfectly appointed breakfast table. As he did so Owen turned back from the open window.

"Another grand morning," he remarked. "More like July than September."

"Very remarkable weather indeed, sir," agreed Watkins. "A trifle belated, if one might use the expression, but none the less agreeable for that."

"I understand you've been having a lousy summer in England."

"Precisely, sir. It is the exact adjective which I should have selected myself."

There was a sound of whistling accompanied by approaching steps, and a second later Joe Anstey marched briskly into the room. In his hand was a small sheaf of opened letters which had evidently arrived by the early post.

"Hello! Beaten me by a head." He tossed his correspondence on to the table and surveyed his guest with an inquiring grin. "What sort of a night did you have? Manage to sleep all right?"

"Not too bad, considering the time we turned in and the amount of whisky you made me drink."

"Feel you can face some breakfast? Let's see what there is." Moving over to the sideboard, Joe lifted up the two covers. "Devilled kidneys and fried eggs and bacon. How about a spot of both? Go splendidly together."

Without waiting for an answer he ladled out a couple of generous helpings, and carrying them across to the table, planted himself down alongside of Owen who had already taken his seat. Watkins, having apparently decided that everything was in order, faded away to his own quarters, closing the door behind him. From outside, four storeys below, the faint hum of the early-morning traffic along Park Lane drifted up in a monotonous rumble.

"Bound to happen just as you blew along." With a disgusted shrug Joe pushed across a cup of coffee. "I've had an S O S from Halsey screaming for my presence at the Works. He's heard from the Ministry about this new scheme of theirs, and he thinks we ought to go into a huddle straight away. Says that if I can manage it he'd like me to run up there to-night."

"Well, you must go, naturally. How long do you imagine you'll be away?"

"Lord knows. Maybe a couple of nights, maybe a week." Joe stabbed viciously at a morsel of bacon and transferred it to his mouth. "Won't interfere with your arrangements, though. You'll stay on, of course?"

"How about Watkins?"

"He'll be delighted. As I told you before, you're the one friend I've got with whom he condescends to be a shade human."

"Makes one feel quite conceited." Owen laughed. "Still, if that's really the case, I think I'll accept your offer. Don't suppose I'd get as good a breakfast anywhere else."

"Splendid. That's all settled, then. If you find it too hot in Town you can always slide down to Playford and have a day on the river. I'll give you a chit to Martin before I go."

"Thanks very much."

"By the way, there's a cover to one of those punts, so if you happen to feel like taking along some grub and camping for the night you've only to mention it to Watkins. He'll fix you up with a hamper."

"Sounds gorgeous." Owen nodded gratefully. "Nothing I'd enjoy more, provided I can get away. Depends upon whether Greystoke has anything to suggest."

"When's your appointment?"

"Eleven-thirty."

"Hope something comes of it. All I can say is that if they don't find you a decent berth they must be a pack of blithering nitwits."

"Can I mention that as being the opinion of an exceptionally acute observer?"

"Certainly. I'll put it in writing if you like." Joe chuckled and glanced across at the clock. "Curse it all, I shall have to be pushing along in a minute or two. I must catch the five-twenty, and there's sure to be a Hell of a lot to do at the office." He spread some butter on to a piece of toast and daubed it lavishly with marmalade. "You'll make yourself at home, won't you? Ask Watkins for anything you want, and give me a ring about ten o'clock to-night. I'd like to hear what's happened. The number's Rockton two six double one: you'll find it written down on the pad beside the phone."

"Don't suppose there'll be any news. Doesn't seem the least likely to me."

"I'm not so sure. I've a sort of feeling that you're going to strike lucky. What would you do if he offered you a job at the Admiralty?"

Owen reached out for the toast-rack. "I'd probably kiss him," he replied cheerfully.

◇◇◇

Though only a stone's throw from Victoria Street, Queen Anne's Gate still retains a good deal of its mellow eighteenth-century charm. Notwithstanding the fact that most of its houses have been altered for the use of government departments, Time and the Office of Works have not yet succeeded in wholly eradicating that gracious atmosphere of a bygone London, towards the final destruction of which their relentless energies are apparently directed. Even to-day the spectacle of a sedan chair in that sedate backwater would seem far more in harmony with the general background than the haughty and contemptuous swish past of the customary Rolls-Royce.

Unlike the majority of its neighbours, number 17A had no official door-plate decorating its discreet but pleasant-looking exterior. It was a narrow, three-storey house with long, old-fashioned windows. The only modern thing about it was an electric bell, and having pressed this, Owen straightened up expectantly and threw away the end of his half-smoked cigarette. For some obscure reason he was conscious of a vague and rather irritating feeling of nervousness.

Almost immediately the door was opened by a middle-aged manservant who had the air and appearance of a retired sergeant of marines. His hard blue eyes submitted the visitor to a swift but searching inspection.

"I wish to see Captain Greystoke." Owen produced a visiting-card. "I have an appointment with him for eleven-thirty."

"Yes, sir. The Captain is expecting you. If you will come with me I will take you up to him at once."

Crossing a circular-shaped hall, they ascended a steep flight of stairs. On arriving at the first landing, the man halted outside a room on the right. In response to his tap somebody rapped out a curt "Come in," and the next instant Owen found himself being ushered into a high-ceilinged, oak-panelled apartment, the bow windows of which looked out over St. James's Park. Its only occupant, who was seated at a table in the centre, pushed aside some papers and rose to his feet.

"Lieutenant-Commander Bradwell, sir."

Captain Greystoke, a short, stockily-built man with a determined mouth and a pair of remarkably shrewd eyes, stepped forward and held out his hand.

"Ah, Bradwell, glad to make your acquaintance." He imprisoned Owen's fingers in a sudden crushing grip, and then, releasing them abruptly, glanced across at his henchman. "I don't want to be disturbed for the next quarter of an hour, Barnes. If anyone rings up put them through to Mr. Everett."

"Very good, sir."

The door closed quietly, and moving back to the table, Captain Greystoke picked up a box of cigars.

"Try one of these, unless you prefer a cigarette. If you do, you'll find some in that box over there."

"Thank you, sir." Owen helped himself to an imposing-looking Cabana, and feeling a trifle surprised at the unexpected friendliness of his reception, sat down in the chair towards which his host had made an inviting gesture. Captain Greystoke resumed his former seat, and for a moment the two of them faced each other in silence.

"I expect you have been wondering why I invited you to look me up." The speaker smiled pleasantly. "The fact is I had a letter from your skipper, my old friend Carmichael. He told me about this unfortunate business of your suddenly going colour-blind. I understand that it happened on your way home from China."

"That's so, sir. Came on without the slightest warning."

"He mentioned that you had been before a Medical Board at Plymouth, and that they were sending you up to Town to consult a specialist."

Owen nodded.

"Have you seen him?"

"I had an appointment yesterday, sir. He examined me thoroughly, and then—well, then he what you might call passed sentence. He told me that my chances of recovery were about one in a thousand."

"Bad as that!" Greystoke leaned back in his chair. "I am sorry—very sorry. Afraid it must have been rather an unpleasant dose to swallow."

"I was more or less prepared for it. I could see what I was up against by the M.O.'s manner at Plymouth."

"Still, I don't imagine it would ease the blow to any great extent."

"Not that you'd notice, sir." Owen smiled crookedly. "When one's whole career is suddenly knocked edgeways—"

"Mustn't talk like that, Bradwell." The elder man shook his head. "I'm not trying to minimise the disaster: it's a heart-rending thing to happen to anyone, especially to a fellow of your age. I realise exactly what it means to you; but as far as its putting an end to your career is concerned—well, that's absolute nonsense. You don't imagine that in the present state of affairs we are going to allow a man with your record to slip through our fingers?"

A tinge of colour mounted into Owen's tanned cheeks.

"You think they could still find some use for me, sir?"

"Plenty of uses. When the balloon goes up—as it very soon will—every experienced officer will be absolutely invaluable. In a sense, Bradwell, you're lucky. If this had occurred five or six years ago you wouldn't have stood a chance. They would merely have opened the door politely and bowed you out. As it is, you can make your mind quite easy. Strictly between ourselves, I have already brought your case to the notice of the Second Lord, and I can guarantee that in a very short while you will find yourself posted to a job ashore in which the trouble with your eyesight won't handicap you in the slightest. I know it isn't the same thing as having a commission afloat, but whatever the work is it will be just as essential to the Service, and, if it's any consolation, you will probably stand just as good a chance of being blown to smithereens. There will be no 'cushy billets' this time—the Luftwaffe will look after that for us."

"It's very kind of you, sir, and I am extremely grateful." Owen paused. "I don't know why you should have troubled yourself—"

"As I mentioned before, I have been in communication with Carmichael." Greystoke tipped off the end of his cigar. "He seems to have rather a high opinion of you, Bradwell. I won't tell you what he actually said or it might make you conceited."

Owen smiled uncomfortably. "That's—that's Captain Carmichael's way, sir. He is always ready to do a good turn to anyone who has served under him."

"I doubt it. I am inclined to give him credit for being a trifle more selective than you appear to imagine. Anyhow, his judgment is good enough for me, and I have reason to assume that it carries a certain amount of weight at the Admiralty. Otherwise. I should not have been empowered to make a certain suggestion which may or may not appeal to you."

Owen's face lit up hopefully. "I should be very interested to know what it is, sir."

"When you were out in China did you happen to hear anything about a man called Medlicot—Lieutenant A. G. Medlicot? He must have been a year or two junior to you."

"I saw that he had died, sir. There was a notice in one of the papers just before we sailed for home."

"Yes, he died rather suddenly. In fact—this is absolutely private and mustn't go any farther—he took his own life by shooting himself through the head."

Owen raised his eyebrows. "What on earth made him do that, sir?"

"I imagine that it was partly remorse and partly because he considered it to be the best way out. If he hadn't committed suicide he would have been arrested and tried for treason."

"Treason!"

"I am afraid that is the only word one can use." The speaker paused. "It was a bad business in every way. Medlicot was a bit of a genius in his own line, and for nearly a year before he died he had been conducting experimental work on some new gadget in connection with submarines. There is no need to enter into further details at the moment. All that matters is that the invention panned out very satisfactorily, and we were just congratulating ourselves that we were one up on the Boche when we learned through an agent that a complete copy of the plans had been sent over to Berlin, and that our Nazi friends were already hard at work on them. As you can well believe, this was something of a facer."

Owen moistened his lips. "You mean that Medlicot had sold them?"

"There was no other conceivable explanation. Only four people had the necessary knowledge, and three of them were men whom it would be quite ridiculous to suspect. Besides"—Greystoke gave the faintest possible shrug—"we have a written confession which settles the matter beyond question. He must have posted it just before he shot himself."

"It seems unbelievable." Owen sat for an instant staring silently at his companion. "I ran across Medlicot once at

Harwich, and he struck me as being a thoroughly decent fellow. What made him do such a damnable thing?"

"Ah! Now we are coming to the point. You know your way about the West End, Bradwell. I don't want you to think that I have been delving impertinently into your private affairs, but I am informed that you are one of those fortunate mortals who are not entirely dependent on their pay, and that when you have a spot of leave you generally put in a day or two in Town. Is that correct?"

Owen nodded. "My father left me quite comfortably off, sir, and I have a good many friends in London. I like to look them up every now and then."

"Quite so. Ever heard of a man named Mark Craig?"

"Mark Craig? Sounds vaguely familiar, but I can't place him at the moment."

"He runs a club in Grosvenor Street—very posh, expensive place where a crowd of rich people go to play poker. It's called the Mayflower."

"Oh, yes, I remember now, sir. I have never been there myself, but I have met blokes who belong to it."

"You have met one, anyhow. Medlicot was a member. If he hadn't enjoyed that distinction he would probably be alive now."

"You mean he had been losing money there, sir?"

"Quite a lot, I imagine. We have no actual proof of that, but everything seems to point to it. I fancy that he was being threatened with exposure, and that in a moment of desperation he sold those plans in order to settle up his debts."

"But couldn't you find out for certain?"

"Not so easy, Bradwell. We did our utmost, of course, but in a case of suicide people are uncommonly shy about giving anything away. Don't want to be dragged into a scandal."

"Wasn't there an official inquiry?"

"A very private one. You see, the mischief was done, and there was no sense in advertising the fact to the whole world. Besides, we had grounds for suspecting a certain highly placed gentleman at the German Embassy. If his name had cropped up the fat would have been in the fire. Our ingenuous government still seem to be under the illusion that they can scrape through without going to war, and to bring a charge of that nature against a prominent Hun diplomat without cast-iron evidence to back it up—well, the mere suggestion would be sufficient to throw the whole Foreign Office into hysterics."

"But surely something ought to be done, sir? If they can get hold of one set of plans—"

"They might be tempted to repeat the experiment? Exactly. You have hit upon the very point which is at present giving my particular department an outsize in headaches. I can assure you that the Mayflower Club and its proprietor are a subject of the deepest interest to us."

"Who is this fellow Mark Craig, sir? Is that his real name?"

"So far as I know. He is an Irish American who has spent most of his early life in the States. He came over here six years ago with a certain amount of cash, and very soon afterwards he launched out in his present racket in Grosvenor Street. He must be a clever devil—I'll give him credit for that. The place was a success from the first, and although the police have been keeping an eye on it they have never caught him out in any actual infringement of the law. All the same, they are convinced that he's a bad lot, and that when he sees the chance he has no objection to doing a bit of blackmailing. My own belief is that he's a Nazi agent, and that he is being subsidised from Berlin."

"Isn't that good enough, sir? Can't you have him arrested and locked up?"

"Might be arranged, but it would only mean that the work would be handed over to somebody else. As it is, we at least have the advantage of knowing where the mischief is likely to be hatched. Unfortunately, if the thing is as well organised as it appears to be, Mr. Craig and his friends are probably pretty well posted with regard to our own activities. I have several first-class men working under my direction, but I wouldn't mind betting a hundred pounds that every one of them is either known or suspected. When it comes to spying the Hun does his job thoroughly."

Owen looked straight into the shrewd grey eyes that were fixed steadily on his own. "I take it that you have some special reason for telling me all this, sir."

"Naturally." The other leaned back in his chair. "I think you might be useful to me, Bradwell. You are being given two months' sick leave, and if you feel like putting your services at my disposal for that period I am quite prepared to accept your offer. The whole arrangement, of course, would be strictly unofficial."

"Sounds all right to me, sir. I don't imagine I should be much good as a detective, though."

"Possibly not. Still, Carmichael is a fairly sound judge of character, and if his statements about you are correct, I believe we are justified in making the experiment." Greystoke gave another of his oddly attractive smiles. "After all, there is a certain amount of scientific evidence in favour of such a proceeding. According to Edridge-Green, who is the principal authority on the subject, people who suffer from colour-blindness are generally above the average in intelligence. Perhaps that is why it is so rare amongst our Cabinet Ministers."

Owen laughed.

"Well, what have you got to say about it? Does the prospect appeal to you?"

"I should be delighted to have a try, sir."

"Excellent. I had better explain what I have in my mind. As I told you a moment ago, we are keeping a close eye on the Mayflower Club, and also on its distinguished clientele. Two of my staff are actually members, but since it's more than likely that our friend Mr. Craig is well aware of the fact, I should imagine that any dirty work he may be arranging to pull off will probably be discussed somewhere else. The most likely place I can think of would be Otter's Holt, the island he owns down at Thames Ferry. Do you happen to know it by any chance?"

"I know where it is, sir. About three miles below Playford."

"That's right." Greystoke nodded. "He bought it last year, and I understand he goes down there most week-ends. Occasionally, I believe, he entertains friends. Now I could have the place watched, of course, either by my own people or by fixing things up with the local police. The trouble is that I daren't take the risk. If Craig is really using it as his private headquarters any hint that we are showing an interest in it would put him on his guard immediately. Whoever I selected myself might be known to him by sight, and in a Thames village a plain-clothes policeman lounging about the towpath would stick out like a lighted buoy. No, what I want is something quite different—some normal, harmless young holidaymaker who will fit naturally into the land-scape. Get the idea?"

"I think so, sir." Owen grinned. "It's a funny coincidence, but I really had some notion of putting in a day or two on the river, and, oddly enough, in that very neighbourhood. I am staying with a pal who has a punt laid up at Playford, and he told me I could borrow it whenever I liked."

"Looks as though Providence were taking a hand in the game. What I am most anxious to obtain is a list of Mr. Craig's visitors. I should be glad to have an accurate description of everyone who sets foot on the island, but the gentleman I am chiefly interested in is our friend from Carlton House Terrace. If there is any further trouble brewing he is pretty sure to be somewhere in the offing."

"What sort of a chap is he, sir?"

"A man of about forty. Tall, long-faced fellow with very thin lips. Generally sports an eyeglass. His name—for Heaven's sake keep this to yourself—is Manstein, Count Conrad von Manstein. He is that unpleasant mixture, a cross between a Prussian Junker and a genuinely fanatical Nazi, about the worst abortion that nature has yet produced. Exactly what his position is at the Embassy I don't know. Some people say that he is Hitler's personal representative, but the only thing I am practically certain of is that he was the moving spirit in the Medlicot affair. I regard him as the most dangerous man we are up against—a cunning, cold-blooded brute, utterly ruthless and without the slightest trace of fear in his whole composition."

"Sounds rather an ugly customer," remarked Owen cheerfully. "Well, I ought to be able to recognise him from your description." He paused. "I think the best thing I can do will be to drift down there Thursday or Friday and hang around doing a bit of fishing below the weir. Lots of people spend their week-ends that way, so it won't attract any particular attention. I've just remembered something else, too. There's a pub in the backwater opposite, and if I keep my ears open I may pick up a few useful hints. Sure to be a certain amount of gossip floating about—always is in those riverside joints."

"Very sound programme." Greystoke nodded approvingly. "You will have to be careful, though—damned careful. Remember that we are dealing with people who stick at nothing, and if it came to their notice that you were asking questions about Otter's Holt it's more than possible that they might turn exceedingly nasty. I should hate to pick up the Sunday paper and read about your body being fished out of the river!"

"I shan't overlook that fact, sir."

"Good! I am not over-sanguine about the business as it is, but you would certainly be no use to me as a corpse. On the contrary, I should find you a confounded nuisance." Pulling a slip of paper towards him, the speaker jotted down a telephone number and passed it across the table. "If you have news for me you can ring me up. Don't say anything over the phone, and don't on any account come here again unless you have a definite appointment. Is that quite plain?"

"Absolutely, sir."

"Then the only other point is the question of funds. As I have said, this little experiment is entirely unofficial, but at the same time it would be unfair to expect you to dip into your own pocket." Greystoke unlocked a drawer and produced a small packet of notes. "You had better take ten pounds to cover your immediate expenses. Judging from my own recollections, riverside inns are apt to be a trifle exorbitant in their charges."

With a word of thanks Owen slipped the money into his pocket, and then, picking up his hat, rose to his feet.

"Very good of you to give me this chance of doing something, sir," he said quietly. "I only hope I don't let you down."

"It wouldn't be the first time I had undergone that experience." The Captain's eyes twinkled, and getting up also, he held out his hand. "If it's any encouragement, though, I have an odd faith in you, Bradwell. I may be superstitious, but I feel that you have been sent along here for this particular purpose." He paused, "And on the rare occasions when I do get a hunch," he added, "it generally turns out to be a winner."

Chapter IV

"More tea?"

"No, thanks." Mark Craig put down his cup and lighted a cigarette. Then, settling himself back comfortably, he half closed his heavily lidded eyes and contemplated his hostess with a kind of slow, sensuous satisfaction.

It must be admitted that Olga Brandon was well worth inspection. Even the ultra-modern room, with its steel chairs, its glass table and its inevitable cocktail cabinet, did little to detract from the dark, exotic beauty inherited from her Romanian mother, for which only a dream palace out of some opium-inspired romance by Mr. Coleridge would really have provided an appropriate setting. That it should triumph so successfully over the chill bleakness of an up-to-date St. John's Wood villa was perhaps the finest tribute that could be offered in its honour.

"Well," demanded Craig, "what's this latest bit of news that you were hinting at? Anything really useful?"

"I guess so." Olga smiled complacently. "Like to have the low-down on a new airfield, wouldn't you, especially if it happens to be on the east coast?"

"A new airfield! Where did you get your information?"

"From a boy I met at a night-club about three weeks ago. He fell for me with a crash, and since then he has been taking me out quite a lot. Seems to have plenty of the needful, so I thought I might as well cultivate him."

"What's his name?"

"Forsyth—Desmond Forsyth. Boring as Hell, but right out of the top drawer—Eton and Oxford and all that sort of stuff. His father has got a big place up in Norfolk—owns about half the county, apparently."

"That must be Sir George Forsyth." Craig nodded. "I know something about him. Goes in for yacht racing, and used to be a Member of Parliament at one time."

"Very likely." Olga shrugged.

"What did this boy tell you?"

"Oh, he was a bit oiled and chucking his money about in the way kids like that do. I asked him whether he could really afford it, and he said that just at the moment he was particularly flush because his old man had pulled off a good deal and sent him along a cheque. Didn't want to talk about it at first, and that made me curious. I jockeyed him into having two or three more drinks, and then out he came with the whole yarn. Seems that the Air Ministry have taken over some of the family property and stumped up handsomely. Very hush-hush affair, of course, and I wasn't to breathe a word to a soul. Wouldn't have mentioned it if he hadn't known that I could be absolutely trusted."

"Did you find out the exact site?"

"Think I'm dumb?" Olga laughed. "It's a three-mile stretch just south of a place called King's Welcome. Nice lonely bit of country as flat as a pancake. They've got a gang of men working there already, railing it off with barbed wire. Going to be one of the biggest aerodromes in England when it's finished—everything O.K. and slap up-to-date."

"Sounds decidedly interesting." Craig gave an approving nod. "I must congratulate you on a smart job of work."

"Thanks, but I wasn't looking for compliments. What I could do with is something a bit more solid. Surely the right dope on a new airfield—"

"You can leave that to me. Our friends are always prepared to pay for what they want. They are too clever to be mean about trifles."

Olga Brandon sat silent for a moment, staring thoughtfully at the speaker's face.

"You believe in them thoroughly, don't you, Mark? You haven't the slightest doubt that they are going to pull it off?"

"None whatever. Within two years at the utmost the Germans will be the masters of the whole of Europe. Nothing can prevent it."

"You will be a very important man." Olga's fingers tightened. "You will have money—money and power."

"A good deal of both if all goes well. One has to take risks, of course."

"How long do you think it will be before things begin to happen?"

"They are happening now. Preparations are going on night and day everywhere." The clock on the mantelpiece tinkled out the half-hour, and glancing across the room, Craig pushed back his chair.

"What's the matter? You're not off yet, are you?"

"I must get along to the Club. I have an appointment for six-thirty. By the way, I believe you've met the man—a fellow called Granville Sutton."

"What does he want?"

"Haven't a notion. He rang up this morning while I was out, and Casey gave him a date. All I know about him is that he's got a bungalow at Playford and that he used to be rather thick with that young fool Medlicot."

"He couldn't make any trouble, could he?"

"Only for himself, I should say." Craig gave an ugly laugh. "It's probably nothing of any importance; still, I thought I had better see him and find out." He moved forward to where Olga was sitting, and bending down, kissed her on the lips. "One-thirty at the Milan to-morrow then, and it's just possible that I may have some good news for you. No, don't trouble to disturb yourself, my dear. I have been here often enough to find my way out."

◇◇◇

The taxi swerved round the corner into Grosvenor Street, and pulled up in front of a house on the north-west side. It was a large, four-storey house with a discreetly prosperous appearance. Neatly kept flower-boxes adorned the lower windows, and on one of the two pillars which sheltered the handsome door in the centre could be observed a small brass plate engraved with the words "The Mayflower Club." Except for this laconic announcement one would have taken it to be the Town residence of some affluent or distinguished family.

"Paper, sir?"

A passing newsvendor halted inquiringly, and purchasing a late *Star*, Craig paid off the driver and moved leisurely across the pavement. The door was opened by a stalwart commissionaire who gave him a respectful salute, and passing through a handsomely furnished hall, he jerked back the gate of an automatic lift. A few moments later he was stepping out on to the top landing—a small private suite shut off from the rest of the establishment which he had had fitted up for his own use.

The apartment he entered was a cross between an office and an expensively equipped sitting-room. At one end of it an American desk and a couple of large filing cabinets took up most of the available space, but everywhere else there was a suggestion of solid—even luxurious—comfort, the most noticeable example of which was the deep, cushion-piled, leather divan that occupied the whole corner between the window and the fireplace. Judging by the pictures that decorated the walls, a generous appreciation of the nude in art was one of their owner's principal characteristics.

Moving over to the desk, Craig glanced through a small pile of letters which had arrived by the midday post. Most of them he tossed into the waste-paper basket, and leaving the remnant to be attended to later on, settled down in the nearest arm-chair and unfolded his copy of the *Star*. Then, pulling out his note-case, he extracted a slip of paper containing a list of the bets which he had made earlier in the day. At that precise moment several thousand other inhabitants of Great Britain were doubtless engaged in the same hopeful occupation.

He was in the act of turning to the racing news when a lavishly splashed headline on the front page suddenly arrested his attention. Almost simultaneously his eyes fell upon the opening paragraph below. The muscles of his jaw tightened, and bending forward over the column in question, he began to read it with a tense and concentrated interest.

DARING ESCAPE FROM DARTMOOR
Convict Scales Prison Wall

Early this morning a convict named James Wilson, who is serving a seven-years sentence for embezzlement, effected what may justly be described as the most ingenious and daring escape from Dartmoor prison that has ever been recorded in the annals of that famous institution. During the summer months from May to September prisoners have their breakfast at six-thirty. The meal is

served in a large building situated in
the main courtyard. It is prepared in a
neighbouring shed some ten yards away,
the trays being carried across by specially selected men, all of whom must
have earned full remission marks for good
conduct before being detailed for this
particular duty. Between each delivery
there is an interval of perhaps twelve
seconds, and throughout the proceedings
an armed warder is constantly patrolling
the yard. Only for one brief period is
he actually out of sight of the short
passage between the two buildings.

Wilson, who was evidently waiting
his chance and must have made his plans
with meticulous care, was released from
his cell at the customary hour of a
quarter-past six. The warder on duty
failed to detect anything amiss, though
a more thorough investigation would
have revealed several highly interesting facts. During the night Wilson had
occupied himself in tearing his under
blanket into long strips and then knot-
ting the ends of them together so as to
construct a rough but fairly service-
able rope. To this he had attached the
strong canvas slip which provided the
covering for his bolster, fastening the
whole contraption round his waist with
such skill that it successfully escaped
the perfunctory examination to which he
must have known from experience that he
would probably be subjected.

On arriving at the cook-house he took
his place among the other men, and in due
course was handed the tray which it was
his duty to carry across to the adjacent
breakfast hall. Instead of doing so he

made his way quickly towards a large heap of gravel that had been deposited inside the yard a few days previously. Here he put down the tray, and having removed the rope which encircled his waist, hastily proceeded to load the canvas bolster slip from the convenient dump beside him. Taking advantage of the moment when the patrolling warder was out of sight he then flung up the weighted bag with such accuracy that it impaled itself upon the iron spikes at the top of the fourteen-foot wall. For an active man the rest was comparatively simple. Within a few seconds the resourceful Mr. Wilson was astride the coping, where, unhooking his amateur rope ladder, he lowered himself by his arms and dropped on the soft turf outside. It is believed that this gymnastic feat must have been witnessed by a fellow convict who was the next to leave the shed, but, true to the proverbial honour that prevails among wrongdoers, the man in question stoutly denies having observed any such dramatic incident. Although one or two local farm hands were in the neighbourhood at the time, the fact that there was a considerable amount of mist would explain why none of them has been able to add anything further to what the authorities already know.

As some ten minutes appear to have elapsed before the alarm was raised, Wilson must have had time to reach the shelter of one of the large straggling plantations that adjoin the prison. Since then nothing has been seen or heard of him. An intensive search of the surrounding moor, however, is now in progress,

and with all the roads watched and every
car and vehicle being held up for examination, it is not considered likely that
the fugitive's spell of liberty will be
of very long duration. Contrary to the
popular belief, founded upon sensational
films and novels, every prisoner who has
so far escaped from Dartmoor has been
recaptured. In the majority of cases men
give themselves up voluntarily on account
of the hunger and exposure to which they
are subjected.

◇◇◇

For several seconds after he had finished reading Craig sat
staring straight in front of him, his underlip stuck out, his
thick eyebrows drawn together in a reflective scowl. Then,
getting up abruptly and moving back to the desk, he pressed
one of the three buttons which stood in a row beside the
large writing-pad. It was apparent that his interest in the
day's racing had been temporarily overshadowed.

After a short interval the door opened quietly, admitting a
dark-haired, sleek-looking man of about forty with an oddly
expressionless face. He was wearing a well-cut morning suit
and had a red carnation in the buttonhole of his coat.

"Didn't know you were back," he observed, glancing at
the opened letters. "I was wondering whether you'd forgotten that appointment with Sutton."

"No, I remembered it all right." Craig paused. "Seen the
evening paper?"

"Not yet. Anything special in it?"

"Have a look at this story on the front page."

Mr. Paul Casey, the highly efficient manager of the Mayflower, took the *Star* which his employer held out to him. The
next moment a low, surprised whistle escaped from his lips.

"Wilson, by all the saints! Done a bunk from Dartmoor, has he? Well, damn my soul, I'd——"

"Read it," said Craig curtly.

Complying with the order, Casey perched himself on the arm of a chair and ran his eye swiftly down the column. That the news had considerably startled him had been obvious from his first reaction, but now that he had had time to recover, his face betrayed no further sign of emotion. Not until he had reached the end did he offer anything in the way of a comment.

"Got more guts than I gave him credit for," he remarked, looking up from the paper. "Never be certain with fellows like that. What do you imagine his game is?"

"I should say that he had only one idea in his head." Craig spoke with complete calmness. "That's to come up here and stick a knife into me. It's what he threatened to do the last time I had the pleasure of seeing him."

Casey raised his eyebrows. "Mean that seriously?"

The other nodded. "I know his type. They're easy enough game, but once they've got hold of the notion that somebody's been leading them up the garden they're apt to go clean off the rails. Wouldn't mind betting that for the last two years Wilson has been sitting in his cell thinking of nothing else but how to get level with us. Became a sort of fixed idea, as the French call it. Otherwise he'd never have been such an idiot as to break out of prison."

"Shouldn't wonder if you're right: you generally are. All the same, I don't think we need lose any sleep over it." Casey shrugged. "It's a longish step from Dartmoor to Grosvenor Street, and——"

"I'm quite aware of that fact, and I'm not in the least worried. The odds are that he'll be inside again within forty-eight hours. Still, there's just the bare chance he might give them the slip; and that being the case, it's only common sense to keep our eyes open. How about Johnson? D'you suppose he'd recognise the fool if he spotted him hanging around here?"

"Bound to, I should think. Shall I give him the tip?"

"No, I'll speak to him myself, that will be best. Don't start talking about it in the Club, but if you should happen to hear any of them airing their views to-night I'd be interested to know what they've got to say." Craig looked at his watch. "Well, it's just on the half-hour, so I suppose this fellow Sutton will be showing up in a minute. No idea what he wants, but he was by way of being a friend of Medlicot, so he may need a bit of careful handling. I'd like you to bring him up yourself and wait in the other room. If I switch on the light it will mean that I've had enough of him and you can come in with a telephone message or something."

"Right you are. I'll go down to the hall and collect him there."

With an understanding nod Casey took his departure, and picking up the discarded paper, Craig settled down again to his interrupted research into the results of the Epsom meeting. The discovery that one of the two horses which he had coupled together in a highly promising double had been beaten in the last stride by a short head was scarcely calculated to improve his temper. Fate at the moment was obviously in a malicious mood; and when the muffled clang of the lift gate suddenly reached his ears, it was with a singularly inhospitable expression that he swung round to face the door.

By contrast, the man who entered in company with Casey seemed to be remarkably at his ease. About thirty years of age, good-looking and faultlessly dressed, he carried himself with that air of slightly insolent confidence which in the case of a large number of women appears to invest its owner with an immediate and almost irresistible attraction. The only blemish to which a captious critic might have drawn attention was the undeniable fact that his eyes were set a shade too closely together.

"Happened to run across Mr. Sutton down in the hall," announced Casey blandly. "He reminded me that he had an appointment for six-thirty, so I've brought him up straight away."

"Ah yes, I've got a note of it here." Without any visible sign of enthusiasm Craig pushed forward a chair. "Won't you sit down and help yourself to a cigarette? I seem to know your name, but I don't think I've had the pleasure of meeting you before."

"Not that I can remember, though, as a matter of fact, we are fairly close neighbours." In a lazily assured fashion the visitor took possession of the proffered seat. "I have a bungalow at Playford, about a couple of miles above Otter's Holt."

"Indeed, is that so?" Craig's voice suggested a certain lack of interest.

"Well, I've plenty to do, so I dare say you'll excuse me." With what was presumably intended to be an affable smile Casey faded out on to the landing. The next instant the door closed softly behind him, and the other two occupants of the room were left facing each other in silence. Craig had resumed his seat and was tapping his leg with an ivory paper-knife which he had picked up off the desk.

"I presume that you wished to see me on a matter of business," he observed. "I haven't a great deal of time at my disposal, so perhaps it would be as well if we came to the point."

"By all means." Sutton took a leisurely draw at his cigarette. "I have a certain proposition I should like to put before you, but, to begin with, I think that a little preliminary explanation might help to clear the ground. It would give you a better idea of my position in the matter, and probably have some effect on your attitude with regard to my suggestion."

"Please yourself; only be as quick as you can."

"About four months ago I had a rather curious and distressing experience." Sutton drawled out the words with what appeared to be intentioned deliberation. "I was going home late one night when I bumped into a friend of mine. It was that poor devil Medlicot who shot himself a day or two afterwards. By the way, wasn't he a member of your Club?"

"Yes, he used to drop in here every now and then." Craig spoke with an admirably assumed carelessness. "Struck me as being a pleasant, attractive sort of chap. Terrible affair his shooting himself like that—last thing in the world I'd have expected from a man of his type."

"Seems to have taken everyone by surprise. Have you any idea what made him do it?"

"Money troubles of some sort, apparently. I only know what came out at the inquest."

"Perhaps I can add a little to that. You see, on the night I met him Medlicot was in a pretty queer state. Looked as if he was badly up against it and had been playing around a bit too freely with the whisky. Thought he'd probably land himself in trouble if I didn't do something about it, so I took him up to my place to give him a chance to cool off. Naval officers can't afford to be arrested in Piccadilly."

"Very sporting of you. It isn't everybody who would be so considerate."

"Always delighted to do a pal a good turn. Besides, sometimes it pays one handsomely. In the present case, for instance, if I hadn't felt sorry for Medlicot and tried to be helpful I shouldn't have enjoyed the advantage of being— how shall I put it—taken into his confidence." Sutton paused. "It's also highly improbable that I should be sitting here at the present moment."

"I fail to grasp the connection between the two events. I liked Medlicot well enough in a way, but he was never an intimate friend of mine. What was your object in coming to me? If you have any inside information why didn't you attend the inquest and give your evidence there?"

"I never act hastily: it's nearly always a mistake. One is so apt to throw away the substance for the shadow."

Once again Craig glanced at his watch. "You must forgive me reminding you that I am a rather busy man. Unless you have something really definite—"

"I have. Extremely definite." Sutton still spoke in the same quiet drawl. "As a result of that little chat with Medlicot, and of certain facts that have come to my knowledge since then, I have arrived at the conclusion that you are playing a highly profitable but, if you don't mind my saying so, a damned dangerous game. To put it quite frankly and precisely, you are working for the Germans."

Except for a slight narrowing of the eyes Craig's face remained absolutely unaltered.

"I don't know whether you are mad or whether this is intended to be a joke. If you are playing the fool, I warn you that there are very distinct limits to what I'm prepared to put up with."

"It would be a pity if you threw me out before I had finished. You would certainly regret it."

"I don't propose to waste my time listening to drivelling nonsense."

"No, that would be too much to expect. Perhaps I can simplify matters by giving you a short summary of what I conceive to be the exact situation. If I am doing you an injustice in any particular detail don't hesitate to correct me."

Craig remained silent, still swinging the paper-knife in his long, powerful fingers.

"By some means or other," continued Sutton, "possibly through the German Secret Service, you discovered that our friend Medlicot was in possession of a set of drawings which the authorities in Berlin were desperately anxious to get hold of. Acting, no doubt, on instructions from your employers, you and some of your crowd worked out a very pretty little scheme for what I believe is vulgarly called 'putting him on the spot.' You knew that he was a keen poker player and inclined to get a bit reckless when he'd had a few drinks, so you arranged for some faked games, in the first two or three of which he was naturally allowed to win. Then, as soon as you'd got him in the right frame of mind, you—well, you pulled your stuff. He dropped four thousand in one night, and when he had to admit that he couldn't settle up you threatened to bring an action against him. That would have meant his being sacked from the Service. At this point, just as he was at his wits' end a certain obliging gentleman butted in and offered to put up the money. The only condition he made was that he should be allowed to take a tracing of the drawings, which, according to his own story, he intended to pass on to the United States Government. Tempting proposal to a man in Medlicot's position. Of course he shouldn't have accepted—very wrong and unpatriotic of him—but still, human nature being what it is, one can't help feeling rather sorry for the poor chap. After all"—Sutton leaned forward coolly and tipped off the end of his cigarette—"however stupid he may have been, he paid for it with his life."

There was a silence which lasted for several seconds.

"Do you really expect me to attach the slightest importance to this rubbish?"—Craig gave a short, contemptuous laugh. "If you do, you must be off your head. Why, on your own showing, all it's based on are the maunderings of a drunken young crook."

"I'd hardly say that. I have taken quite a lot of trouble to verify some of Medlicot's statements, and without wishing to flatter myself I think I can claim to have been fairly successful. Just as a sample, for instance, I can give you the real name of the 'American' gentleman who came forward so conveniently with the cash. It's von Manstein—Count Conrad von Manstein. He is a personal friend of Hitler, and I am rather inclined to credit him with being the head of the whole Nazi spy system in England. Seeing that he has twice been down to Otter's Holt during the last six weeks, I take it that you're on remarkably good terms. Indeed, I shouldn't be altogether surprised if it was you who introduced him to Medlicot."

"You ought to make a fortune with an imagination like yours. Why don't you go along to Scotland Yard and ask them what they will offer you for your story?"

"Because I think I have a better market. I feel certain that when you and your friends have talked the matter over quietly you will realise the advantage of accepting my proposal."

Craig laughed again. "We may as well play the farce out if it affords you any satisfaction. What is this handsome offer which you are kind enough to submit to my consideration?"

"I have no wish to be unreasonable. If you will give me five thousand in one-pound notes you can count upon my keeping my mouth shut. Otherwise I shall feel it my duty to report the facts to the Home Office."

With a contemptuous movement Craig pushed back his chair till it bumped up against the side of the desk.

"You must be an even bigger fool than I imagined. Assuming, for the moment, that there was a grain of truth in all this trash, do you suppose that anyone in their senses would put the slightest trust in a blackmailing skunk like you? What guarantee would they have that you wouldn't turn up the next day and ask for double the amount?"

"That's a difficulty which I think we might be able to get over." Sutton smiled pleasantly. "You mustn't assume that you are the only people in England who are capable of exercising a little intelligence. I, for one, agree with you entirely.

In my opinion this country is finished. We have no Army and practically no Air Force. France is rotten from top to bottom, and as soon as the Germans have settled with her they'll start bombing hell out of us, until we chuck in the sponge and howl for mercy. No good expecting any help from the States: we shall be down and out before they can make up their minds."

"Very interesting," sneered Craig. "So you are a prophet as well as blackmailer! Is that supposed to inspire confidence?"

"It should, in anyone who isn't a nitwit. Like our deceased neighbour the Vicar of Bray, I have a natural preference for being on the winning side. You may point that out to von Manstein, and you can suggest that by securing the use of my services for his organisation he would be making an uncommonly good bargain. I should expect to be treated generously, of course; but I take it that, with so much at stake, money is not a question of primary importance. I think I have already proved that my collaboration might be distinctly valuable. However, if you still have any doubts on the subject, I may mention that I have not quite exhausted my stock of information. I can produce several more curious facts which I fancy you would much prefer that I should keep to myself."

"And what do you expect me to do now?" Craig had risen to his feet and was standing beside the desk. "Pull open a drawer and hand you over five thousand pounds?"

"Nothing as dramatic as that. I realise that you are acting under instructions and that you will have to submit the question to your employers. I suggest that you have a nice heart-to-heart talk with von Manstein, and, if he is sensible enough to accept my terms, that you arrange for us to meet again next week. I have no objection to waiting a few days. I intend to go down to Playford to-morrow, and shall be staying at the bungalow until Monday. I am on the telephone, so you will be able to give me a ring there and let me know what you have fixed up. Perhaps we might lunch together at the Milan. When one is engaged upon these kind of delicate and dangerous negotiations I feel that the easiest plan is to meet somewhere in public. It seems to give both sides a greater sense of security—don't you agree with me?"

Before Craig could reply there was a tap at the door, followed almost simultaneously by the appearance of Mr. Paul Casey.

"Sorry if I'm interrupting you." The manager came forward, holding out what appeared to be a typewritten letter. "It's a rather urgent note from those wine people we wrote to. I think we ought to send them a reply straight away."

"As a matter of fact, I was just going." Sutton rose casually and picked up his hat which was lying on the table. "I fancy we understand each other pretty thoroughly," he continued, turning to his host, "and I shall look forward to hearing from you during the week-end. Sure to find me in any time up till eleven."

"You might take our visitor down with you, Casey." Craig nodded towards the lift. "I'll have a look through this and let you know what I want done about it."

For several moments after the other two had disappeared he stood where he was, scowling thoughtfully at the closed door. Then, giving himself an impatient shake, he sat down in front of the desk, and lifting off the receiver, commenced to dial a number. After a brief interval his efforts were rewarded by a slightly guttural "Hello!"

"Mr. Mark Craig speaking," he announced. "Is that Count von Manstein's flat?"

There was an affirmative grunt.

"Who are you—Frederick?"

"Yes, sir."

"Is the Count in?"

"I am afraid not, sir. He has been out of Town since Tuesday."

"When are you expecting him home?"

"Some time to-morrow, sir. I am not certain when he will actually arrive."

"Very well. I will write a note and send it round. Be sure you give it to him directly he gets back."

"I will do so without fail, sir."

Replacing the telephone and producing a fountain-pen from his inside pocket, Craig pulled forward a sheet of note-paper. It was stamped at the top with the Club address. He began to write slowly, pausing at the end of each sentence as though to reconsider what he had already set down.

My dear Von Manstein,

There has been a very unpleasant and distinctly dangerous development in connection with the Medli-cot affair. I won't enter into details now, but it is most important that I should see you as soon as possible. I had fixed up to go down to Otter's Holt to-night, and as your man tells me that you will not be back in Town until to-morrow there appears to be no point in altering my plans. I should be much obliged, however, if you would give me a ring at Thames Ferry directly you return. Should you be free, why not come down and stay the night? That, I think, would be the best arrangement, but if you are too busy and unable to get away I could, of course, run up to London and meet you either here or at your flat. The matter is most urgent, and we can't afford to waste an unnecessary minute. I am sending this round by hand so as to make quite certain of its safe arrival.

Yours sincerely,
Mark Craig.

Once again he read it through, and then, putting it into an envelope and carefully sticking the flap, pressed the same button by which he had previously summoned Casey. After a longish pause that gentleman presented himself in the doorway.

"Sorry to keep you waiting. Got collared in the hall by that old bore Sir John Tanner. He's thinking of throwing a party here to-morrow."

"That's all right: he can afford to pay for it. See he has everything he wants." Craig held out the letter. "I'd like you to take this round to von Manstein's flat yourself and hand it to his servant. It's too important to trust to anyone else."

The other raised his eyebrows. "Anything to do with our departed friend?"

"Not altogether unconnected. Get back as soon as you can and we will run through these letters before I go."

Taking the envelope without further comment, Casey left the room. As he did so Craig rose to his feet, and walking slowly across to the window, stood gazing down at the passing traffic. Suddenly, and for no apparent reason, a thin, ugly smile flickered across his lips.

"Yes, you'll hear from us sure enough," he muttered. "You can put your money on that, Mr. Granville Sutton."

Chapter V

"Let's see. Watch, money, pipe, baccy, matches, cigarettes—that seems to be the lot." Owen paused reflectively, and then, stepping forward to the dressing-table, picked up an ancient leather wallet containing a cheque-book and two or three letters addressed to himself. "Better not take this—might lose it or drop it overboard." He grinned suddenly at his own reflection. "Besides, if I'm going to be a sleuth, may as well do the job properly. Wouldn't catch Sherlock Holmes cruising around with his name and address in his pocket."

Depositing the wallet in a drawer on top of some more of his belongings, he lifted down a small handbag from the bed, and made his way out into the passage. At the same instant the dignified figure of Watkins appeared from the kitchen. He was carrying a stout wicker-work basket, securely fastened by a leather strap with a convenient handle.

"This is Mr. Anstey's camping outfit, sir," he announced. "I think you will find everything you require except milk and bread. I presume that you will be able to procure them locally. The methylated spirit is in one of the larger flasks."

"Very kind of you, Watkins. Afraid I'm giving you a lot of trouble." Reaching up, Owen unhooked his raincoat from a peg on the hat-stánd.

"Not at all, sir! It's a pleasure. May I inquire how long you intend to be absent?"

"Depends on the weather. Provided it keeps like this I shall stay over the week-end. If it breaks up, that's another matter. Anyhow, should I decide to come back suddenly I'll give you a ring."

"Very good, sir. I hope you enjoy yourself and have some luck with the fishing. I have heard Mr. Anstey say that there are still a few big trout below the weir at Thames Ferry."

"Just where I propose to try." Owen set down his bag alongside the canvas-covered rod on the hall chest, and as he did so the sharp trill of a bell sounded through the flat. It was followed by a vigorous rat-tat on the knocker.

"That will be the car, I expect, sir."

Moving forward sedately, Watkins opened the door. A youngish-looking man in chauffeur's uniform who was standing outside took possession of the basket, and with a final word of farewell Owen gathered up the remainder of his luggage. In another moment or so he was clambering into the comfortable four-seater Daimler which an obliging hire company had placed at his disposal.

"Playford, isn't it, sir? Anywhere special you want to be put down?"

"You know Martin's boat-house?"

"Oh yes—been there several times."

"Well, that's where we're heading. You can take things easy: I'm in no particular hurry."

"O.K., sir."

With a casual nod the driver climbed into his seat, and before Owen had finished lighting his pipe to his complete satisfaction, they were bowling smoothly westward in the direction of Hammersmith.

Now that he had actually embarked on his adventure he was conscious of a feeling of exhilaration to which he had been a stranger ever since that fateful night in the Indian Ocean. With something definite to do, some really important task on which to concentrate his energies, the black cloud of depression so long hanging over his spirits seemed to have been suddenly and miraculously dispersed. The fact that he could still be of use, that he was not a mere piece of discarded lumber, was the precise tonic for which he had been unconsciously craving. It healed and restored his crippled sense of manhood, and as the car slipped across the crowded Broadway a little heart-felt grunt of satisfaction issued from his lips. Yes, it was fine to be on active service again, no matter how fantastically outside his own line this new commission appeared likely to prove.

What sort of figure he would cut as a private detective Heaven alone knew. That he possessed some qualifications must obviously be the opinion of both Captain Greystoke and his late skipper. It was impossible to believe that he would have been selected for a job of this nature without very serious consideration, and fail though he might to achieve anything sensational, he would at least do his utmost to justify their confidence. It was not merely a question of his own future career. By handling the affair successfully he would no doubt increase his chance of being offered further and perhaps more responsible duties, but the principal emotion that dominated his heart and mind was a grim desire to assist in smashing up this gang of spies and traitors whose evil activities seemed to be endangering the very honour and safety of his own beloved Service.

When he thought of Medlicot his lips tightened. Impossible as it was to feel the slightest sympathy for a man who had betrayed his country, such a sordid ending to what had promised to be a brilliant and valuable life could only be regarded as a pitiful tragedy. It filled him with an unspeakable loathing for Craig and the whole rotten crowd who were playing into the Nazis' hands. For vermin of that type merciless extermination was the obvious treatment, and the prospect of lending a hand in this desirable and highly patriotic task sent a warm thrill of pleasurable anticipation trickling down to the very depths of his being.

As to the best way in which to set about his mission, it was too soon as yet to make any exact plans. At present his idea was to drift leisurely down as far as Thames Ferry and establish himself for the week-end somewhere in the neighbourhood of Otter's Holt. The fishing tackle which he had brought with him would provide a plausible excuse for his presence on the spot, and by frequenting the inn and getting in contact with its regular patrons he would at least stand an excellent chance of familiarising himself with the local gossip.

For the rest, things must be left more or less to shape themselves. All he could do was to keep his eyes and ears wide open, and if he could detect the smallest likelihood of picking up any useful information be instantly and resolutely prepared to avail himself of the opportunity. Since that had been the whole essence of his training in the Navy the prospect was not quite so formidable as it might otherwise have appeared.

With this comforting reflection he decided that the most sensible course was to put the problem out of his mind and give himself up to enjoying his journey. It was a long time now since he had experienced the felicity of driving through the English countryside, and once they had turned off the Great West Road and exchanged the monotonous procession of up-to-date factories for green fields and straggling hedgerows, a lazy and restful contentment began to lap him round like an invisible tide. The day was incredibly perfect, one of those warm, still, autumn mornings when the declining year seems to be sitting outside its own front door basking happily in the belated sunshine. A faint scent of burning leaves, the occasional splash of scarlet poppies which had escaped the harvester, the little clusters of midges hovering in the air as though waiting for a breeze to help them on their way, all alike combined to add their own particular touch to the mellow and enchanted atmosphere. That its continued existence should depend upon the whim of an epileptic house-painter appeared at the moment like an unbelievable nightmare.

A glimpse of a signpost bearing the inscription "Playford 1 mile" was the first indication that he was approaching his goal. Cottages and bungalows began to make their appearance, then a square church tower loomed up in the near distance, and through the open windows of a school came a shrill chorus of children's voices. Slowing down as it approached the centre of the village, the car ambled across a sleepy-looking market-place and turned into a narrow, poplar-bordered road that led down to the river. At the bottom of this stood a small, creeper-clad house flanked by a desultory collection of wooden sheds. Moored to the adjoining landing-stage were a number of punts and skiffs, the only living creature in sight being a large and distinctly surly-faced bull terrier, who was evidently keeping a watchful eye upon his master's property.

As the car pulled up, however, an elderly man with a short, grizzled beard sauntered out into the open. His costume consisted of a shirt and a pair of very ancient grey flannel trousers, and to judge by the towel which he was still carrying he had apparently been interrupted in the process of washing his hands. Paying off the driver and lifting out his equipment, Owen stepped hopefully forward.

"Are you Mr. Martin?"

The old man nodded.

"Good. My name's Bradwell. You remember I rang up yesterday and mentioned that I should be coming along."

"That's right. Said something about bringing a letter from Mr. Anstey."

"Here it is. Just a line to say that I can borrow one of his punts. It's the big one I want—going to make a week-end of it, and see if I can catch a few fish."

Very deliberately Mr. Martin read through the note, and then, nodding again as though satisfied with its authenticity, turned round in the direction of an adjacent shed.

"You there, 'Erbert?" he bellowed.

A tousle-haired youth poked his head through the doorway.

"Fetch out that there punt o' Mr. Anstey's, the one with the cover to it. Put the canvas in 'er, and see that the 'oops are all right. Git a move on, now, 'cause the gentleman's waitin'."

"Oh, I'm in no hurry." Owen smiled reassuringly and seated himself on an upturned canoe. "I've come down for a quiet holiday, and I am going to take things as easily as possible. It's the only way on the river if you really want to enjoy yourself."

"I've heard a lot more foolish remarks than that." Mr. Martin tilted back his cap and dabbed his forehead with the towel. "Pity more people don't think the same," he added. "If they did maybe trade would be a shade brisker."

"Had a poor season?"

"Shockin'. Cold as winter most o' the time, and rainin' hard pretty near every week-end. 'Tisn't so much the weather as I'm meanin', though—wouldn't alter things greatly no matter how fine it were. Dead an' done for, the boat business, if you ask me; and what's more, it ain't never likely to pick up again. Played clean out, the same as 'orses an' the music-'alls."

"Bad as that, eh? How do you account for it? There must be some explanation."

"Too slow for 'em, I reckon. Want to be on the move all the time nowadays. Like to 'op into a car and chase off to one o' them road-'ouses where they can dance 'alf the night and fill 'emselves up with gin. No use for lyin' about in a punt. Why, if they feels like a bit o' courtin' all they gotter do is to turn off the road and pull up behind a hedge."

"Sounds a bit cramped and uncomfortable, but perhaps I'm old-fashioned." Owen lit a cigarette and offered one to his companion. "You see, I have been out of England for a couple of years, and no doubt there have been all sorts of fresh developments. Do people still fish, or is that considered too Victorian?"

"We get a few at the week-end—furriners mostly. Find more o' them down Thames Ferry way."

"That's where I'm thinking of laying up. Mr. Anstey says that the most likely place is just below the weir, the farther side of the island. Tells me there's a pub somewhere close by where one can drop in for a pint in the evening."

"He'll be meanin' the Red Lion up the backwater. Aye, you couldn't do much better than stay around there. Old friend o' mine Ted Mellon, the landlord. Just you mention my name, and if there's anything you want he'll fix you up proper."

There was a sudden splashing sound in the direction of the river, and glancing round over his shoulder, Owen saw the nose of a punt emerging from the big shed at the end of the landing-stage. It was being piloted by 'Erbert.

"How about the island?" he inquired. "Do you happen to know who's living there now?"

"Party o' the name o' Craig. Bought it a couple o' years ago when the old General died. Can't tell you much about him 'cept that he's a Londoner."

"What sort of a chap is he? Had any dealings with him?"

Mr. Martin shook his head. "No, nor no one else neither. Don't suppose he's spent a tenner in the place not since he's been here. One of the kind that comes down for the weekend and brings his own stuff with him."

"Hardly the way to make himself popular."

"You've said it." The speaker removed his pipe and spat disgustedly.

"Anyone in the house the rest of the time, or does he just leave it empty?"

"There's the gardener or odd man, or whatever he calls himself. I've seen 'im messin' around when I been going past. Big, hefty-looking bloke with as ugly a clock as I've ever clapped me eyes on. Folks about 'ere say he's a dago and can't even talk proper English."

"Well, I don't suppose he'll interfere with my fishing." Owen laughed carelessly and hoisted himself up. "Anyhow, I intend to hang about off the island, and if he doesn't like it he can go to hell."

With a grim chuckle Mr. Martin stooped down and picked up the handbag.

"Now that's what I calls talkin', " he observed approvingly.

◇◇◇

Somewhere in the distance a clock chimed out the hour of seven. Its sound was just audible above the splashing of the weir, and rousing himself from his half-recumbent position, Owen sat up and began to reel in his line. The sun, now low down in the west, had already disappeared behind the trees on the opposite bank. A faint cooling breeze drifted across the river and sent little eddies and ripples chasing each other over its surface.

As he slowly dismantled his rod his eyes kept on wandering upstream to where the half-hidden chimneys of Otter's Holt peered out through their surrounding foliage. The island, which was perhaps a quarter of an acre in extent, lay about a hundred yards above the spot where he was moored. On one side of it was the weir, while on the other, broken by the narrow entrance to a small backwater, the main stream flowed past in a wide curving sweep. Slightly above this point stood a solitary wooden building with the words "Boats on Hire" painted along its roof.

It was from here, apparently, that a visitor wishing to cross over would be most likely to embark, but during the four hours which had slipped by since his arrival on the scene no such encouraging incident had occurred to break the monotony. Indeed, for all the traces of life it exhibited the island might have been deserted. In spite of the fact that he had been keeping it under careful and consistent observation he had learned absolutely nothing. Even the unprepossessing "gardener," to whom Mr. Martin had alluded, had obstinately declined to put in an appearance.

Feeling a shade disappointed at the negative results of his opening vigil, he uprooted the two poles which had been keeping him in position and began to punt across slowly in the direction of the backwater. He felt that his activities as a fisherman had already lasted long enough, and that for the time being it would be wiser to retire from the immediate neighbourhood. For all he knew, unseen eyes might be secretly observing his proceedings. To continue hanging around after dusk would be bound to arouse suspicion; and since he had no desire to attract more attention to himself than he could possibly avoid, a change of tactics appeared eminently desirable. Besides, regarding it purely from a personal point of view, he was badly in need of a drink. The thought of sitting in a bar with a large tankard of beer in front of him appealed strongly to his imagination, while it also possessed the additional advantage of being part and parcel of his prearranged campaign. After all, the sooner he got in touch with the local gossip the more likely he was to overhear something useful. For the moment, duty and inclination seemed to be pointing towards the same goal; a comforting and convenient arrangement that is too often foreign to their custom.

Passing into the backwater under a small iron bridge, he pushed his way along its winding course, ducking his head now and then to avoid one of the numerous overhanging branches. For about a couple of hundred yards the banks on either side were lined by a thick growth of bushes and willows, and then, as he rounded a bend into a slightly broader stretch, the back garden of the Red Lion made its sudden and welcome appearance.

It consisted of a narrow strip of lawn with an ancient cedar tree in the centre and a few weather-stained chairs and tables dotted about at discreet intervals. The borders were filled with a ragged array of dahlias and chrysanthemums, and at this late hour in the season the whole place presented a forlorn and somewhat neglected-looking aspect. Such encouragement as it offered to prospective customers was contained in the almost illegible notice affixed to a rustic arch which surmounted the landing-stage. So far as it could be deciphered it ran as follows:

YE OLD RED LYON INNE

Fully licensed

Teas Lunches Dinners First-Class Accommodation

There were several boats lying off the steps, and steering neatly in amongst them, Owen hitched up his punt and scrambled ashore. As he did so a small boy, who had emerged from some private hiding-place, came hurrying towards him with an air of hopeful expectancy.

"Look after your things, sir?"

"Who are you?" inquired Owen.

"Ernie Giles, sir. I lives 'ere. My Dad, 'e works for Mr. Mellon."

"Very well, here's sixpence. I'm going inside to have a drink and a bite of grub. If everything's safe and sound when I come back I'll make it a bob."

"Thankye, sir." Ernie pocketed the coin and squared his shoulders. "Don't you worry yerself, sir," he added confidently. "No one won't pinch nothin', not with me around."

Leaving his new-found friend in charge, Owen lit a cigarette and strolled leisurely up the lawn. The back of the inn was screened by a long, creeper-covered veranda, at one end of which was a partly open door with the word "Saloon" engraved upon its glass panel. Stepping through, he found himself in a small, snug, low-ceilinged bar, where a stout, rubicund-faced man who was standing behind the counter polishing a tankard looked up with a genial smile.

"Ah, good evenin', sir. Must 'ave come in through the backwater, didn't you? Thought I heard young Ernie speakin' to someone."

"Been fishing down below the weir," explained Owen. "Suddenly discovered it was seven o'clock and thought I'd slip across for a drink." He seated himself on a tall stool in the corner. "You're Mr. Mellon, I take it? If that's right, Mr. Martin, of Playford, told me to look you up and mention his name."

"Pleased to meet you. Anyone Tom Martin sends along is more than welcome at the Red Lion." The landlord put down his tankard. "Now what's it to be? You're having this one on the house."

"That's very kind of you—a little loose beer, I think." Owen produced a handkerchief and dabbed his forehead. "Thirsty job sitting in the sun, specially when the fish are as sulky as they were this afternoon."

"No luck, eh? Well, that's the way it goes sometimes."
Mr. Mellon filled up a large pewter pot and pushed it across.
"Not but what there's fish about there, you take my word for
it. Why, only last week Mr. Nelson, down at The Moorings,
he pulled out a three-and-a-half-pounder."

"That's encouraging news." Owen took a long, refreshing
draught and sighed contentedly. "Shows that one needn't
give up hope, anyhow. I'll make an effort to get up early
to-morrow, and perhaps—"

"Hullo, hullo—hope I'm not intrudin'!" The other door
of the bar swung open, admitting a breezy-looking, loud-
voiced individual who bore the unmistakable stamp of a successful commercial traveller. For a moment he stood posed
theatrically in the entrance, and then, striding forward to the
counter, thrust out his hand. "Why, Ted, you old scoundrel,
you don't look a day older than when I was in here last."

"Cor-love-my-soul, if it ain't Bert Summers!" The landlord hastened along to where the newcomer was standing,
and the two of them exchanged grips! "Well, well, well,
now—talk about the graves givin' up their dead—"

"Bit of a surprise, what?" Mr. Summers chuckled richly.
"Told me you was still here, and as I was passing pretty close
by I thought I'd switch off and pay you a call. Can't stop
more 'n a few minutes, though—on me way to Reading."

"Well, well, well," repeated Mr. Mellon. "Couldn't believe
me eyes, not when you walked in. Let's see now, must be
gettin' on for five years since we last had a drink together."

"All o' that," assented the other. "And talkin' o' drinks,
how about a couple o' nice doubles? Maybe this gentleman
will do me the honour of joining us?"

"Oh, I'm all right, thanks," protested Owen. "Just got a
whole pint of beer which I haven't started yet."

"What are you doin' in these parts, Bert?" demanded Mr.
Mellon as he splashed out the soda. "Bit outer yer reg'ler

beat, ain't it? Thought you was up in the Midlands some-where—Wolvr'ampton way, if I remember rightly."

"So I was till a couple o' months ago. Had a stroke o' luck then, as you might put it. Bloke who was representin' us in London went and hopped it, and who should drop in for the job but your old pal Bert. Was I glad to get it—oh, boy!"

"Didn't you hit it off with the folks up there, then?"

Mr. Summers shook his head. "No use for 'em," he replied darkly. "Wolvr'ampton by name and Wolvr'ampton by nature."

"That so, eh?"

"Take it from me." The speaker raised his glass. "Here's all the best, Ted, and how goes it with you? What about those two pretty kids o' yours—Gladys and Maysie? Come to think of it, they must be grown up by now."

"Grown up and married, both of 'em."

"You don't say!"

"That's a fact. Done well for 'erself, Gladys has. Got hitched up with a chap in the engineerin' line. Smart young feller and earnin' good money. Took 'er to Paris for the 'oneymoon and stayed at one o' them posh 'otels. Must 'ave run 'im in for a packet."

Mr. Summers clicked his tongue. "Going some, that is."

"You're right."

"Maysie picked a winner, too?"

"Well, in a manner o' speakin'. Leastways 'e's a gentleman. Son of a judge in India or somethin', and went to school at 'Arrer and Oxford. Mind yer, 'e ain't got any brass, not at present."

"How do they get along, then?"

"Managed to fix up with the Brewery to put 'em into a house at Windsor. Nice little place, but no trade worth talkin' of."

'Bit of a climb down for a toff like him."

'No gettin' away from that. Why, on'y the other day he was tellin' me that if six of 'is relations was to go up in an airyplane and that airyplane was to crash and they was all killed, *'e'd be a Duke.*"

'Go on!"

"Gospel truth!" Mr. Mellon paused. "And between you and me," he added wistfully, "it wouldn't be such a bad thing if they did, 'cause 'e's no bleedin' use as a publican."

"Can't have it all ways, not in this world." With a shake of his head Mr. Summers glanced at the clock, and then, raising his tumbler, gulped down the remainder of its contents.

"You ain't goin' just yet?" protested the landlord.

"Got to, I'm afraid. Promised to look in at a meetin' of the Buffs to-night, and I'll be late as it is, if I don't hurry." Once more he thrust out his hand. "Well, cheerio, Ted—treat to see you lookin' so frisky. I'll be droppin' round again one o' these days, and with any luck we'll have time for a proper yarn."

Cocking his hat at a jaunty angle and bestowing a farewell salute on Owen, Mr. Bert Summers moved briskly to the door. In another minute the spluttering throb of a car engine started up outside, and as though suddenly recalled to a sense of his duties as a host, the landlord picked up his glass and moved back along the counter.

"Old friend o' mine," he explained apologetically. "Used to see a lot of 'im at one time."

"Cheery sort of cove." Owen nodded. "Wonder why he's got such a down on the Midlands."

"Too refined for 'em, I reckon. Don't take no stock in good manners up there. Think you're puttin' on airs if you speak civil."

"Well, the best thing we can do is to have another drink. Short one for me this time—gin and orange, please. Any chance of your being able to fix me up with something to eat?"

"Why, certainly. Plenty o' cold stuff in the dining-room. Nice bit o' chicken and 'am, if you fancy that."

"Do me fine."

"Goin' back to Playford for the night, I s'pose?"

Owen shook his head. "I'm sleeping in the punt. It's such grand weather I felt I must have a last week out in the open." He tossed a half-crown across the bar, and took a sip from the small glass in front of him. "I think I'll try fishing a little farther up in the morning, rather closer to the island. By the way, is there anyone living there now?"

"Party o' the name o' Craig. Runs a club in the West End so I've heard tell."

"See much of him?"

"Next to nothin'. Stand-offish sort of cove—too high an' mighty to mix with the likes of us." Mr. Mellon shrugged scornfully. "Wouldn't even know 'e was 'ere, not if 'e 'adn't sent over a message this mornin'. Got a friend comin' down by the last train and wants my man Jim to take 'im across."

Owen's heart gave a sudden jump. "The last train!" he repeated. "Rather a late job, eh?"

"Won't be through till after eleven. Can't be 'elped, though! All part o' the day's work. You see, that's my boat-'ouse opposite the island, and if I started refusin' custom as like as not I'd 'ave trouble over the licence. 'Sides, Jim don't mind, not so long as he gets a good tip."

"Hope he does: he certainly deserves one." Stretching out his arms with a lazy yawn, Owen slid down off his stool. "Well," he demanded, "how about that chicken and ham? Think it will be ready if I drop in now?"

"That'll be O.K., sir. Just step across the passage and you'll find the dining-room right opposite. See you again afterwards per'aps, that's to say, if you ain't in no special 'urry to get off."

A contented smile flickered across Owen's face.

"I'm in no hurry at all," he declared truthfully.

II

Outside the stars were twinkling bravely, but under the thick trees that fringed the entrance to the backwater the darkness was intense. Once within its shelter anyone who was anxious to avoid observation could rest assured that he had achieved his purpose.

Sitting motionless in the punt and steadying himself with the aid of an overhanging branch, Owen stared across in the direction of the island. All he could see was the small, white-painted landing-stage with the black, uncertain bulk of the house looming up behind it. Both above and below the weir the river seemed to be deserted. Except for the steady splashing of the water and an occasional rustling sigh among the tree-tops everything was uncannily still. Even the two stately swans, who had been cruising up and down all the afternoon, appeared to have abandoned their activities and retired to rest.

A glance at the illuminated dial of his watch showed him that it was exactly ten-thirty. Before leaving the inn he had taken the precaution of consulting a time-table; and since, according to Mr. Bradshaw, the last train reached Thames Ferry at seventeen minutes past, it should not be long now before the belated visitor made his appearance. Somehow or other, he had a queer feeling that his luck was in. Though there was no real ground for the assumption, he found himself taking it almost for granted that the stranger would turn out to be von Manstein, that sinister and highly dangerous gentleman in whom the Admiralty were so acutely interested. Mere guesswork though it might be, the prospect of actually witnessing the German's arrival and being able to pass on the information to Greystoke filled him with elation; and registering a vow to make all the use he could of such a

Heaven-sent opportunity, he edged in a shade closer to the bank and patiently resumed his vigil.

After what seemed an interminably long wait the faint sound of footsteps suddenly reached his ears. Then from somewhere in the neighbourhood of the boat-house came a low rumble of voices, followed a minute or so later by the unmistakable splash of oars. Almost simultaneously a black, slowly moving object emerged into view from beyond the opposite bushes. So narrow was the intervening distance that the heads and shoulders of its two occupants could be clearly distinguished. The shorter of the pair, a middle-aged man in a jersey, was pulling away stolidly in the bow: the other sat erect and aloof, the occasional glow of his cigar shining out through the darkness as the boat swayed momentarily sideways under the force of the swiftly running current.

There was a longish pause at the landing-stage while the visitor disembarked, and then, pushing off with what sounded like a mumbled word of thanks, his companion started back on the return journey. In a few minutes he was out of sight again behind the curve of the bank, and after a brief interval the bang of a door, followed by more slowly retreating steps, testified to the fact that he had locked up for the night and was on his way home.

At the very moment Owen leaned forward to pick up his paddle a blurred yellowish gleam suddenly appeared in the centre of the island. As far as he could judge, it seemed to be coming from a window in the upper side of the house. Someone had apparently turned on a light in one of the ground-floor rooms, and in a flash the full possibilities of the situation came home to him with staggering clearness. Gosh, what a chance for anybody who had the nerve to take it! If one could only get across undiscovered and sneak round until one was close enough to see what was going on inside—a soundless whistle framed itself on his lips, and moving aside an obstructing branch, he dug in the paddle and pushed out stealthily into the open. Somewhere farther along the backwater an owl hooted dismally.

Keeping close to the bank and making as little sound as possible, he worked his way gradually upstream until he was abreast of the boat-house. Exactly opposite lay the tip of the island, protected from intruders by a straggling hedge which appeared to extend more or less round the whole property. Right at the extreme point a tangled cluster of trees and bushes jutted out into the water. As a possible landing-place its advantages had already been noted by Owen earlier in the day, and with a swift glance up and down to make sure that the coast was still clear, he swung round the nose of the punt and headed for its shelter.

The light was still showing as he pulled up alongside and made fast to a convenient stump. It obviously proceeded from somewhere directly ahead of him, and edging his way forward through the undergrowth till he arrived at the hedge, he discovered that his original guess had been surprisingly accurate.

He was looking across a lawn towards the side wing of the house, at one end of which a brightly lit french window stood out against the sombre background. In the room behind it, as though he were watching a picture on the screen, he could see a couple of men standing by a table helping themselves to drinks. One of them was wearing a dark suit, the other appeared to be dressed in flannels.

Swiftly but carefully his eyes travelled round the garden. Out to the left, except for a star-shaped bed of standard roses, there was nothing in the way of cover, but on the opposite side, in front of the stretch of hedge overlooking the weir, a thick array of ornamental shrubs ran up to within a foot or two of the window. To Owen they had the appearance of being a direct answer to prayer, and in less time than it takes to write the words he had scrambled successfully over the intervening obstacle and was squirming his way forward through the miniature jungle in front of him.

About ten yards from his goal the foliage became so dense that he was compelled to go down upon his hands and knees. Even then progress was not easy. Despite his utmost care twigs snapped and bushes swayed in the most disturbing fashion, and it was with unspeakable relief that he at last found himself peering out through a gap in the leaves with nothing between his hiding-place and the window but a small tub of flowering chrysanthemums.

His satisfaction, however, was short-lived. Apart from the quick beating of his own heart, all he could hear was a low, unintelligible murmur.

◇◇◇

Von Manstein put down his glass upon the table, and helping himself to a fresh cigar, stared across at his host. Under their sharply cut lids his eyes looked like cold blue pebbles.

"Granville Sutton," he repeated slowly. "So that is the name of the gentleman." Very deliberately he struck a match. "What do you know about him apart from his being a friend of Medlicot?"

"Not very much." Craig shook his head. "He's a good-looking guy who hangs around the West End and seems to be well in with the racing crowd. I guess he lives chiefly on women—anyhow, that's Casey's notion. Kids are his line, silly kids who fall for his man-about-Town stuff. Leads 'em up the garden till they tumble to what he's really like, and then makes 'em pay to keep his mouth shut."

"He appears to be launching out into something a trifle more ambitious." The German paused. "You are convinced that he is really dangerous?"

"Shouldn't have bothered you to come down here otherwise."

"I presume not. It was extremely inconvenient."

"There was no help for it. He wants an answer by Monday, and how the hell was I to act without consulting you? In a jam like this I take my orders from higher up."

"That is quite correct. How much do you think he knows, and how far is he merely guessing?"

"Impossible to say. Medlicot spilt something, sure enough, and ever since then the bastard has been nosing about picking up little bits here and there. If he goes to the right quarter with this story of his—"

"He will never do that. The only point I am considering is the best way to deal with him. He can be removed, of course; but, on the other hand, it is possible that he might be more useful to us alive."

"I doubt it." Craig rose to his feet and paced restlessly across the room. "If I'm any judge, he'd take as much as you were fools enough to offer him and then double-cross you."

"It is more than possible."

"We should be stark, staring lunatics to give him the chance. Why, if he was to do the dirty on us—"

"There is no need to remind me that we are playing for high stakes. I am already aware of the fact."

The smooth, ironic voice brought Craig to a sudden halt, and for a moment he remained eyeing his visitor in a kind of half-resentful silence. Little beads of perspiration were glistening on his forehead.

"What you say, however, is quite true," continued von Manstein slowly. "A man like Sutton might have his uses, but with so much in the balance we cannot afford the luxury of experiments. No; on the whole, I think it would be wiser to eliminate him."

"Same here. But it's not so darned simple, you know. This isn't Germany."

Von Manstein raised his eyebrows. "You are afraid?"

"Hell to that! I'm game for anything so long as it's necessary. What I'm getting at is that it'll need damned careful handling. If you're counting on my putting it through you've got to let me fix the arrangements."

"Quite a reasonable condition."

"I'd want help, for one thing. That guy Kellerman who's so slick with a knife—he'd be the right fellow if you've still got him around."

"Yes, Kellerman can be produced. I was about to suggest that his collaboration might be advisable."

"Could you send him down here by car as soon as you get back?"

"That can be managed easily. I should be interested to hear how you propose to approach the problem."

"There's only one thing to be done—that's to stop the swine's mouth before he has a chance to open it." Once more Craig wandered restlessly round the room, passing his finger along the inside of his collar. "Gee, but it's hot in here—hot enough to stifle one." With an impatient jerk he unlatched the french window, and thrusting it open, drew in a deep breath of fresh air. "My idea is to pay him a visit Sunday night. His place isn't far from here. It's a bungalow called Sunny Bank about half a mile below Playford. Lonely sort of joint at the corner of a lane. Have to make sure there's no one around, of course; but if we wait till it's dark and watch our step"—his lips parted in an evil smile, and tossing away the stump of his cigar, he reclosed the window. "Well, how about it?" he demanded. "Got any suggestions, or are you ready to leave it to me?"

"It sounds an admirable scheme." Von Manstein nodded approvingly. "You will find Kellerman an ideal colleague."

"There's one other point." Craig's eyes narrowed. "I take it that a job like this will mean special consideration from your people. I don't run the risk of shoving my neck in a rope unless I get something out of it."

"You have no need to worry about that. You will be fittingly rewarded, and I will see that a report on your services to the cause is sent direct to the Führer." The speaker paused. "We Germans do not forget. When the New Order is established those who have proved themselves worthy of our trust will be the first to enjoy its benefit." With a short, grating laugh he leaned across and picked up his glass. "To a man who can appreciate the pleasures of power," he added, "the prospect should be a singularly attractive one."

◇◇◇

Inch by inch Owen wriggled his way back into the shrubbery until the bright light that streamed out across the lawn was little more than a vague yellow blur. Then, rising to his feet and exercising the same care that had characterised his approach, he retraced his steps to the point where he had climbed over the hedge. The punt was still there, just as he had left it, and a few seconds later he had pushed out through the screen of overhanging branches and was paddling leisurely and silently in the direction of the backwater.

"Sunny Bank—Sunday night," he repeated to himself. "Sunday night—Sunny Bank. Nice and easy to remember, that's one good thing about it!"

Chapter VI

Punting upstream, especially after a prolonged spell of wet weather, is one of those pastimes which bear an unpleasant resemblance to hard work. To Owen, pushing along doggedly and pausing now and then to mop his forehead, the distance seemed incredibly farther than it had appeared to be on his downward trip. It was a goodish while since he had handled a pole against a stiff current, and by the time he had accomplished three-quarters of his journey he was thankful enough to see the square tower of Playford Church standing up amongst the trees about half a mile ahead. Its bell was just beginning to summon the parishioners to evening service, and a rich air of sabbatical calm brooded over the still and peaceful landscape.

With a suddenly awakened interest he turned his attention to the neighbouring bank. According to the few words he had been able to overhear, the place Craig had been talking about must be somewhere in the immediate vicinity. He had referred to it as a lonely bungalow at the corner of a lane, and following the curve of the towpath, Owen's eyes fell upon a small red-roofed structure which exactly answered to the description. It was some little way back from the river, surrounded by a newly painted fence. This was bordered on one side by the lane in question, while on the other stood a thick plantation of sombre-looking firs which extended along the rear of the premises to within a few yards of the palings. The nearest house, a distressingly garish two-storey villa, was some considerable distance away and completely cut off by the trees.

Anybody wishing to approach the place without being seen would apparently find it a simple enough business. Somewhere farther back, the lane must obviously join up with the road between Playford and Thames Ferry, and by following it as far as the plantation and then taking cover one could negotiate the remainder of one's task in complete and comforting security. Compared with the problems presented by Otter's Holt the thing would be an absolute gift.

Highly satisfied with the result of his preliminary reconnaissance, Owen continued his way leisurely upstream. Now that he was acquainted with the lie of the land there was no point in over-exerting himself. Whatever the object of Craig's visit might be, it was not to take place until "after dark," and although it would be advisable to arrive on the scene of action in good time, that would still mean kicking his heels about ashore for the best part of a couple of hours. Though some of this period might be profitably spent in consuming a meal at the village inn, he had no yearning to attract attention by loafing around the neighbourhood any longer than was necessary. His persistent if somewhat unsuccessful efforts as a fisherman might not have passed unobserved by the residents at Otter's Holt, and if by some unlucky chance the fact of his presence in Playford at this particular juncture should happen to be brought to their notice the coincidence might well strike them as being oddly and unhealthily suggestive. In dealing with gentlemen like Mr. Craig and Count von Manstein it would be suicidal carelessness to neglect the smallest precaution.

As he rounded the last bend and entered the short, straight reach that led up to the boat-house, he caught sight of Mr. Martin leaning forward over the edge of the landing-stage. The old man appeared to be fixing a cover over one of the skiffs, and it was not until the punt was within a few yards that he paused in his operations and lifted an inquiring eye. With a friendly nod of greeting Owen slithered in alongside.

"Oh, so it's you, sir!" The speaker tilted back his cap. "Hope you got on all right and managed to enjoy yourself." Catching hold of the painter, he made it fast to an adjacent ring, and having thankfully shipped his pole, Owen stepped up on to the jetty.

"It's been gorgeous," he replied cheerfully. "Done me a world of good. I've sucked in enough sun and fresh air to last me through the whole winter."

"Aye, you were lucky in your weather. Just got here in time, though, from the looks of it. Wouldn't wonder if we had rain to-night, not from the way the glass is falling."

"That's a nuisance. I don't want to turn it in just yet. Only came along to get a bit of exercise and look up some friends of mine. What I thought of doing was to camp here for the night and slip down to Thames Ferry again to-morrow morning."

"Well, you please yourself, sir. Maybe it won't come to much, and even if it do you won't take no harm, not under that canvas o' yours. If you're in a hurry to be off I'll fix it up for you."

"Thanks very much. Don't want to trail back in the dark and find everything floating about."

"How about the fishin', sir? Did you have any sport down below the weir?"

"Not too bad, taking it all round. Spotted a couple of beauties, but these really big fish take a lot of catching."

"Cunning as bloomin' monkeys—that's what they are."

"So I've been informed." Owen nodded gravely. "There's still time, though," he added. "I'm hoping to have another cut at them before I go back to Town."

Mr. Martin gave a rumbling chuckle.

"That's the spirit, sir," he remarked approvingly.

◇◇◇

Sally buttoned the collar of her thick, oiled-silk coat, and with a final glance at the drizzling rain outside turned away from the window.

"Well, if I'm to get down there by ten-thirty," she observed, "I suppose I'd better be making a start. Not much good waiting for it to clear up—seems to have settled in for the night."

Ruth, who was collecting together the remains of their evening meal, looked up with a frown. "If you take my advice," she retorted, "you'll chuck the whole business."

"But I can't. It wouldn't be fair on Sheila. Besides, the rain doesn't really matter. I shall be quite snug and dry as soon as I'm in the car."

"I wish you'd change your mind and let me come with you. I simply loathe the idea of your going down there alone."

Sally shook her head. "We have had all that out, darling, and it's no use arguing about it again. For one thing, I haven't got the time. It's a longish trip, and if I try to drive fast in the dark I always get the jitters."

"Are you sure you know the way?"

"Oh, yes. Sheila told me in her letter. I take the Thames Ferry road just before I get into Playford and turn up a lane about half a mile farther on. The bungalow is right at the end, facing the river. She says it's perfectly easy and one can't possibly make a mistake."

"She *would*." Ruth scowled. "I still think the whole thing's utterly insane and that I'm a perfect fool to lend you the bus. Until I hear you come in I shall sit here worrying myself stiff."

"Why not go to bed and get some sleep?" suggested Sally. "I'll promise to wake you up and tell you all about it."

Ruth shook her head. "I'm staying put," she declared stubbornly; "and what's more, if you aren't home by one I shall ring up the Playford police and ask them to go round and make sure that you're all right. I'm not joking; I really mean it."

"Then I'd better not dawdle about on the road." With a disarming smile Sally picked up her bag and moved towards the door. "Be good and don't eat all the chocolates," she added. "After hobnobbing with Mr. Sutton I shall want something sweet to take away the taste."

The garage in which Ruth housed her small Morris-Oxford was situated in a blind alley only a short distance from the shop. By the time Sally reached it, however, the rain was already beginning to trickle down her face, so it was hardly surprising that her resentment against the man she was setting out to visit increased steadily with every passing second. Indeed, as she climbed into the driving-seat and started up the engine her feelings attained a point of bitterness which could only find relief in some sort of verbal expression. "Pig!" she muttered to herself with a little half-comical grimace. "I wish someone would walk into your beastly bungalow and jab you in the back with a large, sharp carving-knife."

Whether it was the effect of this slightly bloodthirsty outburst or the mere fact of having to concentrate her attention upon driving, it was comforting to discover that before she was half-way down the King's Road a calmer and more business-like frame of mind was already beginning to assert itself. After all, what was the use of getting rabid and venomous about a complete rotter like Sutton? It only confused one's mind and prevented one from thinking clearly. In order to carry off the interview successfully she would need all the coolness and resolution she had at her command, and now that the critical moment was so rapidly approaching, minor afflictions such as getting a trifle damp must not be permitted to intrude upon the main issue. Eyes on the road and thoughts on the job ahead—that was the correct slogan, beyond any shadow of doubt.

At Hampton Court the rain was easing off, and a faint glimmer of moonlight peeped out from between a rift in the clouds. For a Sunday night there was remarkably little traffic. The customary stream of revellers, who make a habit of running down for a final drink at some riverside inn, had apparently been disheartened by the weather, and freed from the usual procession of blinding headlights, she was able to push along at a considerably faster speed than she would otherwise have attempted. The swift motion seemed to be of help in still further steadying her nerves.

It was exactly twenty-past ten by her wrist-watch when she arrived at the crossroads where Sheila had told her to branch off to the left. With only another half-mile to go this meant that she would be in ample time for the appointment. A vision of Sutton's face when he opened the door and discovered that she had taken control of negotiations brought a momentary smile to her lips, and swinging round the corner in the direction of Thames Ferry, she began to keep a watchful look-out for anything in the nature of a side turning.

In a few minutes she caught sight of what appeared to be the entrance to a narrow lane, where a weather-stained signboard bearing the words "To the Towpath" was affixed to an adjacent paling. If her instructions were correct, all she had to do now was to follow this track until it brought her to the bungalow; a distance, according to Sheila, of not more than two or three hundred yards.

Driving forward slowly and carefully, she passed a couple of iron gates flanked by stone pillars, alongside of which stood a small, neatly kept lodge. Not far beyond rose a gloomy-looking belt of trees. As she advanced she discovered that they formed part of a railed-in plantation, some of the bigger branches stretching out over the lane like queer, fantastic shadows. In the fitful gleam of the moon the effect was curiously sinister.

It was not, however, until a green fence backed by a low, steeply pitched roof loomed up out of the darkness that the first real sensation of doubt and mistrust suddenly assailed her. If this were Sunny Bank—and it certainly answered to the description—a more cheerless place, and one that looked less like expecting a visitor, it would certainly have been difficult to imagine. There was not a trace of light anywhere, and the only sound that broke the inhospitable silence was the faint, steady ticking of her own engine.

Taking a torch from her bag, she climbed out of the car and walked across towards the wooden gate opposite. From here a short path led up to the front door, on either side of which was a small, square-shaped window. As she advanced the depressing stillness seemed to become even more pronounced.

With a slight quickening of her pulse she raised her hand to the brass knocker and gave a loud rap. To her surprise, the door immediately swung open. It was exactly like some rather uncanny conjuring trick, and so startling was its effect that for a moment she stood staring stupidly into the vague blackness of what appeared to be a goodish-sized sitting-room. Then, somehow or other, she managed to find her voice.

"Is there anyone here?" she demanded.

No answer was forthcoming, and suddenly remembering her torch, she pulled herself together and switched on the light. At the same instant her throat seemed to tighten, and before she could choke it back a cry of horror broke from her lips.

Directly in front of her, stretched full length beside an overturned table, lay the figure of a man. One arm was flung out at a grotesque angle, and sticking up between his shoulder-blades was a white object that looked like the handle of a knife. The carpet around him was saturated with blood, a long, straggling trickle of which had already worked its way almost to her feet. Its sickly, unmistakable smell permeated the whole bungalow.

A wild panic took possession of her, and with an involuntary movement she clutched blindly at the side of the door. For a moment or two her heart thumped at such a pace that she felt scarcely able to breathe. All she was conscious of was a frantic impulse to get back to the car, coupled with a horrible weakness that seemed to keep her feet glued to the floor.

Then, very slowly, her courage began to return. By a tremendous effort she forced herself to release her hold, and avoiding the dark sticky mess into which she had so nearly blundered, she moved shakily forward to where the body was lying.

The head was twisted slightly askew, exposing one side of the face. As she had expected, the features were those of Granville Sutton; and although only an hour before she had been wishing for his death, the sight of that white distorted mask sent a cold chill creeping through her veins. In some unreasoning way she felt as though she were responsible for what had happened.

She was still battling against this unpleasant sensation when a deep groan made her start violently. Once more the instinct to run away almost overcame her, but by sheer willpower she succeeded in thrusting it aside. Straightening up, she swung round the torch in the direction of the sound, and there in the farther corner, leaning back against the wall, was the huddled shape of a dark-haired young man, who had apparently just struggled up into a sitting position. He was nursing his head between his hands, and blinking at the light in what seemed to be a kind of vacant bewilderment.

"Hullo!" he muttered. "Where the devil am I?"

Sally came a step nearer, keeping the torch focused on his face.

"Who are you?" she demanded.

"That's—that's just what I'm wondering myself." He made a feeble attempt to sit up a little higher. "All I know is that I've got a peach of a head. Feels as if it was going to explode." A wry smile twisted his lips, and with another involuntary groan he sank back again into the same position.

Sally stood where she was, staring at him silently. As far as looks went he was not in the least like her idea of a murderer. Despite his rain-soaked clothes and a large smear of blood across his forehead, there was something about his appearance which seemed to inspire her with a sudden queer sense of confidence. Anyhow, for some unaccountable reason she no longer felt afraid of him.

"But you must remember your name," she persisted.

"I was trying to when you shoved on that light. It's no good, though—can't think of a damned thing except this foul pain."

"Have you ever heard of a man called Granville Sutton?"

"Granville Sutton? No—what's he got to do with it?"

"This is his bungalow. I had an appointment to meet him at ten-thirty."

The grey eyes stared at her blankly.

"When I got here," she continued, "I found the door open and the whole place in darkness. The first thing I saw was Sutton's body. It's lying on the floor the other side of that table."

"His body!" With a sudden fumbling movement the stranger reached out towards the chair beside him, and grabbing hold of the arm, dragged himself to his feet. The effort seemed to have exhausted his strength, and for a moment he stood there swaying dizzily.

"You mean—you mean that he's dead?"

Sally drew in a long breath. "You can see for yourself."

She turned her torch in the direction of the sprawling figure, and abandoning his grip on the chair, her companion took a step forward. Then, supporting himself by the table, he stood gazing down at the gruesome object in front of him.

"I say, this is a bit grim. Looks as though we'd butted in on a murder." He raised his head and turned slowly towards Sally. "Are you by any chance under the impression that I did it?"

"I was at first: now I'm not so sure."

"Thanks." Another twisted smile flickered across his lips. "Considering everything, that's uncommonly handsome."

"But you're mixed up with it in some way—you must be. What made you come here, and how did you get hurt yourself?"

For a moment he remained silent.

"You can believe me or not, but I haven't the remotest notion. As I told you, I don't even know who I am. All I remember is waking up in the dark with what felt like a red-hot gimlet boring into the back of my head. How long I'd been lying there God knows. Somebody must have given me a clout from behind, and it seems to have wiped everything clean out. I suppose my memory will come back, but—" His face suddenly contracted with pain, and groping for the edge of the table, he sat down abruptly.

"Of course it will, but you oughtn't to try to walk about. I'm sure it's the worst thing you could do." Sally moved a pace nearer.

"I must get the hang of what's been happening here. One can't just sit still gaping at a corpse. For a start, do you mind telling me exactly where we are?"

"We're in a bungalow called Sunny Bank, about half a mile from Playford. It belongs—at least it did belong—to this man Sutton."

"Was he a friend of yours?"

"I hardly knew him. I only came to see him on a matter of business."

"What did he do? I mean, what was his profession?"

"I believe he lived chiefly by blackmailing people."

The stranger gave a low whistle. "Blackmailing!" he repeated. "Well, well, that seems to clear things up a trifle. Tried it on once too often and somebody turned nasty."

"I don't blame anyone for killing him. It's only what he deserved." Sally paused. "In fact, if I knew who it was I—I'd do my best to help him escape."

"Supposing it *was* me after all?" The speaker had swung round again and was eyeing her curiously. "I don't feel like the sort of bloke who goes around stabbing people in the back, but how can I possibly tell?"

"You'd know it instinctively."

"Think so? Well, perhaps you're right."

"I'm certain I am. If you'd killed him, you'd have choked him to death or something like that."

"Sounds more up my street. All the same, one can't get away from the fact that I was lying here right alongside of him. Going to be a bit awkward when people start asking questions."

"You'll have to tell them what you've told me."

"Do you suppose they'll believe me?"

"Not till you have been examined by a doctor. Besides, there's another thing you've got to think about. If you start trying to explain now you may be landing yourself into some frightful mess. You see—you see, in a way, that's how it is with me. I can't tell the truth, because if I did I—I should be letting down a friend."

"But there's nothing to prevent you clearing out."

"Oh, I couldn't run away and leave you like this; it wouldn't be fair. What you've got to do first is to get your memory back. When you know who you are and—and why you came here—"

" 'Fraid it won't work. Before I'd gone a hundred yards I'd just flop down and pass out. That'd make things look fishier than ever."

"I've got a car outside. I can give you a lift."

"But what would you do with me? You'd have to dump me out somewhere. We can't just drive around vaguely waiting for my memory to start functioning."

"No, you must go to bed and rest. If you have a good long sleep you may be all right again by to-morrow."

"That would mean trying to get in at a hotel or a lodging-house."

"I wasn't thinking of a hotel. They'd see that you'd had an accident and they would probably ring up the police."

"What am I to do, then? Crawl up to a hospital and park myself on the doorstep?"

Sally hesitated. "I—I was going to suggest that you might come back to our place. We have a room in the basement where you could stay for the night. It's a kind of workshop really, but there's a big sofa in it, and you would be quite comfortable. I should have to explain to my partner, of course. You see, we live together above the office, and she'll be waiting up for me."

"That's damned sporting of you." The stranger paused, surveying her with a kind of puzzled admiration. "I wonder if you quite realise how much you're risking. You know, it's a pretty serious business hiding a bloke who may have committed a murder."

"But you haven't." Sally shook her head firmly. "I'm positive of that now or I shouldn't have suggested it."

"You certainly have the knack of encouraging one."

"I feel that we're both in a horrible jam and that we ought to help each other. You must have had some reason for coming here, and you must know what happened before you were knocked down and stunned. As soon as you're better you'll remember all about it, and then we can decide what we're going to do. We shall have to talk it over with Ruth. She's my partner, and she's frightfully sensible and level-headed."

With a wan smile and a faint shrug the other dragged himself to his feet. "I'll leave it to you," he observed wearily. "I oughtn't to let you stick your neck out like this, but I feel too groggy to start arguing. By the way, have you any objection to telling me your name?"

"It's Deane, Sally Deane. Ruth and I run a decorating business. We've got a place in the King's Road, Chelsea, and that's where I'm going to take you." She switched the light back upon the body, and repressing an instinctive shudder moved reluctantly towards it.

"What are you doing?"

"I came to see him about a letter, a letter he was using to get money out of a friend of mine. It may be in one of his pockets."

"I'll have a look. You stay where you are." Bending down shakily, the stranger made a hurried search through the dead man's clothing. In a few seconds he had completed his task. "Nothing here," he announced. "At least, only a cigarette case and a lighter. Somebody's been through him already, and done the job pretty thoroughly."

"Damn!" Raising the torch, Sally glanced hastily round the room. For the first time she realised that the whole place was in a state of wild disorder. Every drawer and cupboard appeared to have been wrenched open, and a large proportion of their contents lay scattered about the floor. She stared at the wreckage with a feeling of sick dismay.

"We can't search through all that stuff: it would take ages. We must get away at once before anyone comes along and finds us." Without waiting for a reply, she put her hand on her companion's arm. "The car's quite close—just the other side of the lane. You'll be able to manage that, won't you? Hold on to me, and I'll help you if you feel faint."

◇◇◇

Slumped down in the corner of the back seat, his eyes closed and his head still throbbing with a dull, persistent ache, Owen battled valiantly against a strong inclination to be sick. The effort of crossing the road and climbing into the car had left him completely exhausted. He felt so ill and dazed that any further attempt to wrestle with the incredible situation in which he found himself seemed for the present to be utterly beyond his power.

From one fact alone he was able to derive a certain definite comfort. Whatever effect the injury had produced upon his memory, it had not altogether robbed him of his wits. The events of the last ten minutes were at least perfectly clear and distinct. He could recollect everything that had occurred from that first bewildering moment when he had recovered his senses, and grimly fantastic as the whole business was, he could see no substantial grounds for questioning its reality. The man in the bungalow had undoubtedly been murdered, and judging by the circumstances, it was quite conceivable that he himself had committed the crime. For some reason, however, this girl, Sally Deane, who had made such a timely and miraculous appearance on the scene, was evidently convinced of his innocence. Anyhow, she was prepared to run the risk of sheltering and concealing him until his memory returned, and in his present state of physical prostration that was the only matter which seemed to be of immediate importance. What he needed was sleep—a long spell of deep, refreshing sleep, from which he would wake up into a sane and familiar world.

After a little while the feeling of nausea became rather less acute, and in spite of the swinging and bumping of the car he began to drift into an uneasy, half-conscious doze. He was vaguely aware of the fact that the fields and hedges had given place to rows of villas, and that these in turn were being superseded by long vistas of closed and depressing-looking shops. Buses and trams loomed up out of the darkness and clattered past the window, while every now and then an abrupt halt in front of some forbidding traffic-light sent a fresh spasm of pain shooting through his head.

At last, just as he was recovering from a particularly vicious jolt, the car swung round a corner and glided forward into what appeared to be a narrow and ill-lighted alley. In another second it had pulled up, and before he had had time to rouse himself properly, the girl in front had slipped down from her seat and jerked open the door.

"Here we are," she announced with a reassuring smile. "It's quite close to my place, so you won't have far to walk. How are you feeling now—any better?"

"Just a shade, I think—still a bit wobbly about the knees." By a colossal effort he succeeded in scrambling out.

"Well, sit down on that step while I shove the car in. It's quite all right: no one's the least likely to come along."

Obediently as a child he parked himself in an adjoining doorway, from which position he looked on in a sort of vague trance until his companion had completed her task. She was in the act of closing the garage door when a neighbouring clock chimed out the hour of twelve.

After that things became a trifle blurred. He had a confused impression of being helped to his feet, guided out into a deserted side street and shepherded towards another and broader thoroughfare, up and down which a certain number of belated vehicles still appeared to be making their way. Ten yards beyond the corner, in front of an old-fashioned shop window, obscured by a drawn blind, a warning pressure on his arm brought him to a standstill. There was a brief pause followed by the click of a key, and the next instant he found himself stumbling forward through an open doorway with a small determined hand still directing his progress.

"Stop where you are," came a low whisper. "You'll knock something over otherwise."

A sudden rose-shaded glow flooded the apartment, revealing various pieces of attractively arranged furniture and casting its soft, becoming light on the face of his companion. For the first time the fact that she was adorably pretty began to dawn slowly upon his muddled brain. Almost immediately, however, she was back again at his side, and before he quite realised what was happening he was being piloted carefully down a short flight of steps and ushered into a long, low-ceilinged room which seemed to be provided with an inordinate number of shelves and cupboards. Up against the wall in one corner stood an ancient but comfortable-looking divan.

"This is the place I was telling you about. You will be absolutely safe here. Now what you've got to do is to lie down on this couch and keep perfectly still and quiet. I'm just going to run up and fetch Ruth. I shall be back again in a moment, and then I'll have a look at your head. I'm sure it ought to be sponged and bandaged."

"Feel I'm being a crashing nuisance." He sank back gratefully against a pile of cushions, and looked up into the beautiful but troubled blue eyes that were anxiously studying his face. "Nice name, Sally," he murmured drowsily. "Just right for a guardian angel."

◇◇◇

Ruth awoke with a guilty start and scrambled up hastily out of the big arm-chair in which she had been dozing.

"Oh, it's you, darling! Thank goodness you're back." She came forward, fastening her dressing-gown which had fallen open. "Well, how did you get on? Is he going to accept your offer?"

Very slowly Sally removed her hat.

"He's dead," she announced.

"*Dead!*"

"Dead," repeated Sally. "Somebody came into the bungalow and stabbed him."

There was a profound silence which lasted for several seconds.

"Gosh!" muttered Ruth huskily.

"Don't look at me like that. I didn't do it."

"Of course you didn't." Shaking off her momentary paralysis, the other dragged forward a chair. "Sit down," she commanded, "sit down there, and I'll get you a drink. You—"

"I don't want a drink: I just want you to listen. I *must* tell you all about it. It's—it's so frightfully important."

Her partner gave a brief nod. "Go on," she remarked.

"When I got down to the bungalow it was all dark and there didn't seem to be anybody about. Then I suddenly found that the door was open. I—I walked in and put on my torch, and—oh, Ruth, you can't imagine the horrible shock I got. There he was lying on the floor in a great pool of blood with the handle of a knife sticking up between his shoulders."

She gave an involuntary shiver and covered her face with her hands.

"It must have been ghastly. What did you do?"

"I was so flabbergasted I nearly passed out. I had to hang on to the door for a moment or two. Then, just as I was feeling a little better, I heard a sort of groan, and I saw that there was someone else there as well."

"Someone else! You mean the murderer?"

"I thought so at first, naturally. It was only when he began to talk that I felt I must be wrong."

"Who was he?"

"He didn't know himself. Couldn't even remember how he got there. Somebody had hit him on the head, and he'd completely forgotten everything."

"*What!*"

"Oh, of course it sounds phoney—horribly phoney—all the same, I'm quite sure that he was speaking the truth."

"How can you tell?"

"He wouldn't stab a man in the back: he isn't that sort." Sally swallowed nervously. "If—if I wasn't absolutely certain I shouldn't have brought him here."

"*You—wouldn't—have—brought—him—here.*" The words came out in a slow, stunned whisper.

"Oh, Ruth, don't be angry. What else could I do? Whoever he is, he's quite decent and nice, and I couldn't just walk out and leave him. If they'd found him there like that they'd have been bound to arrest him."

"But—but—oh, my God!" A trifle unsteadily Ruth walked across to the sideboard and tilted herself out a splash of whisky.

"You see, even if he's innocent," continued Sally, "it would have been impossible for him to explain. He can't account for anything until he gets his memory back. That may happen all of a sudden—directly it does—"

"He'll probably grab hold of another knife and stick it into us." Ruth gulped off a mouthful of neat spirit and put down the glass. "You're bats, darling—absolutely bats. Don't you know that hiding a murderer—"

"He's not a murderer: I don't care what anyone thinks." Sally laid a hand on her partner's arm. "Come and see him for yourself," she begged pleadingly. "It's the only way you can possibly judge."

"Where is he?"

"In the workroom lying on the sofa. I told him I was sharing the place with a friend and I promised I'd bring you down as soon as I'd had a chance to explain."

Ruth gave a sort of half-despairing shrug. "All right," she said dully. "We may as well make a night of it now we've really started."

"Just a second while I collect one or two things. I must bandage up his head before he goes to sleep."

Hurrying into her bedroom, Sally came back with a sponge and bottle of iodine and a round, paper-covered packet. These she handed to Ruth, and then, crossing over to the fireplace, picked up a small brass kettle which was simmering away gently on the gas-ring.

"That's all we shall want," she announced. "There's a clean towel down there, and we can use the basin out of the lavatory. Won't matter if it gets a little bloody."

"Not in the slightest."

With the resigned air of one to whom the worst has already happened, Ruth stepped out on to the landing. From here a winding flight of stairs ran down to the ground floor, terminating at a curtained arch which gave access to the shop. In another minute the two of them were standing in the narrow stone-flagged basement, where a shaft of light from the half-open workroom streamed out against the opposite wall.

"He's still awake: I can hear him moving about," whispered Sally. "Wait here while I get the basin."

She disappeared through a doorway on the left, and emerging a moment later with an enamelled tin bowl tucked under her arm, led the way briskly up the passage. Looking rather like Lady Macbeth in the sleep-walking scene, Ruth followed in her wake.

When they entered the long, somewhat ill-ventilated apartment their guest was in the act of settling himself back on the couch. His shoes and his rain-coat were lying on the floor alongside, and in his hand was a slightly battered silver cigarette case.

"What have you been doing?" demanded Sally. "I told you to lie perfectly still." She marched forward to the couch, and with a disapproving frown put down the basin and the kettle.

"Sorry." The speaker forced a penitent smile. "Felt I'd better get out of these before you came back. Didn't know I was so wet and dirty."

"You've got to be good and obey orders." Sally picked up a towel which was lying on the table. "This is Ruth," she added. "I've explained everything, and she's been fearfully nice and sporting about it."

"You're both marvellous! I—"

"Don't talk. Just lie down and let me have a look at your head. It's got to be washed and bandaged."

Without protesting the patient turned over on his side, and having rolled up her sleeves to the elbow, Sally set to work. Except for an occasional word to Ruth, who stood by acting as "dresser," she conducted her ministrations in silence.

"There!" she observed, straightening up with a relieved sigh. "That will keep it clean and stop it from bleeding. You've got a nasty bruise and it's begun to swell a little, but I don't think there's any very serious damage." She paused. "Why are you holding that cigarette case? Do you want to smoke?"

"Thought I might find out who I was, so I had a run through my pockets. Only thing I dug up was this."

Sally leaned over him and scrutinised the monogram in the centre. "Looks to me like an O and a B. I expect they're your initials?"

"Ought to be. Doesn't seem to help, though." The stranger wrinkled his forehead.

"How about Oliver?" suggested Ruth.

"Oliver will do for the time being." Sally took the case from his hand and placed it on the table. "Don't worry yourself by trying to think," she continued: "it will all come back to you suddenly without the slightest effort. The only important thing now is that you should get off to sleep."

The grey eyes which were looking up into hers closed wearily.

"O.K., angel," murmured their owner.

Taking charge of the discarded coat, which she hung over the back of the chair, Sally picked up the basin and moved towards the passage. Ruth, who meanwhile had collected the remainder of their medical equipment, followed in silence. At the last moment she turned to cast a final glance at the recumbent figure on the couch, and then, switching off the light, closed the door and turned the key. The latter object she transferred to the pocket of her dressing-gown.

"Well, darling," whispered Sally eagerly, "what do you make of him? He doesn't look a bit like a murderer, does he?"

Ruth shook her head.

"I think he's rather a pet," she admitted. "All the same, I'm glad we had that lock mended."

Chapter VII

Clattering noisily down the long slope, and crossing the stone bridge, the big, clumsy-looking farm lorry continued its journey up the opposite rise. Little by little the sound of its wheels faded into a low rumble, and raising his head, Mr. James Wilson was just in time to see it disappearing round the base of a distant tor. Then once again the bleak vista of rock and heath was as deserted and silent as ever.

A forlorn enough figure, with his drab prison clothes and his unshaven chin, Wilson stood there amongst the thick cluster of brambles and gorse, where for the past fourteen hours he had been patiently waiting for another spell of darkness. As a hiding-place, which at the same time possessed all the advantages of an observation post, the spot had undoubtedly been well chosen. On one side it commanded an uninterrupted view of the road for the best part of a mile, while on the other, where the moor made an abrupt and precipitous descent, a wide panorama of lush meadows and dark-green splashes of woodland unrolled itself peacefully in the warm September twilight. It resembled one of those alluring railway posters which invite the prospective traveller to spend his holiday in "Glorious Devon."

At the present moment, however, Wilson's eyes were gazing in the contrary direction. They were fixed upon a small, solitary, granite-built house, standing in an ill-kept kitchen garden about twenty yards from the near end of the bridge. Adjoining it was a low outbuilding that looked like a garage, and from there a roughly made gravel track, bordered by a row of stunted fir trees, ran down to a wooden gate facing the roadway. The whole property was surrounded by a wire fence, several strands of which were obviously in need of repair.

All day, except for a few odd intervals when he had fallen asleep through sheer weariness, he had been peering across hungrily at that lonely and somewhat forbidding homestead. An inhabited house, with its owner temporarily absent, was the very object that he had been yearning to come across ever since his escape from the prison. Now at long last it seemed as though his unspoken prayer had been answered. Twice during the course of his vigil he had seen a would-be visitor hammer on the door without evoking any response, and the belief that here, almost within a stone's throw, lay the Heaven-sent chance of obtaining those two vital necessities, food and a change of clothes, had been steadily deepening as the long hours wore gradually on.

Several times, indeed, he had been sorely tempted to creep out of his refuge and investigate for himself. Being fully aware, however, that the whole countryside was only too anxious to assist in his recapture, the danger of attempting such a feat by daylight had been sufficiently obvious to restrain his impatience. From any one of those rocky crests keen eyes might be keeping watch upon the surrounding moor. A single suspicious movement would be enough to attract their attention, and once the alarm was given it would mean a speedy ending to his desperate bid for liberty. Before nightfall he would be back again in that cursed cell, with a bitter sense of failure and frustration added to the corroding hatred that already filled his heart.

Taking from his pocket the last of the sour and rather hard apples which he had filched from a cottage garden during the previous night, he settled down again grimly to await the oncoming darkness. Despite his hunger and fatigue he was obsessed by a kind of savage happiness. In the teeth of almost impossible odds he had at last succeeded in carrying through the first part of his programme, and now that Fate, in the shape of this deserted house, had seen fit to step in and lend him a helping hand, the chief problem that still confronted him appeared to be on the point of solving itself. To his half-insane mind, warped by interminable months of solitary brooding, such a state of affairs was in no way surprising. A passionate conviction that the longed-for hour of revenge would eventually arrive had never deserted him, and as he lay there chewing slowly and staring up into the dark-blue vista above, a wave of fresh and exultant strength seemed to come flooding back into his tired and aching limbs.

Very gradually the long streaks of crimson and gold faded out of the west, while one by one the more distant peaks became merged in the gathering dusk. High overhead an army of stars was already beginning to invade the sky. The moment for action was at last drawing near, and rising to his feet again with a purposeful deliberation, Wilson commenced to push his way stealthily through the tangled screen of brambles. Gripped in his right hand was the broken strip of iron railing which had been lying beside him in the grass.

He had advanced as far as the last bush, and was just straightening up to make a final cautious inspection, when the unmistakable hum of a motor-cycle suddenly broke the silence. His lips tightened and his whole body became tense and motionless. Almost simultaneously a yellow light swept up over the crest of the slope, and sailing down the road like some gigantic firefly, came to an abrupt halt exactly in front of the wire fence. In another moment the rider had dismounted and was pushing open the gate.

With a sickening feeling of disappointment Wilson stared across at the burly, leather-coated figure which had so shatteringly broken in upon his plans. Of all conceivable mischances, this last-minute return of the owner of the house had been the one which he had least expected. Only a minute ago everything had appeared to be perfectly clear sailing, and now—a whispered oath broke from his lips and the fingers that were clutching the rail tightened in convulsive fury.

Pursuing his way up the gravelled track and unlocking the door of the garage, the intruder wheeled his machine inside and propped it against the wall. The headlamp was still on, and from across the road he could be seen removing his coat and unstrapping a goodish-sized parcel from the luggage carrier at the rear. This he placed carefully upon a bench, and then, leaving the light still blazing away unchecked, stepped out again into the open and vanished up a narrow path which appeared to lead round to the back door.

Imminent danger, as Doctor Johnson has pointed out, has a remarkably bracing effect upon the intellect. After that first spasm of almost uncontrollable rage Wilson's mind had been working at top speed. The sight of the motor-cycle had opened up a whole fresh world of possibilities, and as the figure of its proprietor melted into obscurity, a sudden desperate resolve crystallised in his heart. It was obviously a question of now or never.

Stealthily as a panther he slid out from behind the bush and keeping his head well down, darted across the rough stretch of grass that separated him from the road. In a few minutes he had arrived at the gate. On one side of the short ascent lay a belt of black shadow cast by the line of fir trees, and taking advantage of this to cover his approach to the garage, he tiptoed silently across the intervening path and flattened himself stiffly against the front wall of the house.

He had hardly taken up his new position when an indifferently whistled rendering of "Annie Laurie" began to filter through the night air. Almost at the same instant there was a crunch of approaching steps. Nearer and nearer they came, advancing leisurely along the narrow passage, and then, with the last unfinished note still issuing from his lips, the unsuspecting soloist suddenly made his appearance.

Whack!

The iron rail thudded down on to the thick leather cap, and crumpling at the knees, its wearer slumped forward like a pricked bladder. As he fell the top of his head struck against the low stone parapet that bounded the garden.

It was obviously no moment for dawdling about, and in any case indecision was not one of Wilson's failings. Dropping his weapon and grabbing hold of the prostrate body by the ankles, he hauled it unceremoniously across the gravel and dragged it into the garage. The heels flopped down upon the concrete floor with a dull clatter, and in less time than it takes to write the words he had swung home the heavy, stoutly hinged door and was leaning against the bench panting for breath.

As soon as he had sufficiently recovered, the first object to which he turned his attention was the large square package beside him. It consisted of a wooden box covered by a thick layer of brown paper, and on wrenching away the latter he found himself confronted by what appeared to be the fruits of a day's marketing in some neighbouring town. For a moment he could scarcely believe his eyes. With fumbling haste he pulled out two loaves of bread, a slab of cheese, a tin of biscuits and a carton of lump sugar, and then, resisting a clamorous urge to satisfy his hunger straight away, picked up the discarded coat which its owner had also flung down upon the bench.

A hurried search through the pockets brought to light two more heartening discoveries. One was an unopened packet of twenty cigarettes, the other a tattered wallet with five new, crisp, clean one-pound notes tucked away in a separate compartment.

A trifle dazed by this staggering rush of good fortune, he stepped forward and peered down at the sprawling figure in front of him. By the light of the lamp reflected from the end wall he could see that the man was still alive. Thanks to the thick cap, the blow which would otherwise have fractured his skull had apparently only succeeded in stunning him, and with a grunt of relief, for he no longer felt the faintest animosity against his victim, Wilson turned quickly to examine the motor-cycle. To his unspeakable joy the tanks proved to be nearly half full.

II

"So!"

Von Manstein removed his eyeglass and polished it carefully with a silk handkerchief. Then, replacing it in position, he once more picked up his evening paper and concentrated his attention on the double-headed paragraph at the top of the right-hand column.

```
MURDER AT A THAMES BUNGALOW
Well-known Sportsman Found Stabbed

   Early this morning the body of Mr.
Granville Sutton, a familiar figure on the
racecourse and in the West End of London,
was found lying on the floor of his riv-
erside bungalow which is situated about
half a mile below Playford. Mr. Sutton had
been stabbed between the shoulders, and
```

death must have been practically instantaneous. The discovery was made by a lad named George King, who was engaged in his customary task of delivering milk. King immediately raised the alarm, and within a few minutes Superintedent Fothergill, of the local police, had arrived upon the scene and taken charge of the investigations. The disordered condition of the bungalow points to robbery as having been the probable motive of the crime. There were signs which suggested that the murderer arrived and escaped by car, and it is considered not unlikely that this clue will be of considerable assistance in establishing his identity. Anyone who may have noticed a motor-driven vehicle either entering or turning out of the Playford-Thames Ferry Road between the hours of ten and midnight is requested to communicate with the police at the earliest possible opportunity.

"Mr. Craig."

Frederick, the wooden-faced manservant who had opened the door, moved stiffly to one side, and following close on the announcement of his name, Mark Craig walked into the room.

"Sorry to be late. Had a spot of trouble with the car." The visitor glanced back as though to satisfy himself that the door had been properly closed, and then, with an abrupt change of expression, advanced towards the easy chair from which his host had made no attempt to get up. "You have read the evening papers?" he demanded.

Von Manstein nodded. "It appears that you are to be congratulated. You seem to have handled the affair most successfully."

"Glad you think so." Craig sat down heavily on the big ottoman that jutted out from the corner of the fireplace. "There's a lot more to it, though, than they've got hold of yet." He paused. "Something has happened that no one on God's earth could have possibly foreseen."

"Indeed!" The Count raised his eyebrows. "Nothing that might lead to any unpleasant consequences, I hope?"

"On the contrary, it may turn out devilish useful."

"I'm relieved to hear it. You had better help yourself to a drink and tell me the whole story."

Accepting the invitation, Craig turned to the small inlaid table at his elbow, where the necessary ingredients, in the shape of a syphon and a decanter of whisky, had already been set out. There was a brief silence, and then, relinquishing his half-emptied glass, he looked up again to face the cold, watchful stare of his companion.

"Wasn't any fault of ours: the plans I'd made worked out perfectly. We got there soon after it was dark, and I'll take my oath no one had spotted us. It had been raining like hell for the last two hours. Sutton opened the door himself, and I guess from his face he'd been expecting someone else. I'd got my piece ready, though; and as soon as he tumbled to the idea that we'd come over to talk business he made no trouble about letting us in. I could see he was carrying a gun in his pocket, but it was about as much use to him as a sick headache. That guy Kellerman is as quick as a cat. Never seen a smarter bit of work in my life."

"What did you expect? We are not in the habit of employing bunglers."

"I'd say not!" Craig picked up his tumbler and took another long gulp. "Next job was to go through the bastard's papers, but before I started in I sent Kellerman outside just to make sure that I wouldn't be interrupted. I told him that if anyone came snooping around he was to lay him out with that rubber cosh of his. We'd left the knife in the body on purpose. It was one I'd specially fixed up—cut some initials on the handle so as to give the cops something to get busy on."

"An admirable idea." The speaker nodded approvingly.

"Well, I was just about through when I heard the bump. Seems that a guy had come sneaking out from some trees at the back and got over the fence. Meant to have a squint through the window, I guess. Kellerman had fixed him right enough, and it didn't take us long to cart him inside. He was out to the world, and I'll lay odds he never even knew what hit him."

The listener frowned.

"Describe his appearance to me. It is possible that I may know him."

"He was a biggish guy, over six foot, I'd say. Might have been out abroad from the way he was sunburned. Looked a bit like Gary Cooper and had a small scar on the corner of his forehead. I'd put his age at about twenty-six or twenty-seven."

"I do not fancy I have the pleasure of his acquaintance. You searched him thoroughly, of course? Was there nothing in his pockets which would help our people to identify him?"

"Only a cigarette case with the initials O.B. on it. If you ask me, I'd say he was the fellow Sutton was looking out for, and that he'd called round to make himself mighty unpleasant."

"Is that a mere guess, or have you any definite reason for thinking so?"

"Wait till you've heard the rest and you'll be able to judge for yourself." Craig paused. "Seemed like the best notion was for me and Kellerman to clear off and leave our pal to do the explaining. So I grabbed up the stuff I'd collected and we slid out quick. As I told you, there's a whole lot of trees at the back, and we'd just got in amongst 'em when we suddenly saw the lights of a car coming round the corner. Put the wind up both of us for a moment. It stopped dead opposite the bungalow, and the next moment out hopped a skirt. Just the sort of smart-looking kid Sutton used to trail around with. Must have got the surprise of her life when she shoved open the door and walked in."

Von Manstein's eyes narrowed. "And what happened?"

"We heard her let off a squeal, and then after a bit—six or seven minutes, I reckon—out she comes again with that big stiff holding on to her arm. Guess his skull must be made of cast iron. She helps him into the car, nips in herself, and before you could say Jack Robinson they were chasing away back up the lane. She's got guts, that kid, whoever she is—"

"A very interesting development." Von Manstein stroked his chin, meditating. "What do you make of it yourself?"

"I'd say that Sutton had been doing the dirty on her, and that this guy had come down to beat him up. Like as not she tumbled to what was going on and thought she'd better butt in and stop the rough stuff."

"That is possible. Let us hope you are right."

Craig glanced at his companion a trifle uncertainly. "You don't figure that he could have been one of Greystoke's bunch?"

"It is a point that we must keep in mind. I certainly cannot place him by your description, but there is always a chance that the worthy Captain may have been enlarging his staff. You are positive you left no finger-prints?"

"Is it likely? Never took off our gloves the whole time."

"Well, we must trust that your private vendetta theory will turn out to be correct. In any case, Mr. Sutton has been successfully eliminated, and that is the matter with which we are chiefly concerned. You have brought the papers with you?"

Diving into his side pocket, Craig produced a square packet tied up with string which he handed over to his companion. "That's all I could find. There's a sort of diary there that might be helpful. Tells what he was up to and puts down one or two names and addresses. They may mean something to your crowd."

"In a case like this the more information we can get the better." Von Manstein laid the packet on the table beside him. "Permit me to congratulate you again. You have acted with enterprise and judgment, and you may rest assured that the Reich will not be unmindful of the fact. I will make it my business to see that your services are suitably recognised."

Craig's heavy-lidded eyes brightened, and finishing his drink, he hoisted himself up off the ottoman.

"O.K., Count," he drawled. "I guess that's good enough for me."

◇◇◇

"Mark!"

Olga Brandon started up abruptly, spilling the ash of her cigarette on to the carefully polished parquet floor. With a reassuring smile her visitor closed the door and came forward to where she was standing.

"Couldn't make it any sooner. Been having a talk with von Manstein." He took her hands, and giving her a quick kiss, drew her down beside him on to the sofa. "You got my message from the Club?"

"Yes. Florrie told me as soon as I came in. I have been waiting for you ever since." She drew in a long breath. "I have read what it says in the paper, Mark. What does it mean? Has it—has it anything to do with you?"

Craig patted her arm. "It's all right, honey. The whole job's finished, and you can take it from me there's no call to get rattled. That bastard Sutton just got what he was askin' for."

The girl stared at him for a moment in silence.

"Did you kill him yourself?"

"Would it put the wind up you if I had?"

"You know me better than that. It's you I'm thinking about." She laid her hand on his sleeve and gripped it fiercely. "Tell me, Mark—tell me the truth. I'd never give anything away, not even if I was tortured. I'm all for the Germans. I'd love to see them smash hell out of these stuck-up swine."

"Yes, I reckon we think along the same lines." He ran his stubby fingers caressingly over her bare throat and neck. "Well, why not. You get around quite a lot, and maybe you might have heard something useful. Anyhow, I guess there's no harm in putting you wise."

Speaking in quick, broken sentences, he proceeded to explain why the removal of Sutton had become absolutely essential, and then, not without a certain boastful satisfaction, described the flattering confidence exhibited by von Manstein in entrusting him with the full responsibility for carrying out the necessary arrangements. In almost the same words that he had used half an hour earlier he went on to repeat his account of what had taken place at the bungalow, making no effort to excuse or conceal his own share in the deliberately planned murder. Kellerman's swift and efficient work with the knife, the hurried search for incriminating papers, the sudden scuffle outside, and the unexpected complications which had subsequently developed—the whole macabre story came tumbling out with complete and revolting frankness. All through, the girl sat motionless and silent, her dark eyes riveted upon his in a fixed, unwavering stare.

"Haven't figured out exactly what the two of 'em were up to," he finished, "but I guess it was some private affair of their own and nothing to do with us. Anyhow, it'll keep the cops busy. There'll be finger-prints and tyre-marks for 'em to play around with, and while they're getting ahead on that line we can just sit back and take things comfortable. Might even spread ourselves a trifle so long as the Count stumps up handsomely. How would you fancy a week in Paris and a spot of shopping to furbish up the wardrobe?"

"It would be great. How much do you think he'll be good for?"

"A decent packet. The Boche pays well when you give him the real goods. What matters, though, isn't the dough we can collect right now: it's how things will be in another year's time. Wait till Hitler's in Buckingham Palace and these darned Britishers are crawling around on their bellies."

"I'm not forgetting. All the same, there's no harm in drawing a bit on account."

"Say, that reminds me." Pulling out a leather wallet, Craig extracted a folded sheet of note-paper. It was covered on all four sides with straggling writing in an obviously feminine hand. "I found this in Sutton's pocket, and I didn't see any reason for handing it over to von Manstein. Struck me that the party who wrote it wouldn't exactly like to have it floating around loose. Might be willing to cough up in order to get it back. Only snag is that she hasn't put her address, and dames called Sheila are just about as common as dirt."

With an eager movement Olga took possession of the letter, and before she had finished reading the first page a wicked smile was already playing round her lips. Leaning forward Craig watched her closely.

"By gosh, you've got something here, Mark." Her voice had a ring of malicious triumph. "There's only one girl who could have written this, and that's Sheila Deane. I knew she was drifting around with Sutton up till a few months ago."

"Who is she?"

"No one in particular. Just one of those dumb good-lookers that artists and photographers go potty about. There were two pictures of her in the Academy last year."

"Has she got any brass?"

"Shouldn't think so. I believe her father was a country doctor, and the sister runs a furnishing shop or something of the sort down in Chelsea. I went there once with Lottie Gray."

"Doesn't sound too hopeful."

"I'm not so sure. There's a rumour that she's engaged to Julian Raymond, and if that's the case you can bet your life that she'd manage to find the needful. Wouldn't surprise me if Sutton was trying to put the black on her himself."

Craig whistled softly. "Looks as if we'd struck oil. Think she could have been the one who butted in with the car?"

"Didn't sound like her from your description."

"Well, there's money in it, that's a cert. Have to back pedal for a time, of course. Too damned dangerous to start anything at present."

"There's no hurry. Let her get on with it and marry the fool. She'll be splashing in it then, and you can take it from me that she'll be just as ready to fork out."

"You've hit it, honey." Craig grinned appreciatively. "Not the sort of dope a dame would like passed on to her hubby."

"You had better let me keep it. It will be safer here. If there was a raid on the Club and they happened to run across it—"

"Yeah—I guess you're right." As he spoke Craig's eyes travelled across to the clock on the mantelpiece, and after a confirmatory glance at his own watch he hoisted himself to his feet. "Gee, I must be getting along. How about to-morrow? Like to lunch with me at the Milan and drink the health of the happy pair?"

"Seems only fair." Olga refolded the letter, and with a contented yawn stretched out her arms. "After all," she added venomously, "they'll have to pay the bill."

Chapter VIII

Ding-dong. Ding-dong. Ding-dong.

A metallic boom floated vaguely into his consciousness, and with a protesting grunt Owen rolled over on to his elbow and reluctantly opened his eyes. His first sensation was one of utter bewilderment. For a moment or two he lay staring round the unfamiliar room with its long array of shelves and cupboards, and then, flinging off the rug that covered the lower part of his body, he struggled up stiffly into a sitting position. Where the deuce was he, and why— His hand went up to his head and his exploring fingers encountered a bandage. The effect was what is sometimes described as "electrical." It was just as though he had pressed a button and some obstructing curtain had been suddenly whisked aside.

"My holy aunt!" he muttered. "The angel's workshop, of course!" Like a queer unrolling film the events of the previous night began to crowd back into his mind. Curiously enough, they seemed to be taking place in reverse order. From the moment when Sally had spread the rug over him and told him to go to sleep his memory travelled in swift stages through what seemed to be a positive nightmare of strange and almost incredible experiences. Only when he arrived at the point when he was sitting dazed and half-conscious in the darkness of the bungalow did the stream of recollections suddenly peter out. Cudgel his brains as he might, all his further efforts were useless. Beyond that, everything was still a complete and maddening blank.

Getting off the couch a trifle unsteadily, he picked up his watch, which was lying on the table. The hands were pointing to three o'clock. The next instant he realised that he had omitted to wind it, and laying it down again with an impatient frown, he crossed over towards the small window opposite and peered out between the protecting iron bars.

He found himself gazing into a miniature back yard, the distinguishing feature of which was a large, rather dilapidated dustbin. The place was enclosed by a high, dirty-looking brick wall, with a flight of steps leading up to a door in the centre. Above this barrier rose an irregular line of chimney-pots, their black shapes standing out fantastically against a narrow strip of leaden-coloured sky.

As to what time of day it was, or how long he had been unconscious, there was nothing to afford the remotest indication. It was true that he was distinctly hungry, but since his last meal must be verging upon ancient history, such a state of affairs was only to be expected. The one fact about which there could be no question was that the rest and sleep had done him a world of good. Apart from a slight headache he felt in astonishingly good shape.

A gilt-framed mirror hanging on the wall suddenly caught his eye. With a certain hopeful excitement he walked towards it, but at the first glimpse of his own reflection the same chill feeling of bewilderment swept over him again with renewed force. This sunburned unshaven face, crowned by a slightly dishevelled bandage, might, for all it suggested, have been the property of a complete stranger. It was the uncanniest sensation he had yet experienced.

Before its full effect had had time to wear off there was a gentle tap on the door. He jerked round sharply and there, in the dim light that filtered in through the yard window, stood the blue-eyed, smiling figure of Sally Deane.

"Oh, you *are* awake at last and actually walking about!" She surveyed him with an air of professional gratification. "How's the head, and how are you feeling generally?"

"Ever so much better." He grinned cheerfully as though in support of his assertion. "You know, you ought to set up as a doctor. I'd make a grand advertisement for you."

"I must have a look and see whether you're telling the truth." Switching on the light, she advanced towards the couch, and having seated himself in the required position, Owen remained passively silent while she removed the bandage. The touch of her fingers and the sound of her soft breathing as she bent over him sent a queer thrill of pleasure trickling down his spine.

"Not too bad," she announced with a satisfied nod. "It hasn't bled any more, and the swelling seems to have gone down quite a lot. On the whole, I think we've made a pretty good job of it."

"I'm glad you approve." He looked up and let his eyes rest on the small, heart-shaped face with its adorably curved lips and firm, resolute little chin. "I'm terribly grateful for all you've done for me," he added. "I don't believe I thanked you half enough last night."

"Well, you informed me that I was your guardian angel. What more could you say than that?"

"Heaps." With a gingerly movement he explored the lump on the back of his head. "What time is it?" he demanded. "My watch has stopped and I haven't the shadowiest notion."

"Just on seven in the evening."

"Gosh—have I been out as long as that?"

She nodded. "I've been down once or twice to see how you were getting on, but each time you were still fast asleep. Your pulse seemed to be quite steady and regular, so I thought I'd better not disturb you. I was just a bit worried, of course, but I couldn't very well send for a doctor. He would have started asking questions, and—and that might have got you into trouble. All I could do was to wait until you woke up and see how you felt then!"

"I feel as right as rain except for my wretched memory. I know exactly what happened after you walked in, but the devil of it is that that's where everything seems to start off. As to who I am or how I got there, or whether I really stuck a knife into that blackmailing twirp—"

"Don't worry: it will all come back before very long." She patted him encouragingly. "What about some food? I expect you're quite hungry?"

"I wouldn't say no to a large chunk of bread and cheese."

"Oh, we can do better than that. I was just going to cook something for Ruth and myself, and it will be perfectly easy to make it enough for three. Would you prefer to have it down here, or do you feel well enough to come up and join us? We—we shall be very pleased if you would."

"It's terribly decent of you to ask me. Of course I'd much rather make a party of it: that's to say, if you don't object to my revolting appearance. I've been having a squint at myself in the glass, and—"

"You think you could do with a shave?" She put her head on one side and contemplated him gravely. "Yes, that occurred to me when I came in this morning, so I slipped out and bought you a brush and a safety razor. I've put them on the shelf in the lavatory, and you'll find a piece of soap and a towel there as well."

"But this is altogether too much. You leave me simply speechless with gratitude."

"That's all right. Both Ruth and I like strong, silent men."
She laughed mischievously. "I'll bring you down some hot
water, and then you can toddle along and make yourself
beautiful. You needn't hurry over it, because it will take at
least twenty minutes to get dinner ready. By the way, do you
remember whether you like mushrooms?"

"Mushrooms?" Owen paused and wrinkled his forehead.
"I think I must," he said slowly. "Anyhow, I can feel my
mouth watering."

◇◇◇

Ruth deposited the syphon and the bottle of whisky in the
centre of the table, and then stood back to survey the effect.
At the same instant Sally appeared in the doorway. She was
carrying a tray containing three portions of iced grapefruit,
the faint perfume of which drifted pleasantly across the
small sitting-room.

"Here we are," she announced. "All ready to start off. Do
you mind trotting down and fetching Oliver?"

"Why don't you go yourself?" objected Ruth. "He's your
property, not mine."

"But I want you to get to know him. You'll have a much
better chance if you talk to him alone."

"I'm not keen on taking chances with people who've
probably committed a murder." Ruth's lips twitched. "However, as you've done the cooking, darling, I suppose I must
humour you. If you happen to hear a strangled scream, fling
open the window and yell for the police."

Without further protest she stepped out on to the small
landing, and making her way downstairs and across the
dimly lighted shop, pulled up at the head of the short flight
that connected it with the basement.

"Hullo," she called out in her deep, rather husky voice.
"Dinner's ready if you've finished shaving. I've come along
to show you the way."

"That's very nice of you." Looking surprisingly clean and respectable, Owen emerged from his subterranean retreat and mounted the steps. His appearance was so improved that Ruth raised her eyebrows. "What have you been doing to yourself?" she exclaimed. "Why, I hardly recognised you."

"Only had a wash and a scrape. Marvellous the difference it makes." He smiled. "I may be wrong, but I'm beginning to hope that I'm not quite such a complete thug after all."

Ruth studied him for a moment in silence.

"Were you telling Sally the truth?" she demanded. "Can't you remember anything, not even your name?"

He shook his head. "Sounds like a fairy tale, I know; but, all the same, it's an absolute fact." He frowned. "Look here, let's get this quite straight. I don't blame you in the least for being suspicious: it's only natural. If anyone handed me out a yarn like that I'd feel dead sure he was lying."

"Well, I thought you might be last night. You see, I know Sally, and I know how generous and impulsive she is. Anybody can impose on her if they make out that they're in trouble."

"So I should imagine." Owen nodded. "I'll bet there isn't one girl in a million who'd have been kind and plucky enough to haul me out of that mess and bring me back here. I was so groggy last night I hardly realised what was happening. Now I've had a spot of sleep things are starting to sort themselves out."

"What do you mean by that?"

"Merely that something will have to be done about it. I may have killed Sutton or I may not, but in any case I can't possibly go on hiding in your basement. If I'm really a murderer and the police get on my track—"

"We shall both find ourselves being hauled off to Bow Street." Ruth shrugged. "Well, I've pointed out that pretty forcibly already, but it doesn't seem to cut any ice with Sally. Perhaps she'll be more disposed to listen to you."

"She'll have to."

"We shall see." With an enigmatic smile Ruth turned towards the staircase. "Come along up, anyhow. It's no use standing around here letting things get cold."

She motioned Owen to precede her, and leading the way up the staircase, he found himself confronted by a narrow landing with an open door exactly opposite. After the comparative gloom of the lower regions the small, cheerfully lit room, with its cream-coloured walls and neatly laid table, gave him the sudden feeling that he was stepping into a new and enchanting world. The illusion was distinctly heightened by the presence of Sally, who, in a plain green linen frock and with her copper-coloured hair gleaming in the lamplight, looked even more adorably beautiful than when he had last set eyes on her. He had a wild impulse to stride forward and snatch her up in his arms.

"Well," she observed demurely, "this is our chaste little attic. What do you think of it now you've got here?"

He looked round slowly, taking in all the various details. "Except for the absence of harps," he replied, "it's exactly my idea of Heaven."

"We've got a wireless," remarked Ruth dryly. "I can turn it on if you like."

"No, you don't," declared Sally. "I object to being crooned at while I'm eating grapefruit." She pulled out a chair. "Let's sit down and begin, anyhow. I had no tea and I'm simply ravenous."

They took their places at the table, and a brief, slightly embarrassing silence descended upon all three of them. It was broken by Ruth, who was watching the other two with what appeared to be a spice of half-malicious amusement.

"Oliver has got something to say to you, darling," she announced. "He has suddenly gone all noble and thinks he ought to clear out. I feel he's absolutely right, myself, but I told him he had better discuss it with you."

Sally turned to Owen. "Is this a fact?" she demanded, "or is Ruth just trying to be funny?"

"The nobility part's all bunk," he replied, "but the rest of it's true enough. I've been thinking it over while I was shaving, and I see now that it's the only possible way out. Matter of fact, I ought never to have come here."

"Don't be so stupid," returned Sally. "You were much too ill to look after yourself. Besides, where else could you have gone at that time of night?"

"I should have stopped where I was until someone rolled up and fetched the police!"

"Nonsense. They would have arrested you right away."

"Well, if I'm guilty, I'm ready to face up to it. In any case, I'd no right to plant myself on you."

"But you didn't. I had practically to carry you. My arm's still aching even now."

"That's not the point," objected Owen. "By skulking around here I'm putting you two into a fearful jam, and—"

"Now listen to me." Sally waggled her spoon at him. "I explained it all last night, but I suppose you were too fuddled to take it in. To start with, I don't believe that you killed Sutton. I think somebody banged you on the head and left you there purposely just to give that impression. All the same, you would probably have been arrested for it, and no matter who you are, or what your profession is, being tried for murder isn't exactly the sort of thing that does one any particular good. Even if one gets off, there are always a lot of kind people who run around saying that one ought to have been hanged."

"But supposing I really *am* a murderer?"

"It wouldn't make the slightest difference." Sally shook her head. "On the contrary, instead of being merely sorry for you I should be frightfully grateful as well. If ever anyone wanted killing it was that pig Sutton. I'd have done it myself cheerfully if I'd thought I could have got away with it."

Owen set his lips obstinately. "I'm afraid that doesn't help much; at least, not from my angle. My job is to clear off and keep you two out of it. If I didn't I should feel an unutterable squirt."

"Very well." Sally shrugged her shoulders. "In that case, as soon as you leave here I shall go straight to the police station and tell them everything. I shall be arrested too, and it will mean that my—my friend's story will be splashed around in all the newspapers and that she'll probably commit suicide. Perhaps that will satisfy you?"

"Bit difficult to manage, isn't she?" Ruth looked at Owen's face and smiled mockingly.

"Oh dear, don't let's start squabbling; at all events, not till we've finished eating." Sally jumped up and began to collect the plates. "I've done some lovely cutlets with mushrooms and sauté potatoes; we can't enjoy them properly if we're all arguing our heads off. I vote that just for the present we forget about last night and talk of something else."

"I second that." Ruth held up her hand. "Debate to be postponed until the arrival of coffee."

"I suppose I shall have to support the motion." Owen made a gesture of surrender. "Can I do anything in the parlourmaid line?"

"Certainly not: you're the guest." Sally picked up the pile of plates and turned towards the kitchen. "Have a cigarette and help yourself to a whisky," she added. "It won't hurt you if you put plenty of soda in it."

Accepting her invitation, Owen remained obediently in his seat. After a brief interval the second course made its appearance, and at the appetising odour which suddenly filled the room a faint nostalgic memory seemed to stir vaguely in the depths of his being. Somewhere in his obliterated past mushrooms had apparently occupied an important and prominent place.

"This," remarked Ruth, "is entirely in your honour. Sally's a topping good cook, but nine times out of ten she shoves it off on me. She always pretends she's too tired."

"So I am, as a rule. When you've been climbing ladders and measuring curtains and soft-soaping clients all day, you feel you've a sort of right to sit back and be waited on. At least, that's one way of looking at it. Of course the real truth is that Ruth spoils me horribly."

"You must both be desperately clever to run a show like this," observed Owen. "How long has it been going?"

"Just fourteen months." Sally smiled proudly. "Last week Ruth got out our first balance-sheet, and after paying our own salaries and putting a bit by for interest on capital, we found that we'd actually made a profit of twenty-five pounds. We were so bucked we rushed out and bought a couple of new hats."

"What does an interior decorator do?" enquired Owen. "Sounds as if it was something like goldmining."

"Oh, it's quite easy and simple. You merely get hold of people with money who want to be thought artistic and clever, and then you persuade them to let you do up their flat or their house. Of course, if it's a big job you have to work in with a proper builder and go shares, but Ruth's desperately smart about fixing up anything of that sort. She handles the whole business side. I just sketch out the ideas and puddle around with a foot-rule and a pot of paint."

"Don't you believe her," interrupted Ruth. "Sally's a genius in her own line; and what's more, she can twiddle a customer round her little finger. I sometimes sit and blush at her sheer damned cheek."

With obvious relish she proceeded to narrate stories illustrating her statement, and before long Owen was laughing so heartily and feeling so completely at home that for the time being the grim problem presented by his own extraordinary situation more or less faded into the background. It was only when Ruth had brought in the coffee and Sally was engaged in filling up the three dainty little Wedgwood cups that he forced himself half-reluctantly to return to the main issue.

"I'd hate to shove a damper on the party," he observed, "but there's no sense in trying to put things off any longer. We've simply got to get down to brass tacks." He paused. "What's been happening at Playford? Has anyone been along there and found the body?"

Sally passed him across a cup and nodded gravely. "Yes, there's a paragraph about it in the *Star*. She leaned back and picked up a paper which was lying on the sofa. "Here it is on the front page," she continued. "I was going to show it to you, but I thought I'd wait till we'd finished our dinner. I wanted you to have something to eat before I sprang it on you."

Swiftly and silently Owen read through the half-column and then, with a gathering frown, looked up to encounter the watchful eyes of his two companions.

"I don't like it," he said, shaking his head. "Especially that bit about the tyre-marks. Supposing they were to come round here and ask to see your car?"

"We should have to show it them, of course, but it wouldn't prove anything. There must be millions of half-worn Dunlops about."

"You're quite sure you left nothing in the bungalow?"

"Positive. All I'm worrying about is the letter. If they get hold of that and found out who the writer was, some wretched inspector would roll up and ask all sorts of horrible questions. I wish to Heaven I knew what had happened to it."

"I'd sell my soul if I could only remember how I got there." Owen clenched his fists. "I must have had some special reason for going to the damned place—"

"Not necessarily." The interruption came from Ruth.

"How do you mean?"

"You might have been walking past, and have heard Sutton scream out for help or something."

"That's an idea!" Sally's eyes brightened. "There may have been two or three of them on the job, and if you came charging in at the wrong moment—"

"They'd naturally knock you on the head to save their own skins." Ruth leaned back and puffed out a cloud of smoke. "At least, that's what I should have done," she added.

"You may be right. I'd love to think you were." Owen paused. "Sutton was certainly asking for it, and I dare say there are quite a lot of people who wanted him out of the way. Perhaps he got too fresh and started in on some crowd a bit tougher than himself."

"Serve him right," declared Sally. "I'd sympathise with them entirely if they hadn't left you to hold the baby. That was a rotten trick."

"I'm not really defending them," explained Ruth. "All the same you can't expect people to be too particular when they've just committed a murder. Why, if anyone tried to blackmail me I should simply see red."

A queer, half-stifled exclamation escaped from Owen's lips. "See red," he repeated slowly. "*See red.*" Little beads of perspiration broke out upon his forehead, and putting down his cup, he sank forward over the table and buried his face in his hands. Sally jumped up instantly.

"What is it? Are you feeling bad again?"

"No, no. Don't talk—for God's sake don't talk. It's coming back—it's all coming back to me now!"

"You—you mean your memory?"

He raised his head, and for several dragging moments the tension seemed almost unbearable. Then, with an abrupt movement, he thrust back his chair.

"A telephone," he muttered. "Is there a telephone in the place?"

Ruth opened her mouth as though to reply, but before she could speak Sally was already pointing towards the desk in the corner.

"Right in front of you," she announced. "If you want the directory, it's on the shelf below."

In a couple of swift strides Owen crossed over and took off the receiver. The two girls remained where they were, watching him in breathless silence as he hurriedly dialled a number.

"Is that Whitehall two six eight one?...I should like to speak to Captain Greystoke, please...Bradwell...No, I want to talk to him personally...Oh, hell—any chance of my being able to get in touch with him?...Not till then?...Yes, if there's the least likelihood of it I should be greatly obliged. Will you say that unless I hear to the contrary I will come to his office at three o'clock to-morrow...Yes, he has my number...Thanks very much."

The receiver clattered down on to its stand, and drawing the back of his hand across his forehead, the speaker turned round and shrugged wearily.

"That," he observed, "is precisely what would happen."

Sally stepped forward from the table, and taking hold of his arm, shepherded him towards the sofa.

"Give him another whisky," she commanded, "a good strong one." Quietly but firmly she drew him down beside her, and then, stretching out her arm, relieved Ruth of the hastily replenished tumbler. "Here you are," she continued "Drink this and sit still for a minute."

A trifle unsteadily, he took the glass and drained off its contents.

"You must have thought I'd gone crackers hurling myself at the phone like that." He smiled apologetically. "If it's any relief, I can assure you that I'm perfectly sane. You see, the whole thing came back to me in a sort of blinding rush, and all I could think about was getting hold of a friend of mine whom I'd promised to ring up. It's—it's desperately important that I should see him as soon as possible."

"Well, it's no use upsetting yourself. If he's away you will just have to wait till to-morrow."

"What I want to know," remarked Ruth bluntly, "is whether you killed Sutton. That seems to be the really essential point."

"I should say it was highly improbable, but I'm not absolutely certain. I remember climbing over the fence and crawling up towards the back window, but after that everything suddenly fades out. Looks as though I'd collected my packet somewhere in the garden."

"But why—"

"Don't keep on chucking questions at him," protested Sally. "Let him tell us in his own way."

Owen extended his hand. "Give me another cigarette first; it will help to clear my head. Thanks." He lit it slowly and sat for a moment staring at the smouldering tip. "Suppose I'd better begin by introducing myself. My name's Bradwell—Owen Bradwell. I'm a Lieutenant-Commander in the Navy."

"Might have guessed that. It's exactly what you look like." Ruth nodded.

"Shut up," said Sally crisply.

"I'm on leave at the moment, what's professionally called 'sick leave.' I was coming home after a couple of years on the China station, and one night—out in the Indian Ocean it was—I suddenly found that I'd gone colour-blind. Couldn't spot the difference between a red and green light. Just about as devastating a thing as could happen to anyone up my street." He took a long, vicious pull at his cigarette. "Went before a Medical Board when I got to Plymouth and they packed me off to Town to consult a specialist. I've been staying with a pal called Anstey who has got a flat off Park Lane. I saw the Harley Street merchant last week, and he practically told me that as far as active service is concerned my career as a dashing N.O. was finished and done with. All I should be any good for in future would be some pottering job ashore, sitting on a stool in a dockyard office and keeping a weather eye on a lot of pot-bellied contractors." He gave a short, mirthless laugh and leaned back against the cushion.

"I am so sorry." Sally's blue eyes were full of sympathy. "It's—it's sickening bad luck, but you never know how things are going to turn out. Perhaps they'll offer you something more interesting and exciting."

"I rather doubt it. You see, I've had my chance, and I appear to have messed it up pretty thoroughly."

"Had it anything to do with what happened at Playford?"

"It had everything to do with it." He frowned. "I can't tell you very much, because it's the kind of affair that has to be kept quiet; but thanks to my skipper, who's in touch with some of the Big Noises, I was offered a job by a friend of his at the Admiralty. If I'd managed to pull it off it would have sent my stock up with a jump."

"Is that how you came to get knocked on the head?" It was Ruth who put the question.

"Maybe. Anyhow, it was why I was scouting around outside the bungalow." With an impatient jerk he flung his half-smoked cigarette into the fireplace. "Don't get hold of the idea that I'm just thinking about myself. My own private affairs don't matter a hang. What's worrying me is that I ought to bung in a full report straight away, and as the chap I'm working for is out of Town I can't possibly do anything about it until to-morrow. Makes one want to blaspheme."

"Can't you talk to somebody else instead?"

"That's the devil of it! I've strict orders to deal with no one except my own particular boss, and even then I'm supposed to use the telephone. Until I've seen him and explained the whole business I daren't open my mouth. Absolutely washes out any idea about going to the police."

Sally wrinkled her forehead. "Well, there's only one thing for it, you'll just have to stop here and hide in the workroom."

"Nothing I'd enjoy more if I could choose for myself. As it is, I'm afraid I shall have to get back to the flat."

"But why?"

"I must be there in case this bloke rings me up. There's a faint possibility that he may get into touch with his office, and if he does they've promised to pass along my message."

"I don't expect we shall be separated for very long," observed Ruth. "We shall probably meet again in the dock at Bow Street to-morrow morning." She shrugged resignedly. "Lucky we bought those new hats, isn't it?"

"Half a moment: I've got a brainwave." Owen straightened up in his seat and turned to Sally. "My appointment isn't till three o'clock, so why shouldn't we all have lunch somewhere? We ought to celebrate an occasion like this. It's the first time I've ever been knocked on the head and rescued by a couple of interior decorators."

"Really!" Sally opened her eyes. "I thought that sort of thing was always happening to Lieutenant-Commanders."

"I wish it was. Life would be a lot brighter and more stimulating." He looked smilingly from one to the other.

"Well, what do you say about it? Let's go to the Milan and do the job in style."

"It's a lovely idea, but I'm afraid it won't work. One of us must stop here. We can't drift out like that and leave the business to run itself."

"Don't worry," remarked Ruth. "I'll stay and look after the shop."

"Not on your life," declared Sally determinedly. "We'll either toss up for it or—"

"Don't be mulish, darling. I'm not throwing a Christian martyr act. This ghastly mess we've got ourselves into is all your doing, and like a respectable, clean-living girl I prefer to keep out of it. I should hate to be tapped on the shoulder by a policeman just as I was swallowing an oyster."

"Suppose we make a compromise," suggested Owen. "Sally can come to-morrow, and as soon as the real murderer has been discovered I'll invite you. Then you can eat as many oysters as you like in perfect peace."

Sally laughed. "You don't know what you're letting yourself in for. The last time we went out to lunch together—"

"Dry up." Ruth's green eyes twinkled mischievously. "If you don't," she added, "I'll tell him about that corn on your little toe."

Chapter IX

Setting his teeth savagely, Owen took another frantic pull at the oars. The boat lurched forward a couple of feet and then slid back again into its previous position. With an anguished cry Sally leaned forward from her seat in the stern.

"Oh, go on, go on," she moaned. "You'll be late for your appointment."

"Blast my appointment!" A gust of impotent rage swept through his heart. "How can anybody row when the damned sea's full of treacle?"

"It's not treacle: it's *blood*."

The glare of a torch streamed out through the darkness and there, sprawled grotesquely right in front of his feet, lay the dead body of Granville Sutton. Sticking up between his shoulder-blades was the crooked handle of an umbrella.

"Blood, blood, blood," wailed Sally. "It's getting into the frying-pan and spoiling the mushrooms."

A deluge of water surged over the boat, knocking Owen backwards and wrenching the oars from his hands. He was conscious of struggling wildly in a cold, suffocating blackness, and then by some astounding miracle he found himself sitting up in bed with the impassive figure of Watkins standing sedately at his elbow.

"I am sorry to wake you up, sir, but a gentleman has just been enquiring for you on the telephone. I informed him that you were still asleep, and he asked me to give you a message."

"A message?"

"Yes, sir. He said that he wished to confirm your appointment for three o'clock this afternoon. He declined to leave his name."

"Thanks. That will be all right." Jolted back suddenly into complete consciousness, Owen rubbed his eyes and glanced round the room. Through a narrow gap at the side of the drawn blind a thin shaft of sunlight flickered across the carpet and played fitfully round the base of the wardrobe. "What time is it now?" he demanded.

"Ten minutes past twelve exactly, sir."

"Holy Moses! Why didn't you rout me out sooner?"

"You had left no instructions as to when you wanted to be called." Watkins gave a discreet cough. "I regret that I was out when you returned last night, sir," he continued, "but not having been notified of your intentions I had arranged to spend the evening with some friends. By the time I arrived back you had already retired. I have looked in on several occasions this morning, but since you were still sleeping soundly I assumed that you would prefer not to be disturbed."

"Very thoughtful of you." Owen's eyes twinkled. "Just in case of any misunderstanding, though, I should like to mention that I had not been out on the binge. I had had a long and rather exhausting day and I was simply dog tired."

"Just so, sir. That is precisely what I imagined." Crossing over to the window, Watkins drew up the blind. "I trust you enjoyed your week-end, sir? A pity the weather was not a trifle more settled."

"Oh, it wasn't too bad, on the whole. Sunday night was certainly a bit of a wash-out, but, taking it all round, I think I was remarkably lucky."

"Would you care for a cup of tea, sir?"

"No time, I'm afraid. I've got a luncheon engagement at one o'clock, and I must hurry up and get dressed."

"Very good, sir. I will put your bath on straight away."

◇◇◇

Handing over his hat and pocketing the ticket, Owen stepped back out of the cloakroom into the luxuriously carpeted vestibule of the Milan. As usual at this hour, the place was crowded. In every direction little clusters of people were sitting or standing about waiting for some belated friend, while through the constantly revolving door an apparently endless stream of fresh arrivals kept drifting in to swell the already imposing throng. The air was filled with a buzz of conversation, punctuated now and then by a mechanical voice bleating out the number of some resident guest.

He had produced his case and was about to light a cigarette when he suddenly caught sight of Sally. She had been completely concealed behind an enormous overdressed woman who had come in a moment before, and at the first glimpse of her standing there and looking around in search of him, his heart gave such a disconcerting jump that he nearly disgraced himself by shouting out her name. The next moment he had pushed his way forward and they were shaking hands.

"You're beautifully punctual," he observed. "I suppose that comes from running a business?"

She smiled. "It comes from the fact that I'm fearfully hungry. We both overslept ourselves this morning and there was no time to have a proper breakfast."

"Let's go in at once, then. I rang up and reserved a table."

"That was very nice and thoughtful of you."

She nodded approvingly, and steering a course for the entrance to the dining-room, Owen mentioned his name to the stately attendant who was functioning in the doorway. The latter consulted his list, and the next moment they were being conducted across the vast restaurant in the direction of the long array of flower-banked windows which looked out towards the Embankment.

"This is topping. Hope I'm not too dowdy compared with all these gorgeous females." Sally settled down into her chair. "How do you like my new hat?" she demanded.

"Terrific! Knocks spots off anything in the place."

"Thank you. Now I feel more at home." She waved aside the menu which the waiter was presenting to her. "I'd rather you ordered the lunch," she continued. "When there are such a lot of things to choose from I can never make up my mind what I'd like best."

Owen reached out for the card and for several moments looked over it thoughtfully. "How about beginning with some *pâté?*" he suggested. "Then we might have a couple of young grouse and finish up with Pêche Melba." He beckoned to the wine waiter who was hovering in the background. "Bring us a bottle of really good Burgundy," he added. "You know what you've got better than I do."

The man made a gratified bow. "M'sieur may leave it to me with complete confidence."

"Does that meet with your approval?" Owen turned back to Sally, who was surveying him with a sort of grave amusement.

"Speaking professionally, I should describe it as a perfect piece of interior decoration." Her lips twitched. "I think you ought to come into partnership with us."

"That's not a bad idea. After the bungle I've made of my present job I shall probably be looking out for a new profession."

"But are you sure you've bungled it?" Sally's face had

suddenly become serious. "Of course I—I don't know what it's all about—"

"And I can't explain, I'm afraid: at least I can't give you any details." He frowned. "What it amounts to, however, is that I've got to go along to the chap I'm working for and tell him that just as I had a chance of collecting the information he wanted I was fool enough to get knocked on the head and lose my memory. Not what one would call a pleasant prospect, but the thing's so damned serious I've no other choice."

"Then it will all have to come out, I suppose? I mean about that wretched letter and my reasons for going to the bungalow."

"Not necessarily. I've been thinking it over, and I believe I can square that all right."

"Won't you have to explain how you got away and what you've been doing ever since?"

"I certainly shall."

"What are you going to say?"

"Wait till we've been served. Here's our man coming back now."

They sat silent while racks of crisp brown toast accompanied by delectable-looking slices of *pâté* were ceremoniously deposited in front of them. On the farther side of the room the orchestra broke out into the latest heart-stirring masterpiece recently imported from Broadway.

"That business of yours has nothing whatever to do with what I'm working on." Owen had lowered his voice and was leaning forward across the table. "If I can, I want to keep you out of it altogether."

"But how?" persisted Sally. "You've got about twenty-two hours to account for, and you must have spent them somewhere."

"I could have spent them lying in a ditch or hidden away under a hedge. Suppose you hadn't turned up, and suppose

I'd recovered consciousness say about midnight. You know the state I was in—half dazed and not able to remember a blessed thing. It's quite possible that I might have walked out of the place and blundered along vaguely in the dark until at last I collapsed again through sheer weakness. I might easily have lain there in some out-of-the way spot until four or five the next afternoon. Then, as soon as I came to my senses and realised what had happened, my first idea would naturally have been to stagger back to Town and get in touch with Greystoke. I could pretend that I caught a train at some station up the line and went straight home to my flat, where I rang up his office."

Sally stared at him for a moment before replying.

"This job you're on is really important—something connected with the secret service, isn't it?"

"Yes, in a way."

"And are you proposing to tell all these lies merely to oblige me?"

Owen contented himself with a nod.

"Then the whole notion is just fantastic. To start with, it wouldn't hold water for a minute, not if it was looked into properly. They would know you'd invented it for some reason of your own, and after that they wouldn't believe a single word you told them."

"It's more than possible," admitted Owen.

"Well, do you imagine I'd sit down quietly and let you do anything so idiotic? I—I know it's terribly decent of you to suggest it, but—" She paused, her lips slightly parted and a sudden determined light shining in her eyes. "Oh, it's no good trying to hide things any longer; at least, not from you. We're all in this together, and the sooner you know the whole truth the better."

"Go ahead. I'm listening."

"It was Sheila, my sister, who wrote that letter to Sutton. The only excuse I can make for her is that she must have been utterly infatuated at the time. Later on she found out what he was really like and refused to have any more to do with him. A little while ago she got engaged to somebody else. He's quite a well-known man in politics, and he'd be terrified of any sort of scandal which might interfere with his career. I've no use for him myself, but Sheila is desperately keen on marrying him because he can give her exactly what she wants. I'm making her sound horrid, but that isn't fair. There's nothing really wrong with her. It's merely that she has always been spoiled because she's so beautiful."

"Is she like you?"

"I've got a faint look of her, at least so people say—only just enough to show that we're sisters. Why, if she was here now every man in the room would be goggling at our table."

"What a revolting idea!" Owen gave a slight shudder.

"I think this will meet with M'sieur's approval." The wine waiter was standing at his elbow proffering a bottle for inspection. "It is a Nuits George, twenty-nine—a remarkably fine vintage."

"Good work! Shove it on the table and we'll help ourselves." He slid half a crown into a conveniently receptive hand, and waiting until they were alone again, helped himself to a fresh piece of toast. "I gather the proposal was that she should buy this letter back? How much was the swine asking for it?"

"A thousand pounds. He swore that unless she paid up he'd put it in an envelope and send it to her fiancé. She'd have been fool enough to do it too, if she could have managed to raise the cash. As it was, all she could get hold of was five hundred. She came to me in such a state of jitters that I felt I had to do something about it. I knew it was no use her trying to bargain with him, so I offered to take on the job myself. He'd arranged for her to bring the money to the bungalow at ten-thirty, and I thought the simplest way would be to go down and have it out there and then, I loathe putting off anything nasty of that sort: it only makes it seem more difficult."

Very deliberately Owen filled up a glass and passed it across.

"Seems to be a hobby of yours, rescuing people who've got themselves into jams!"

"Oh, I had to help Sheila. I promised my mother that I would always look after her."

"Then what do you want me to do? If I tell the truth—"

"It will just have to come out, that's all. Sheila knows what's happened. She looked round last night after you'd gone, and I explained the whole situation."

"As a matter of fact, it isn't Sheila I'm worrying about—it's you."

"Me?"

Owen nodded. "In a murder case the police suspect everybody. I shall be a hot favourite, of course; but when they learn that Sutton was blackmailing your sister and that you went there to try to get hold of the letter, they're dead certain to rope you in as a promising alternative. You'll be questioned and requestioned till you don't know whether you're on your head or your heels, and—"

"I'm not afraid." Sally squared her shoulders defiantly. "I don't mean to say that I should like it; but if there's something going on that's got to do with the safety of the country, one can't just think about oneself."

"That's a pretty fine way of looking at it, if you don't mind my saying so."

"Nonsense," retorted Sally. "Anyone who didn't feel like that would be a complete twirp." She picked up her glass, took a sip of its contents and smiled at him encouragingly. "That's settled then; you must tell this friend of yours everything, and if he doesn't believe you he can come and talk to me."

"Thanks. It will certainly make things a heap easier." Owen hesitated. "I—I wish I could tell you how grateful I am, but I'm a shockingly bad hand at expressing what I feel. I think most sailors are."

"The Silent Service they call it, don't they?" Sally's eyes twinkled mischievously. "I expect it comes from being so much on board ship and seeing so few women. You ought to find some nice girl and get her to give you a course of lessons. If you like, I'll put up an advertisement in the shop."

"That's a grand notion. May I come and sit there and interview the applicants?"

"You'll have to ask Ruth: she's the managing director." There was another pause as the waiter arrived to remove their plates, and then, with a quick return to her former seriousness, Sally suddenly broke the silence. "When can I see you again? I shall be dying to know how you got on."

"What are you doing after lunch? Going back to Chelsea?"

"Not just yet. I want to look in at one or two places and see if I can match some materials. It will probably take me a couple of hours."

"Well, why not come along to the flat and have some tea with me?"

"I'd love to, but suppose you're not back?"

"That's all right. If there's any chance of my being late I'll ring up Watkins and tell him to look after you. He's Joe Anstey's retainer, and you'll feel as if you were being waited on by an Archbishop."

"Sounds a bit alarming, but I don't mind risking it."

"Splendid!" Owen sighed contentedly. "Now we've fixed that," he added, "I can do justice to the grouse."

II

"Not a bad wine, though I'm damned if it's worth thirty shillings a bottle." Mark Craig took another sip and then resumed his attack on the Sole Colbert. "However," he continued, "seeing that our friends are paying for it, I guess we needn't excite ourselves. Between you and me, honey, I don't mind admitting that they've coughed up handsomely."

"Why, that's grand." Olga gave a satisfied nod. "Then I take it that the trip to Paris is definitely on?"

"You bet it is. Nothing like a holiday after one's pulled off a good deal."

"How soon can we get away?"

"Better make it the week after next. I'd rather hang around for a few days just in case anything breaks."

"Yes, perhaps it would be as well. They don't seem to be handing out any dope to the newspapers; at least, there was nothing fresh in the *Mail* this morning." The smooth brow contracted into a slight frown. "I'm not exactly worrying, but I'd feel more comfortable if I knew what they were up to."

"All set trying to locate that car and identify the knife." Craig gave a short chuckle. "Couple of nice fat clues served up hot on a plate. Just what a cop dreams about when he's tucked up in his little cot."

The girl glanced at him admiringly. "You're a great man, Mark, and you'll go pretty far with your brains and your nerve. Reckon I'd be glad to work with you even if there was nothing else in it." She raised her glass, and then, replacing it on the table, leaned back with a sort of insolent grace and allowed her eyes to wander round the room.

"Come to that, my dear, you're not exactly dumb yourself." Craig drawled out the words, contemplating her lazily from under his half-closed lids. "If anything happened along that called for guts and—" He broke off abruptly. "Say, what are you staring at? Someone you know over there?"

"It's Sheila Deane's sister, the girl who runs that decorating joint in Chelsea. She's lunching with a fellow at one of the tables in the window. Looks as if he might be a barrister or a naval officer."

"That so!" With a leisurely movement Craig glanced round over his shoulder, and at the same instant the muscles of his jaw stiffened abruptly.

"What's the matter?"

He turned back slowly, and reaching out for the bottle, refilled his glass.

"It's the guy Kellerman slugged; and unless I'm drunk or dreaming, that's the dame who butted in and carted him off."

Olga drew in a sharp breath.

"You're sure?"

"Sure enough to stake my life on it."

They sat for a moment facing each other in silence.

"What are you going to do? Can you find out who he is?"

"We must. Von Manstein has an idea that he might be one of Greystoke's bunch." The thick fingers that were holding the fork tightened viciously. "How about her recognising you? Any chance of that?"

"Shouldn't think so. I was only in her place once, and all the time I was there she was talking to Lottie; I just strolled around and looked at the stuff."

"Well, keep an eye on them, and let me know soon as they start getting ready to quit."

"You mean to follow them?"

"Sure. I'm just sticking to that son of a bitch till I see where he fetches up. The girl don't matter now we know where we can collect her."

"Any way I can help?"

"Maybe—later on."

"If there is, you can count me in." Olga flung another quick glance at the distant table. "You can count me in to the limit—you know that, Mark."

Chapter X

In response to Owen's ring, the door of number 17a Queen Anne's Gate was opened by the same burly, keen-eyed individual who had escorted him upstairs on his previous visit. His arrival was evidently expected, for with an inviting gesture the man stepped aside to make way for his entrance.

"Captain's engaged at the moment, sir, but he will see you as soon as possible. Perhaps you wouldn't mind waiting in here."

Crossing to the other side of the hall, he ushered his visitor into a small, severely furnished room, the windows of which also looked out on to the Park. The only effort at decoration was an enlarged photograph of one of his Majesty's battleships forging ahead under full steam into what appeared to be the teeth of an Atlantic gale. It hung above the mantelpiece, with a date, Nov. 13th, 1934, scribbled boldly across the bottom left-hand corner.

Left to his own devices, Owen seated himself at the bare, gate-legged table and pulled out the long envelope that was encumbering his inside pocket. From this he extracted the thin wad of foolscap paper which contained his report. It was the fruit of two hours' concentrated work the previous night, work which he had not dared to put off until the morning in case his recently recovered memory should again play him false.

Slowly and carefully he read through the whole eight sheets. As a straightforward statement of the facts it appeared to be a fairly satisfactory composition; but apart from this slightly redeeming merit, all that it really amounted to in the cold light of day was an elaborate confession of failure. What were Greystone's comments likely to be when he had to admit that as far as the key incident of the whole affair was concerned his mind was still a complete blank? Whatever gleams of intelligence or enterprise he might have displayed during the earlier part of his investigations, the crass stupidity of permitting himself to be knocked senseless at the crucial moment would be more than sufficient to offset any possible credit that might otherwise be due to him. For such clumsiness there could be no excuse. Fate had tossed the ball straight into his hands, and like a blundering fool he had allowed it to slip through his fingers.

Well, it was done now, and sitting staring at those closely written pages wasn't going to mend matters in the slightest. He shrugged grimly. He had been given his chance, and if he had merely succeeded in proving himself unfitted for the work entrusted to him there was nothing for it but to face up to the consequences. After all, it was just possible that what he had seen and overheard on the island might be of some assistance to the Authorities, and if that were the case the personal interests of Lieutenant-Commander Owen Bradwell were not a subject of the remotest importance. In the Navy the only thing that mattered was the job. It was an axiom which had been hammered into him ever since the day when he had first set foot in Dartmouth, and, like other lessons learned in the same stern school, it had long ago become an unquestioned part of his professional creed.

He had folded up his report and was in the act of return-ing it to its envelope when the man who had admitted him suddenly reappeared in the doorway.

"The Captain is free, now, sir. If you will come with me I will take you to his room."

Leading the way up the staircase, he ushered Owen into the now familiar apartment on the first landing, where, as before, the sturdily built figure of Captain Greystoke was seated at the large table in the centre. On this occasion, however, the host made no attempt to rise. Contenting himself with a nod and a curt gesture towards a vacant chair, he resumed his perusal of a typewritten letter which he was holding in his hand, and feeling unpleasantly like a guilty schoolboy who had been summoned to an interview with his headmaster, Owen stepped quietly forward and sat down. As he did so the door closed behind him.

For an appreciable interval the silence remained unbro-ken, and then, having signed his letter, Greystoke placed it on one side and straightened up in his chair.

"This request of yours for a personal interview was a trifle unexpected, Bradwell. My instructions were that for the present you were to confine your communications to the telephone. Has that escaped your memory?"

"No, sir."

"Then perhaps you will be obliging enough to give me an explanation."

Taking out the envelope again, Owen laid it on the table. "It's here, sir. This is a full report which I drew up last night. I don't know whether you would prefer to read it or whether—"

"If you have anything to tell me that is really urgent and important I would rather hear it from your own lips."

"Very good, sir."

"And—er"—the frosty expression on Greystoke's face momentarily relaxed—"you can smoke if you like, Bradwell."

He pushed across the silver box in front of him, and with a murmur of thanks Owen helped himself to a cigarette. Somehow or other, this unexpected invitation did much to restore his self-confidence.

"I'm afraid it's rather a long story, sir, but I'll do my best to make it as concise as I can."

Beginning with a short account of his arrival at Thames Ferry and his abortive vigil off the island in the guise of a fisherman, he went on to describe his visit to the Red Lion and the instructive conversation which he had enjoyed with its landlord.

"You had told me to use my own judgment, sir," he continued, "and since it seemed possible that this bloke who was coming down from Town might be von Manstein, I thought I'd better stick around and have a dekko at him. It was close on eleven when he showed up. I was lying low behind some bushes at the entrance to the backwater, and I could just see him being ferried over to the landing-stage. The light had pretty well gone by that time, and all I could make out was that he was a tallish, upright sort of cove and that he was smoking a cigar. Struck me that if I wanted to find out any more my only hope was to slip across on to the island."

Greystoke, who up till then had offered no comment, nodded approvingly.

"There was a sort of thicket at one end of the place, so I made for that and worked the punt in under the trees. When I got ashore I found that I was looking across a stretch of lawn slap into a lighted room on the ground floor. The two of them, Craig and this other merchant, were both in there yapping away to each other, and feeling that you would probably like to know what they were discussing, I slid in amongst some shrubs and worked my way up to the French window. Unfortunately the damn thing was shut. Seemed at first as if there was nothing doing, but after about five minutes I had a stroke of luck. One of them opened it, to let in some fresh air, I suppose, and I managed to overhear two or three sentences. They were fixing up to go to Playford Sunday night and drop in on a chap who lived in a bungalow called Sunny Bank." He paused. "I don't know whether the name suggests anything to you, sir?"

"Sunny Bank!" Greystoke had stiffened abruptly. "Go on," he rapped out.

"I thought it was obviously part of my job to be present at the meeting, so I punted up there Sunday afternoon and had a look at the place. It's a lonely sort of shack at the corner of a lane about half a mile down the towpath. I hung around till it was getting dark, and then I did a little trek across country and hid up amongst some trees at the back of the garden. According to my watch, it was nearly six minutes past ten when the balloon went up. I saw Craig and another fellow climb over a stile into the lane and knock at the door. I don't think the second man was the one I'd seen on the island—he looked a bit shorter. Anyhow, somebody let them in, and I decided that it was up to me to keep tabs on what was going on. I had a sort of idea that there was trouble in the offing."

"From what I've read in the papers your idea appears to have been well founded." Greystoke drummed softly on the writing-pad. "Am I to understand that you were within a few yards of the place when this fellow Sutton was murdered?"

"Apparently, sir."

"What do you mean by apparently?"

"It's the only word that seems to fit." Owen took a long breath and summoned up his courage. "I made a mess of it, sir. Tried to work the same stunt again, and this time it didn't come off. One of those beauties must have slipped out without my spotting him and have been lying up in the dark with a rubber cosh or something of the sort. All I remember is crawling along as far as the fence and climbing over into the garden. I haven't the slightest notion what hit me, but whatever it was it knocked me stone cold. For the next quarter of an hour I was out to the wide."

Greystoke raised his eyebrows. "And then——?" he asked quietly.

"I came round with an appalling head on me and found myself in pitch darkness. Everything was an absolute blank. I hadn't the foggiest recollection of what had happened, and I couldn't even remember my own name. Just as I was trying to sit up someone switched on a light. I was in a room, a strange room I had never seen before, and there was a girl in a wet mackintosh standing right in front of me shining a torch on my face. She asked me who I was and what I was doing there, and when I explained that I hadn't the remotest idea, she—well, she introduced me to Mr. Granville Sutton. He wasn't a pretty sight. He was lying on his face with the shaft of a knife sticking up between his shoulders."

For a moment Greystoke stared at his visitor in silence.

"He was dead by then—you are quite certain of that?"

"Not a doubt of it, sir. The only question was which of us had killed him. The girl appeared to have pitched on me as the guilty party, and as I wasn't in a position to contradict her I lay low and let her get on with the talking. She was astoundingly cool and calm about it all. She told me she had driven down from Town by appointment to buy a letter with which Sutton had been threatening to blackmail a friend of hers. According to her story, the door of the bungalow had been open—she had found the pair of us lying on the carpet. Knowing the sort of skunk Sutton was, she seemed inclined to think that anyone who had had the enterprise to jab him in the back must be a public benefactor. To show her gratitude she suggested taking me back to her own place and hiding me away from the police until I was fit enough to carry on for myself. It was a mad notion, of course, but I was feeling so rotten I simply hadn't the strength to argue about it. Before I quite realised what was happening she had lugged me out into the lane and helped me into the car, and after what seemed to be a hell of a long drive we fetched up at a garage. It was somewhere in Chelsea, where she and another girl run a kind of decorating business. They've got a shop in the King's Road with a small flat up above and a workroom in the basement. By the time I'd staggered round there I was just about all-in. I've a vague recollection of lying on a sofa and having my head bandaged, and then I must have dropped off and slept like a log. They tell me I never blinked an eyelash till seven o'clock yesterday evening."

"Is that when you recovered your memory?"

Owen shook his head. "It was a bit later, sir. Sally Deane, the girl who had brought me there, invited me to come up to the flat and have some food. You see, by that time she had rather altered her opinion. She had begun to think that someone else might have committed the murder and that I'd been planted there to hold the baby. Of course we started talking it all over again, and while we were in the middle of it the other girl, whose name's Ruth Barlow, said something about 'seeing red.' That was what did the trick. The moment I heard the words the whole business about my going colour-blind suddenly came back to me. In another minute or two I'd remembered everything, and it struck me pretty forcibly that the sooner I got in touch with you the better. There was a telephone in the flat, so I rang up straight away. When they told me that you wouldn't be here until this afternoon I thought the wisest plan was to ask for an appointment. I knew I was disobeying orders, but I felt that before I said anything to the police it was my business to let you know what had happened."

"You were perfectly correct." Greystoke rubbed his chin meditatively. "What is the exact position with regard to those two young women? I mean, how far have you taken them into your confidence?"

"They know nothing beyond the fact that there's a good deal more behind it than the killing of a scug like Sutton. I had another talk with Miss Deane this morning, and she admitted to me that the girl who had been blackmailed was her own sister. She had naturally wanted to keep that to herself, but if it's got to come out she says she is quite prepared to make a full statement."

"H'm! You appear to have been singularly fortunate in your choice of a rescuer."

"I quite agree, sir." A faint flush stole into Owen's face. "I am sorry I put up such a poor show myself. I am afraid I have let you down rather badly."

"On the contrary, taking it all round, I think you are to be congratulated." Greystoke picked up the envelope which was lying on the table. "You tell me that this report of yours is absolutely complete?"

"As far as I can make it. I have left out nothing that seemed to be of the slightest significance."

"It should be an interesting document, especially to our friends the police. As soon as I have read it I will get into communication with the Home Office. At the moment the situation seems to be a trifle complicated, but I have no doubt that we shall be able to agree upon some course of action. In the meantime—" He paused. "Well, in the meantime I am inclined to think that the best thing you can do is to go back to your own flat and stay there quietly until you are sent for. After a crack on the head like that, another day in bed isn't likely to do you any harm."

"Very good, sir." Getting up obediently, Owen retrieved his hat.

"And—er—there is no need for you to feel too depressed, Bradwell." The speaker smiled again and held out his hand. "As I said just now, I am far from dissatisfied with your efforts. If they only result in our being able to hang Craig you will at least have rendered the country a notable and salutary service."

<h1 style="text-align:center">II</h1>

Just as Owen was withdrawing his latch-key the kitchen door opened and Watkins appeared in the passage.

"There is a young lady waiting to see you, sir. She informed me that you were expecting her, so I showed her into the study."

"All correct, Watkins. Think you could rake us up a cup of tea?"

"Certainly, sir. It will be ready in a few minutes. I took the liberty of ringing up Dobson's, the confectioners, and they have sent down some crumpets and a cake."

"Splendid! You must be a thought reader."

With an approving nod, Owen jerked open the door on his left, and as he did so Sally jumped up from the low, cushion-strewn couch in front of the window. The next moment her hand was in his and he was looking down into her smiling, upturned face.

"Lovely to find you here," he observed. "I hope Watkins has been taking care of you."

"He's been most attentive!" Her eyes twinkled. "All the same, I think he was just a trifle suspicious—not quite certain whether I wouldn't sneak into the dining-room and pinch the spoons!" She paused. "How did you get on? I am sure you must have some good news or you wouldn't be looking so cheerful."

"That's nothing to go by. I always look cheerful when there are crumpets for tea." A trifle reluctantly he released her hand. "Mind if I sit down? I've been talking straight on end for the last hour and—"

"Why, of course," exclaimed Sally penitently. "I was quite forgetting about your poor head."

With solicitous care she piloted him across to the couch, and disregarding his half-hearted protests, insisted on propping him up comfortably against a lavish background of cushions. Then, pulling forward a chair, she seated herself beside him.

"That's better," she remarked. "But whatever you do you mustn't overtire yourself. Perhaps you ought to wait till you've had your tea."

"Certainly not," declared Owen firmly. "If I let myself be pampered like this I shall probably get to like it."

"Would that matter?"

"Might make me soft and ruin my career." He wriggled back into a still more luxurious position. "The real truth is that I'm feeling extraordinarily bucked. Instead of being flayed alive, as I fully expected, I've crawled out with what precisely amounts to a pat on the back. Seems almost too good to be true."

"I'm so glad. Do tell me all about it."

"Unfortunately that's just what I'm not allowed to do. Strict orders to lie low and keep my mouth shut."

"Oh, well, it's only what I expected." Sally gave a resigned shrug. "Still, it sounds hopeful," she added. "If I can assure Ruth that we're not going to be lugged off to prison—"

"No chance of that. The trouble is that I'm afraid you'll be asked a lot of awkward questions. You see, I had to come out with the whole story. I hated doing it, but—"

"Nonsense, you couldn't help yourself." Sally shook her head. "It's Sheila's own fault for being such a colossal idiot. I wanted to keep her out of it, naturally, but if it's as important as you say, we must just face up and take what's coming. I've made that quite clear to her already."

"May not be as bad as it looks." Owen paused. "My boss is going into a huddle over it with the police, and if they're satisfied that this business about your sister had nothing to do with the murder they'll probably be quite ready to hush it up. It's the line they generally take in cases of blackmail."

"You're very comforting. I—"

The intrusion of Watkins armed with a large silver tray put an abrupt end to the discussion. With an imperious, "You stop where you are and I'll pour out," Sally rose from her chair, and lying back in semi-recumbent ease, Owen contented himself with watching her appreciatively while she manipulated the tea-pot.

"Two lumps of sugar," he announced, "and a good large slab of crumpet. I like the under bit best, there is usually more butter on it."

"Here you are, greedy, and be careful you don't mess the cushions." Coming back to the couch, Sally presented him with a cup and a plate. "I'm glad you're getting a little more confidential," she added smilingly. "You know, apart from the fact that you're in the Navy and that you've gone colour-blind, that's the first thing you've really told me about yourself."

"Haven't had much chance to pour out my heart yet." Owen took a large bite of crumpet. "Still, if you'd care for a few biographical details I'm quite willing to provide them. That's to say, if you've no objection to my talking with my mouth full."

"I think I can bear it."

"Well, to start with, I'm rather what you might call 'on my own in the world.' My governor, who was a grand chap, was badly wounded at Jutland, and he pegged out when I was a kid of seven. The mater didn't live very long after that: I—I don't think she really wanted to. I was brought up by my grandmother, and somehow or other I managed to scrape into Dartmouth. Passed out at the end of twenty-seven, and for the last eleven years I've been knocking about various parts of the world, trying to learn something about my job. When I'm on leave I generally put in a few days with my granny at Tonbridge Wells, and then jog up to Town and do a round of the theatres. Nice, healthy, innocent sort of life, but not very exciting when you describe it to anyone else."

Sally surveyed him thoughtfully over the rim of her teacup.

"You're terribly keen on the Navy, aren't you? I mean you simply hate the idea of leaving it?"

"It would be a bit of a wrench. You see, I've been in it all my life, and I really haven't very much in the way of interests outside. I suppose I could take to keeping rabbits but even then I should probably go wrong when it came to sorting out the colours."

"You've certainly had your share of trouble and bad luck. I wish there was some way in which I could help you."

"Help me! Why, you've been doing nothing else for the last two days." Owen wiped his fingers carefully, and then, leaning across, patted her on the shoulder. "Suppose we give my affairs a rest and talk about you instead. I'm simply thirsting to hear all about your past life."

"Oh, it's very ordinary and dull, I'm afraid." Sally hesitated. "I have just one thing in common with you: both my parents are dead too. Daddy was a doctor in Suffolk, and he was killed in a motoring accident. Until my mother died we lived on in a small house in Ipswich. I was nineteen then and Sheila was a year younger. She had about a couple of hundred a year of her own which had been left to her by an aunt, but it was all in the hands of trustees and she couldn't touch the capital. Still, it was better than nothing, and she was so beautiful to look at that as soon as we came up to

Town people simply raved about her, and she soon began to make quite a lot of money sitting for artists and photographers. I got a job drawing designs for a firm of decorators in Kensington. That's how I met Ruth. She was a customer of ours, and she was so pleased with some work I did for her that she offered to put up enough cash to start a little show of our own. Of course I jumped at the idea. We had a bit of an uphill fight to begin with, but Ruth's a splendid organiser and awfully clever at business, and last year, as I told you, we actually made a profit. It was only natural that she should feel worried when I brought you back. You see, if we had been arrested for hiding you from the police it would all have come out in the papers, and everything would have gone to blazes!"

"You both behaved like a couple of grand sports," declared Owen. "My boss thinks the same, and if there's any way of keeping your names out of it you can bet your life he'll fix it up for us. He's having a consultation with the Home Office, and we must wait and see what they decide to do."

"How about you?" enquired Sally.

"My orders are to stop here until I'm sent for. The tragedy is that I shan't be able to get down to Chelsea."

"That will be very good for you. The quieter you keep, and the fewer people you talk to, the better." Sally put down her cup and glanced at the clock.

"I say," pleaded Owen, "you're not thinking of going just yet? Why, there's a whole crumpet left, and all that beautiful cake."

"I must get home. Mrs. Higgins, our char, is away for a couple of days, and I promised Ruth faithfully that I'd be back by five. I've got to help her clear up the shop."

"This is very distressing. I've got so used to having you around it's become an absolute necessity."

"But you didn't know I existed until a couple of days ago."

"Oh, yes. I knew you existed, though I'd never had the luck to run across you."

"You're talking dreadful nonsense. I expect it's that knock on the head. It often leaves a patient with a touch of delirium."

"Is there any cure for it?"

Sally hesitated an instant, and then, stooping down, quietly just brushed his forehead with her lips.

"That's all I can think of," she said.

"Marvellous!" Owen closed his eyes and sighed blissfully. "I suppose you couldn't repeat the dose?"

"Not to-day." She straightened up again, flushed and smiling. "It only works properly when it's taken in extreme moderation."

III

"You are certain there is no mistake?"

"I tell you I'd recognise the guy anywhere. Why, wasn't I with him long enough to know his blasted face again if I happened to run across it?" With an impatient jerk Craig flung away the stump of his cigar. "As for the girl—well, I can't be so dead sure about her; but, all the same, I'm ready to lay ten to one, though, she's the same party. Something about her chin and the way she holds her head—obstinate-looking little bitch, if ever there was one."

"Go on," ordered von Manstein curtly.

"Thought you'd be interested to know a bit more about his lordship, so as soon as they'd finished their lunch I slid out after them. They didn't stick together, not for long. When they got to Trafalgar Square the girl sheered off, while her bright boy friend headed round into Whitehall. Directly he crossed over I guessed he was making for Queen Anne's Gate, and sure enough, that's where he fetched up."

"Number 17A?"

"You've hit it. He's one of Greystoke's lot, that's a dead cert, and like as not the girl's in the same racket." Craig paused and moistened his lips. "Damn them both," he added viciously. "I wish to God we'd stopped their mouths when we had the chance down at the bungalow."

"It might have been advisable." The Count remained silent for a moment, staring meditatively at his carefully polished finger-nails. "I thought I knew all Greystoke's men, but I may be mistaken. From what you tell me, it looks as though he were a new hand at the game, and that he has been set to work on the Medlicot business. If so, it means that they suspect Sutton of being mixed up in it, and that's getting too near the truth to be altogether healthy. It is a matter on which we must obtain some definite information as soon as possible."

"What would it be worth to me if I was to dig it out for you?"

"I don't think we should quarrel about the price. When the safety of our organisation is in question money is of no consequence."

Craig leaned forward, an ugly gleam in his heavily lidded eyes. "Well, the girl's our mark, if you ask me. She's his fancy piece, and I guess she knows all about it. What we've got to do is to grab hold of her and make her talk."

"Quite a promising idea." His companion nodded slowly. "How would you suggest putting it into execution?"

"I've thought of a way it might be done, so long as your people will play straight. I ain't risking my neck again, not for the mere fun of it."

Von Manstein stiffened. "We Germans do not betray our friends. When the Reich makes a promise, that promise is carried out."

With a furtive movement Craig drew his chair a shade closer.

"Then listen," he said softly.

Chapter XI

Dusk was beginning to settle down over the surrounding forest when the bus from London came to a halt outside the timbered front of the Chigbury Arms. Gathering up her well-stocked shopping-bag, a pale, quietly dressed woman rose from the front seat, and following in the wake of one or two of her fellow passengers, stepped out on to the narrow pavement. She had barely alighted before the bus was again in motion, rumbling off along the peaceful village street and disappearing down the long, white, level road which stretched away to Epping and Chelmsford. It was the last journey of the day, and neither the driver nor the conductor was in any mood to dawdle about unnecessarily.

"Good evening, Miss Wilson." The stout, cheerful-looking landlord, who was standing in the doorway of the inn, raised his hand in a friendly salute. "Thought you must have gone up to Town, seeing as there weren't no one at the 'Ollies."

"I had to visit my dentist, so I took the chance to do a little shopping." The speaker displayed her bag. "Did you want to see me about anything?"

"It was only that bottle of whisky and the syphon you ordered. I sent my lad along with them after we closed, and he couldn't get no answer. Didn't like to bring 'em back, so he slipped round behind and shoved them in the toolshed."

"Oh, that will be all right. I don't suppose anybody has stolen them."

The landlord shook his head doubtfully. "'Tain't too safe nowadays, not with all these 'ikers and motorists about. Why, the number o' glasses I've had pinched outer the bar this year is enough to drive a man to drink."

"I expect that comes from being so close to London. Still if we weren't, you wouldn't get so many customers."

"That's true, Miss. Can't have it both ways, as my old dad used to say."

"Well, good night, and thank you very much." Catherine Wilson cast an apprehensive glance at the thick layer of cloud which was stealing up from the west. "Looks as though we were going to catch it," she added, "so I think I had better hurry home before I get drenched."

Turning into a lane a little way past the inn, she struck off briskly along its deserted course. On either side lay flat stretches of rough turf where a few rather meagre-looking ponies were enjoying a belated supper. Some three hundred yards farther a dark, straggling line of foliage marked the outskirts of the forest, and by the time she had covered about half the intervening distance a thin, driving rain was already beginning to fall. Quickening her pace, she pressed on through the gathering dusk, and at last, just as the drizzle was developing into a steady downpour, the dim outline of a cottage suddenly appeared amongst the surrounding trees.

It stood in the middle of a small clearing, hemmed in on three sides by bushes and undergrowth. At the back was a circular patch of kitchen garden, while in front a strip of lawn, with broad, carefully tended borders, ran down to within a few paces of the road. Except for a white-painted wooden gate in the centre the whole place was enclosed by a stout hedge of thickly growing holly.

Making her way hastily up the path, the owner produced a key and unlocked the front door. It led straight into what was evidently the main room of the cottage, an oddly shaped, low-ceilinged apartment with two diamond-paned windows and a large, old-fashioned, red-brick hearth. Stretched out luxuriously on the rug lay a big half-Persian tabby cat, with an empty saucer reposing alongside. Roused by the sudden intrusion, it rose leisurely to its feet, and arching its back, emitted a long, plaintive, reproachful miaow.

"Was he left all alone then, and had he finished up his milk?" Bending down over her offended pet, Catherine stroked him caressingly. "Never mind, Pushkin," she added, "I've brought you back a nice tin of salmon, and if you're good and patient for a few minutes you shall have some for your supper."

Having lighted the lamp and thrown off her wet coat, she passed through into the small kitchen at the back. Her first action was to fill a kettle and put a match to the oil stove, which, like everything else in the place, was spotlessly clean. Then, returning to her bag which she had deposited on the table, she set about unpacking and sorting away its contents. All the while the cat, which had followed her in, was circling round ingratiatingly and rubbing itself against her legs.

It was just as the last article, a half-pound of freshly ground coffee, was being emptied into a tin that she suddenly remembered about the whisky. With a frown of annoyance at her own forgetfulness, she turned back towards the sitting-room in quest of her coat. At the same moment the thing happened. Startlingly clear above the patter of the rain came a quick, insistent tapping at the side window.

A stifled gasp, in which relief and terror appeared to be equally blended, escaped from her lips. In a sort of stumbling run she hurried across towards the back door, and with shaking fingers wrenched aside the stiff bolt. There was a shuffle of footsteps, and out of the wet gloom a leather-coated figure slipped past her and tripped blunderingly over the frightened cat.

"Jim!"

"Shut that damned door!"

Like a person in a dream Catherine did what he commanded, and then, facing round, leaned back with her hand pressed against her heart.

"How long have you been here?" she whispered.

"God knows. I thought you were never coming back." Tugging off the thick peaked cap that partially concealed his features, James Wilson flung a quick, furtive glance in the direction of the sitting-room. "You're all alone? No chance of anyone barging in?"

His sister shook her head. "Oh, Jim, what made you do it? Why did you try to escape? They are sure to find you again, and then it will be worse than ever."

"Never mind that now." The speaker gave a sudden shiver and drew his wet sleeve across his forehead. "A drink's what I want—that's if you've got any."

"There's a bottle outside: I'll fetch it for you. You had better come into the other room. It's more comfortable there, and you'll be quite safe."

Unresistingly Wilson allowed himself to be conducted through the doorway and shepherded towards the small sofa alongside the fireplace. Regardless of the damage inflicted by his muddy boots, he slumped down wearily upon the clean chintz covering, while, crossing to the nearest window which looked out upon the lane, his sister hastily pulled the curtains.

"I will get you something to eat at the same time. I'm sure you must be starving."

Without waiting for a reply, she hurried back again into the kitchen, and as though too exhausted to concern himself with the direction of affairs, the fugitive rolled over on to his side and began slowly unbuttoning his coat. Dirty and unkempt, with a three days' growth of beard disfiguring his chin, he looked a grimly incongruous object against that peaceful and orderly background.

Lying there in the softly-shaded lamplight, his eyes wandered round the room till they came to rest on a framed photograph which stood in solitary state on top of the writing-desk. It was a portrait of himself at the age of five, a chubby, curly-headed boy in a white sailor suit, clutching a bucket and a spade and seated upon an obviously imitation rock. Although it had been taken nearly twenty-five years ago, he could still vaguely remember the queer smell of the studio and the reassuring face of his mother as she had stood behind the camera smiling at him encouragingly. His lips parted in a bitter smile, and fumbling in his side pocket, he dragged out a crumpled, half-empty packet of cigarettes and looked about him in search of a match.

He had sunk back again against the cushions and was staring up blankly at the thin trail of smoke rising towards the ceiling when Catherine reappeared in the doorway. She was carrying a tray which, in addition to the whisky, contained a leg of cold chicken and several thick slices of bread and butter. She placed it on a small stool at the head of the sofa.

"Sit up, Jim, and eat a little of this. You will feel better after you've had some food."

With an unsteady hand Wilson reached out for the tumbler, and lifting it shakily to his lips, gulped down the greater part of its contents. A long sigh of satisfaction testified to the success of the experiment. His eyes brightened, and rousing himself stiffly, he turned his attention to the tray.

For a while his sister stood beside him watching him in silence. He ate fast, hacking off large chunks and swallowing them greedily, and it was not until the first edge of his hunger showed signs of becoming blunted that she made any attempt to renew her questions.

"How did you get here?" she asked. "Was it on the motor bicycle that you took from that house on the moor?"

He contented himself with a nod.

"What have you done with it?"

"Shoved it in a pond the other side of the forest. Walked the last five miles, and a hell of a job it was to find the way." He put down his knife and fork and drained off the remainder of the whisky. "What happened to that chap I bashed over the head? Has there been anything about it in the papers?"

"He's in the hospital at Okehampton. The doctors think that he'll probably die."

"I'm sorry for that. I didn't mean to kill him. I only wanted to lay him out."

Catherine's fingers tightened. "But why did you come here? Don't you realise how dangerous it is? They know you're my brother, and—"

"Don't worry: I shan't be inflicting myself on you for very long. If you'll help me I'll promise to clear out of this by to-morrow night."

"What do you want me to do?"

"Go up to Town in the morning and buy me one or two things I've got to get hold of. I'll let you have the money."

"What sort of things?"

"Clothes. I can't move a step in this blasted rig-out. Every copper in England has got a description of it by now."

For a moment Catherine sat staring at him, her wide-open eyes full of doubt and fear. "Yes, I—I could do that, but what use would it be? Where can you go afterwards, and how will you manage to live?"

"That's my affair." With an angry scowl Wilson picked up the empty glass. "If you buy the stuff I can look after myself all right. Give me another drink first, and I'll make you out a list."

II

Ruth stuck up the envelope which she had been addressing and glanced impatiently at the clock on the mantelpiece.

"I wish Mrs. Higgins would hurry up. She promised to be here by two, and I'd like to see her before I go out."

"Anything you specially want done?" enquired Sally.

"She'd better clean up the flat first: the whole place is in a filthy mess. I haven't even had time to wash the breakfast things."

"I'll tell her to get on with it. She said she'd be able to stay late to-night, so we can leave the shop till after tea. By the way, what time will you be back?"

"Round about four. Sorry to leave you all on your own, but I must see Jackson to-day and fix up that Pelham Crescent business. It's no use writing to him: he'll take a week to answer."

"I shall be all right," declared Sally. "I've got a couple of sketches I want to finish, but I can bring them upstairs and do them here. I don't imagine we shall be flooded out with customers."

"How about our Lieutenant-Commander?" enquired Ruth. "Any chance of his dropping in?"

Sally shook her head. "His orders are to stick around the flat in case they send for him. If there's any fresh news he has promised to give me a ring."

"Well, I hope I shan't come home and find the place lousy with policemen. I've been expecting them to roll up the whole morning."

"Don't worry. If it's really as important as Owen says, everything will be done very quietly. Of course they are bound to send someone to ask questions, but I shouldn't imagine he'd be in uniform. He'll probably look more like a doctor."

"So it's Owen now!" Ruth grinned and raised her eyebrows. "I hope you aren't going ahead too rapidly, darling. These sailors—"

With a sudden jerk the door of the shop swung open and the familiar figure of Mrs. Higgins loomed up in the entrance. She was breathing heavily and looking a trifle flushed.

"Hullo, so you've got back safely." Ruth rose from the desk.

"Yes, thank you, Miss. Sorry if I've kept you waiting, but the train was a bit late getting in." Putting down a string bag on the table and straightening her hat, the speaker fanned herself vigorously with her disengaged hand. She was a stoutly built woman of about fifty, with one slightly drooping eyelid, and a small, tight-lipped mouth that reminded one of a mutinous child.

"How did your niece's wedding go off?" enquired Sally.

"Oh, that was all right. Emma looked lovely, though I says it myself. All in white, she was, with a big bunch of roses pinned to 'er frock."

"I suppose you enjoyed every second of it."

"That's just what I didn't," was the unexpected answer.

"Why, what was the trouble?"

"It was the lodgings I was in." Mrs. Higgins sniffed bitterly. "They may well call it *Stony* Stratford; I was 'alf bitten to death by fleas."

"Good heavens!" Sally made a desperate attempt not to giggle.

"It's a fact, Miss. Five shillings a night I was paying, too, and fourpence hextra for a cup of tea in the morning. Scand-'lous, I calls it."

"Positively criminal."

"Hope you haven't brought any of them along with you," remarked Ruth.

"No fear, Miss. Stripped meself to the skin soon as I got home, and went through me things most careful."

"In that case we may as well go up, and I'll show you what I want done." Stifling a grin, Ruth turned towards the staircase. "Better pop down and collect your stuff, Sally," she added. "You'll just have time before I go out."

◇◇◇

Tring—tring—tring.

The telephone bell at her side suddenly broke into action, and laying down her pencil and ruler, Sally leaned across and picked up the receiver. The time was just on a quarter to four, and from one of the rooms above the energetic hum of an Electrolux floated down the stairs.

"Hullo!" she observed. "Barlow and Deane speaking."

"Hullo, Sally! This is Owen."

"Yes, I thought it was."

"You sounded frightfully crisp and business-like."

"Have to be when I'm in charge of the shop. How are you, and what's the news?"

"None at present. I've been sitting here all day waiting for something to break. Beginning to get a bit tedious."

"What do you think they're doing?"

"Talking it over and fixing up what line they're going to take. Anyone been round asking questions?"

"Not yet."

"Is Ruth there?"

"No, she's gone off to interview a builder. I'm all on my own except for Mrs. Higgins."

"Damn! I was hoping you'd be able to come round to tea again and cheer me up. I'm desperately in need of another dose of tonic."

"Can't be done, I'm afraid. You'll just have to carry on bravely and uncomplainingly."

"How about dinner? Watkins would arrange something for us. He's a marvellous cook."

"That's no use, either. We're going to have a regular clean-up this evening. Mrs. Higgins has been away for a day or two, and everything's in a fearful muddle."

"This is hideously depressing. Looks as if I shall have to fall back on the wireless."

"And very good for you," Sally laughed. "The Children's Hour comes on at five; you'll enjoy that."

There was a chuckle at the other end of the phone. "Listen, angel. I'm going to be serious for a moment—dead serious. I've got a desperately important problem I want to ask your opinion about."

"I'm listening."

"Suppose you were a rather ordinary, uninteresting chap with no particular prospects and you suddenly fell madly in love with the most beautiful girl in the world. You knew you weren't fit to black her boots, and yet you adored her so frantically that every minute she wasn't with you seemed a positive agony. Well, how would you face up to it? Would you have the nerve to tell her, or would you behave like a perfect gentleman and just fade away gracefully out of her life?"

"I don't think that's the sort of question one ought to discuss over the phone," objected Sally.

"Why not?"

"It might embarrass the operator."

"Not if she has any decent human feelings."

"They aren't allowed in government offices."

"This is no time for jesting. Don't you realise that my whole future happiness is trembling in the balance?"

"Well," began Sally slowly. "If I found myself in that position—" She broke off abruptly and glanced towards the entrance. "Oh dear, what a nuisance! Here's someone coming in."

"Don't ring off, for the love of Mike."

"But I must. I can't offend customers. It wouldn't be fair to Ruth."

"You might at least give me a hint."

"Not now: there isn't time. I'll turn it over in my mind while I'm having my bath!"

With another laugh and a faint tinge of colour in her cheeks which made her look prettier than ever, Sally put down the receiver. At the same instant the door opened, and a smartly dressed girl, who had emerged from the car drawn up outside, walked into the shop and advanced towards the desk. She was strikingly handsome in a warm, dark, slightly exotic style, and carried herself with an air of easy assurance.

"Oh, good afternoon." The greeting was accompanied by a friendly smile. "Am I speaking to Miss Barlow or to Miss Deane?"

"I am Miss Deane." Sally stepped forward from the table at which she had been working. "My partner is out at the moment, but if you want to see her she will be back about four."

"I believe you do the actual designing and all that sort of thing, don't you?"

"Yes, it's my special department."

"Well, isn't that lucky now!" The visitor paused and glanced about her with evident interest. "My name's Tregellis," she continued, "and I'm the sister of Mrs. Gerald Freeman. As you've probably seen in the papers, she has just bought Merton Lodge, that lovely old house at Hampstead that used to belong to Sir George Vernon. It all wants doing up, of course, but she and my brother-in-law have set their hearts on getting in as soon as possible, and when they're both of the same mind things are apt to move pretty quick.

That's why I thought I'd better slip in to-day on the off-chance of catching you."

Sally experienced a little exultant thrill. "You mean you wished to consult us professionally?"

"Guessed you might be interested. Some of my friends have been saying nice things about your work, and I suggested to my sister that before she fixed up definitely with anyone else it might be a good idea to get you to come out there and give us your opinion. Don't know how the proposition strikes you? I can't promise for certain that she'll offer you the job, but as it would be taking up your time she would naturally be prepared to pay a reasonable fee. Shouldn't like you to feel we were just trying to suck your brains."

Sally laughed. "I should be very pleased, of course. When would you like me to come?"

"That's just the trouble. If you ask me, I guess it's a case of now or never. Fact is, my sister has made an appointment with some other people to-morrow morning, and she's in such a tearing hurry it wouldn't surprise me if she settled the whole business straight away. On the other hand, if you cared to come along right now in the car we could all three run up there together, and you might take a look round and let her have your ideas. She's staying with me at my house in St. John's Wood, and I told her that, provided you were disengaged, I would try to collect you on my way back. The only snag is that she's dining with some friends to-night, so if we propose to do anything about it we shall have to hustle. Afraid I'm giving you rather short notice, but it only came into my head this morning, and I just thought it might be worth trying."

"It was most kind of you, and I'm very much obliged." Sally glanced at the clock. "Yes, I can manage it. My partner will be back almost directly, and it won't matter closing up the place for a few minutes. If you'll excuse me, I'll just run upstairs and explain things to our domestic help. Shan't keep you more than a second or two."

"Why, that's fine! Had a sort of hunch I was going to be lucky!"

With another of her engaging smiles Miss Tregellis sauntered across to inspect the Chinese cabinet against the opposite wall, and leaving her in possession of the establishment, Sally made her way hastily upstairs. In the open doorway at the head of the flight Mrs. Higgins was standing beside the discarded Electrolux. Judging by her attitude, she had apparently been listening to the conversation.

"I 'eard what you was saying, Miss," she announced in a stage whisper. "Sounds like a good job, don't it? You go along with the lady, and I'll keep an eye on the shop till Miss Barlow gets back."

"Thanks, Mrs. Higgins, that's exactly what I want." Sally turned into her bedroom and made a rapid dash for the dressing-table. "Tell her that I've gone out to look over a house at Hampstead, and that if there's anything doing I'll probably give her a ring. I shall be locking up when I leave, but if any customers should happen to roll along you can let them in and ask them whether they would care to wait. It will be quite safe so long as you're around yourself."

"Very good, Miss, you leave it to me."

Pulling on a hat and taking a final glance at herself in the mirror, Sally slipped into a loose summer coat and hurried back down the staircase. As she reappeared her visitor, who was still admiring the cabinet, looked up with an expression of surprise.

"Well, well," she observed, "I must say you've been pretty slick. Can't think how you managed it in such an amazingly short time."

"I often have to pop out unexpectedly, so I'm getting quite an expert as a quick-change artist."

Leading the way forward, Sally slid forward the bolt of the safety catch, and waiting until her companion had passed through, closed the door firmly behind her. A moment later she was stepping up into the comfortable padded front seat, where the owner of the car had already established herself at the wheel.

"I hope to goodness something will come of it," remarked the latter, as they headed away in the direction of Sloane Square. "It would be just too bad if you were to have all this trouble for nothing."

"It wouldn't be the first time," Sally smiled. "In a business like ours blighted hopes are just part of the day's work."

"There's one thing you needn't worry about in this case, and that's the question of expense." Miss Tregellis gave a faint shrug. "My sister has oceans of money, so if you've any brilliant suggestion to make you can trot it out freely. In fact, between ourselves, the more it costs the better she'll probably like it."

"Thank you for telling me. It sounds exactly the chance I've always been looking for—a sort of decorator's dream suddenly come true. All I'm afraid of is that I shall wake up with a start and find myself in bed."

Proceeding rapidly up Park Lane and Baker Street and crossing the Marylebone Road, the car swung round the corner of Lord's into the still pleasant, if sadly disfigured, district of St. John's Wood. Not wishing to distract her companion's attention, Sally made no attempt to renew the conversation, and it was not until they came to a halt in front of a small, neat, stucco-fronted villa that Miss Tregellis herself again broke the silence.

"This is my modest shack," she announced. "Come along in and have a cocktail before we start off."

Without waiting for an answer she stepped out on to the pavement, and following her up the short path that led to the front door, Sally found herself being conducted into a miniature, oval-shaped entrance hall. A partly open door on the left revealed a very modernly equipped sitting-room, the furniture of which appeared to consist principally of chromium and glass.

"I expect my sister is upstairs." Peeling off her driving-gloves, the speaker tossed them carelessly on to a table. "If you'll go in and make yourself comfortable I'll run up and tell her you're here. You'll find cigarettes and matches in that box on the mantelpiece."

She turned towards the staircase, and as unsuspiciously as a duck entering a decoy, Sally moved forward into the apparently deserted apartment. It was almost the last action of which she was properly conscious. A brutal clutching hand on the nape of her neck wrenched back her head, and at the same instant something that felt like a wet and sickly-smelling towel smothered the sharp cry of pain that forced itself from her lips. For a second or two she fought desperately, wriggling and twisting like a trapped animal. Then came a sudden merciful blackness, and with a little choking sob she ceased to struggle.

Chapter XII

"I thought you might like some fresh toast with your marmalade, sir."

Depositing a rack on the breakfast table, Watkins deftly removed an empty dish which had recently contained eggs and bacon.

"Thanks." With an appreciative nod Owen laid aside his paper. "Don't know why I'm so infernally hungry this morning, but I suppose it's because I overslept myself. By the way, has the post come yet?"

"Nearly two hours ago, sir. There were no letters for you."

"Hm! That's annoying."

"How about lunch, sir? Will you be taking it here, or—"

"Lunch! What, on top of a colossal feed like this! Why, if I were to eat anything else before—"

"Excuse me, sir."

The jarring trill of a telephone bell was echoing through the room, and replacing the dish, Watkins turned towards the instrument.

"It's all right: I'll answer it. I'm expecting a call."

Jumping to his feet and crossing over hastily, Owen lifted up the receiver, only to be greeted by the unexpected voice of his absent host, Joe Anstey.

"Hullo, hullo! That you, Owen?"

"It is. You've just torn me away in the middle of my breakfast."

"What, at this hour! Dammit, you seem to be taking things pretty easy."

"Of course I am. I came here for a rest cure."

"Hope it's doing you good. Watkins looking after you all right?"

"Splendidly. Do you want to speak to him? He's in the room."

"No, you can tell him. Say that I'll be back some time to-morrow morning, probably before midday."

"That's fine. I'll make a point of waking up a bit earlier."

"What have you been doing with yourself? Did you get down to Playford?"

"I did, and had a delightful week-end. Very nearly caught a trout."

"What's this yarn in the papers about somebody being bumped off in a bungalow? Must have happened while you were there."

"So I gather. Fellow called Sutton, apparently. Ever run across him?"

"Not to my knowledge. Have they any idea who did him in?"

"Couldn't tell you."

"Well, as long as they don't suspect you, that's O.K." Joe chuckled at his own jest. "How about the bloke you were going to see at the Admiralty? Anything come of it?"

"Several possibilities in the offing. Expecting to hear from him to-day."

"Good. I felt certain they'd fix you up somehow. Can't afford to chuck away Lieutenant-Commanders with a world war lurking round the corner."

"You haven't changed your opinion, then?"

"Not likely. From what I've learned up here—well, perhaps we'd better leave it at that for the moment. See you to-morrow, old man, and hope to hear that you've pulled off a really top-hole job. By the way, don't make any engagement for the evening. I've been working like a galley slave the last few days, and I feel like going out somewhere and having a little mild dissipation. Can't talk any longer now, I'm afraid. Too busy. Cheerio!"

The line went dead with a sharp click, and making his way back to his interrupted repast, Owen leisurely resumed his seat.

"That was Mr. Anstey: he'll be home some time to-morrow morning. He says you needn't bother about dinner, because we shall both be feeding out."

"Very good, sir."

Taking the empty dish with him, Watkins retreated to his own quarters, and having opened out the *Daily Mail* at a fresh page, Owen propped it up against the coffee-pot and proceeded with his breakfast.

He had consumed two slices of toast and marmalade, and was in the act of helping himself to a third, when a sudden ring, followed by a loud rap on the front door, caused him to sit up with an abrupt jerk. The next instant he had pushed back his chair and was listening expectantly.

From the hall came a subdued murmur of voices, punctuated by the familiar rumble of the descending lift. Then the door of the room opened, and with what appeared to be a slightly disapproving expression Watkins re-entered and closed it carefully behind him.

"It's a person from Scotland Yard, sir. A detective-sergeant, I understand."

"Scotland Yard!" Owen tried to appear suitably surprised. "What the devil does he want?"

"He informs me that he would like to have a word with you, sir."

"Really! Well, in that case you had better show him in. One can't refuse to see a policeman: it might hurt his feelings."

"Quite so, sir."

Still looking a trifle scandalised, Watkins departed on his mission, and in another moment a red-haired, alert-eyed young man, dressed in a well-cut lounge suit, stepped briskly across the threshold.

"Lieutenant-Commander Bradwell?"

Owen nodded. "That's correct."

"I am Detective-Sergeant Campbell of the Criminal Investigation Department." The visitor glanced round swiftly, as though to satisfy himself that they were alone. "I am sorry to disturb you in the middle of your breakfast, but my instructions are to bring you along to Headquarters at once. I was to inform you that Captain Greystoke and the Chief Inspector are awaiting your arrival."

Owen raised his eyebrows. "Sounds as though it would be advisable to get cracking. I'll ring down and tell the porter to stop us a taxi."

"There is no need for that: I have a car outside."

"Really! You do things pretty handsomely."

"It all depends." The other smiled dryly. "Quite a number of our clients have to make the journey on foot."

"I can only say I feel deeply honoured."

Leading the way out and picking up a hat as he passed through the hall, Owen came to a momentary halt in front of the half-closed kitchen door.

"I am going out for a little while, Watkins," he announced. "If Miss Deane should happen to ring up, you can tell her that I shall be getting in touch with her later."

"Very good, sir," came the impassive reply.

An interested expression flickered across the sergeant's face, but it was not until they had descended the staircase and were passing out through the main entrance that he suddenly found his voice.

"Miss Deane?" he repeated. "I take it that must be the young lady who runs the decorating business in Chelsea? I was down there yesterday afternoon interviewing her partner. Unfortunately she herself happened to be out."

He stepped across the pavement and unlocked the door of the four-seater Hillman which was drawn up in the roadway.

"What time was that?" demanded Owen as he clambered into the front seat.

"I got there about twenty past four." Moving round to the farther side, the sergeant took his place at the wheel.

"You were out of luck. She was in at a quarter to, because I was talking to her on the phone."

"Have you spoken to her since?"

"No. I was just going to have a shot at it when you turned up. Why? Nothing wrong, is there?"

"Not that I'm aware of." Gliding forward into the turmoil of Piccadilly, the car swung eastward in the direction of the Circus. "Merely means that I shall have to repeat my visit and ask a lot of the same questions all over again. Nothing new about that: seems to be the general rule in our line of business."

With a resigned shrug the speaker once more relapsed into silence, and continuing their progress down the Haymarket, across Trafalgar Square and out on to the Embankment, they turned in through an open gateway flanked on either side by a stalwart and apparently rather bored policeman. From its neighbouring eminence Big Ben was hammering out the hour of eleven.

Pulling up on the near side of a grey, cheerless-looking courtyard, the sergeant leaned across his companion and pressed down the latch.

"This is where we disembark," he observed curtly. "My orders are to take you in straight away."

Before there was time to offer any comment Owen found himself marching down a long, distempered corridor, which in some vague way reminded him of a hospital. At the third door on the left his companion halted. The discreet tap that followed was answered by a muffled grunt from inside, and the next moment he was being ushered into a large, well-lighted room where three men of notably different appearance were grouped round a table, plentifully littered with papers and documents.

"Lieutenant-Commander Bradwell."

"All right, Campbell."

The door closed quietly, and the grim-faced, heavily built man who was sitting nearest hoisted himself to his feet.

"I am Chief Inspector Elliot," he announced with a slight touch of North Country accent. "I understand that you are already acquainted with Captain Greystoke." His eyes travelled to the third member of the party, a tall, lantern-jawed individual who was thoughtfully caressing his chin. "This is Superintendent Fothergill of the Berkshire County Police. He is in charge of the investigations concerning the death of Mr. Granville Sutton."

"Take a seat, Bradwell." Captain Greystoke nodded encouragingly. "There are several matters I wish to speak to you about, but before we come to these the Superintendent has some questions he would like to ask with relation to your statement. You can answer him with absolute frankness."

Stepping forward obediently, Owen took possession of a vacant chair. The Chief Inspector resumed his seat, while, having produced a large note-book which he laid open on the table in front of him, the lantern-jawed man straightened up stiffly and cleared his throat.

For about ten minutes a stream of queries followed each other in rapid succession. From his arrival at Playford right up to the time of his second visit to Queen Anne's Gate point after point in the written report which Owen had so laboriously compiled was brought out again for further elaboration. Now and then, in response to some reply, the Superintendent would pause to make a brief addition to his notes. Apart from this, however, the catechism proceeded without interruption, both Greystoke and the Chief Inspector sitting by in silence, as though awaiting the conclusion of a necessary but slightly tedious overture. At last, with the air of one who has unflinchingly discharged his duty, Fothergill laid down his pencil and turned to meet their gaze.

"It certainly looks as though your theory were correct, sir," he observed, addressing himself to Greystoke. "We should like to have secured a personal statement from Miss Deane, but I take it that that will be obtained to-day?"

"I am sending Campbell down there again now." It was the Inspector who answered.

"Then I think the position is perfectly straightforward. As soon as I have communicated with the Chief Constable, I feel certain that, in view of the—hm—somewhat unusual circumstances, he will raise no objection to handing over the whole affair to Scotland Yard."

"It would undoubtedly simplify matters," remarked Captain Greystoke.

"Quite so, sir." The Superintendent gathered together his papers. "I will ring up Colonel Anstruther immediately. I need hardly add that if there is any further way in which we can be of assistance the whole of our local resources will be entirely at your disposal."

"Thank you, Mr. Fothergill. Your collaboration will be most welcome." The Captain smiled pleasantly. "Before you return to Playford we will draw up a detailed plan for tonight's operations, and I know that any arrangements which have to be made on the spot can be confidently entrusted to your hands. Please tell Colonel Anstruther how deeply I appreciate his helpful and considerate attitude."

Radiating an aura of efficiency and self-importance, the Superintendent retired from the room, and with the ghost of a smile flickering round his lips Greystoke glanced at the Chief Inspector.

"All very satisfactory," he observed. "Considering every-thing, our friend seems to have accepted the situation remarkably well."

"Bit disappointed, of course. Nasty jolt to have a topline murder case snatched out of one's hands." The big man shrugged. "Still, he's a sound, experienced officer, and we can rely on him not to let us down."

"Good. That's all that matters." For a moment Greystoke sat frowning thoughtfully at the closed door, and then, with a characteristically abrupt movement, he turned his atten-tion to Owen.

"How are you?" he demanded. "Quite got over that tap on the head?"

"Quite, sir."

"Pleased to hear it. I shall want you to-night, but it's not going to be exactly a job for an invalid."

Owen's face brightened hopefully. "I think I can keep my end up, sir."

"I had better explain. We have been looking into a number of matters during the last forty-eight hours, espe-cially with regard to Mr. Sutton's antecedents. He appears to have been a pretty distinct blot on the landscape, and we can regard his removal as an act of public sanitation. The most interesting point we have unearthed is the fact that he was on friendly terms with Medlicot. We don't know precisely how far the intimacy went, but it's more than possible that

Sutton may have persuaded the young idiot to talk about his work. In that case, there are two alternative theories, either of which might account for the murder. Sutton himself may have been one of von Manstein's protégés, and working in collusion with Craig. Thieves do occasionally fall out, and with a crowd like that it frequently means that someone ends with a knife in his back."

"Pity it doesn't happen more often. Save us a world of trouble." Chief Inspector Elliot shrugged regretfully.

"Personally," continued Greystoke, "I am inclined to believe that Sutton was working on his own. We have undoubted evidence that he was a blackmailer, and if something he ran across at Playford put him on to the idea that Craig was in the pay of the Huns, it wasn't the sort of chance that a gentleman with his tendencies would be likely to neglect. My own guess is that he was trying to put the screw on a bigger ruffian than himself, and that, for once in a way, he got what he was asking for."

Elliot nodded his agreement. "That's my opinion, too. Much more in keeping with a chap of his type."

"From our angle the point is of minor importance." Greystoke turned back to Owen. "What we wanted was some legal excuse for arresting Craig and going through that damned house of his from top to bottom. Now, thanks to you, we have got our chance. With the reluctant approval of the Home Office I propose to pay a call at Otter's Holt this evening, and to spend what I hope will be a profitable two or three hours over checking up on its owner's effects. My impression is that if he has any incriminating stuff tucked away, that's where we are most likely to find it. Whether there will be definite proof of his connection with von Manstein is another matter. Our friend the Count probably knows his business too well. I am hoping, however, that as a result of our little expedition he may consider it healthier to pack his traps and clear out of the country. If we can get rid of him and hang Craig we shan't have been wasting our time. At all events, I, for one, shall be able to sleep with considerably more comfort."

"There is just one point that has occurred to me, sir." Owen paused.

"Go on, then. Let us have it."

"If the man I saw through the window talking to Craig really was von Manstein, wouldn't there be sufficient evidence to rope him in as an accessory?"

"In normal circumstances, yes. With things as they are, however—that's to say, with a government that still believes in the possibility of appeasement,—the answer's a wash-out. If I understand anything about the political situation, the idea of arresting von Manstein on the unsupported statement of one of my own agents would be turned down flatly by the entire Cabinet. I should be informed that it was quite unjustified, and that we should be merely playing into the hands of the anti-British elements in Berlin. Before our people would agree to take such a step we should have to present them with a cast-iron, watertight case. It's just possible that we shall be able to do so, but, for my part, I am not particularly optimistic. I shall be well satisfied if I know that the blackguard is safely back in his own unspeakable Fatherland."

Owen's lips hardened, but he made no attempt to offer any comment.

"Suppose we return to our arrangements for this evening. I have decided to take you along with us for two reasons. In the first place, if he happens to be around, you might be able to identify the man who went into the bungalow with Craig. We want to get hold of him rather badly. In the second, I feel it's only fair that you should be in at the death. If you like, you can look on it as an award for distinguished service."

"Thank you, sir."

"Be here at ten o'clock sharp. We shall go down by car and contact the local men at Thames Ferry. By the way, have you got anything in the shape of a gun?"

Owen shook his head. "I'm afraid not, sir. I left mine at Plymouth with the rest of my gear."

"Well, I dare say Elliot will be able to fix you up with one. No harm in being on the safe side."

"That'll be all right, sir," declared the Chief Inspector. "I'll see that he's properly looked after."

"Then I think that's about all for the present." Greystoke glanced at his watch. "You had better get along home, Bradwell, and stick around there till it's time for you to come back." He smiled and held out his hand. "I'd like to be certain where you are, just in case there's any change in the programme."

◇◇◇

Watkins shook his head.

"No, sir. There has been no call from Miss Deane or anyone else. I have been here the whole time."

"I suppose the line's in order." Looking a trifle worried, Owen moved across the hall in the direction of the telephone. "By the way, Watkins, I shan't be going out again until this evening. Don't want any lunch, as I told you, but perhaps you could let me have a bite of something about eight o'clock? Hope it's not putting you to a lot of trouble."

"Not at all, sir. There's a nice fresh sole in the larder which I intended to grill for your breakfast to-morrow. I'm afraid it will mean your having eggs and bacon again for breakfast."

"That will do me splendidly."

With his usual impassive bow Watkins retired into the kitchen, and picking up the first volume of the directory, Owen began to search down the long column of Bs till he arrived at the entry he was looking for. "Barlow and Deane, Decorators, 57a, King's Road, Chelsea, S.W."

He was half-way through dialling the number when he was interrupted by a sudden clamorous knocking. He straightened up impatiently, and with a muttered "Damn!" put back the receiver in its cradle. The next instant he had crossed over to the front door and jerked it open.

"Ruth! Well, that's amazing! I was just—"

"Is Sally here?"

"Here!" he repeated. "No, of course not." A queer, apprehensive chill seemed to gather round his heart. "Why, what's the matter?" he demanded.

"She has disappeared—vanished. She went away yesterday afternoon and no one has seen her since."

There was a brief silence.

"Come in." Owen's voice was oddly quiet. "Come along in and tell me exactly what has happened."

As he spoke he took hold of her arm, and without waiting for a reply led her across the hall and into the study. It was a typical bachelor's "den," a snug, comfortable room, permeated by a faint odour of cigar smoke and old leather.

"Sit down." He pulled forward a chair and closed the door behind them. "Now," he continued, "what do you mean when you say that she's 'disappeared'?"

Ruth moistened her lips. "According to Mrs. Higgins, a woman called at the shop yesterday at about a quarter to four and asked whether one of us would come out to Hampstead and give her an estimate for doing up a house. I'd gone along to see a builder, and Sally was all on her own. It sounded like a good job, though, and I suppose she was afraid of missing it. Anyhow, she evidently made up her mind to take it on. She left a message for me with Mrs. Higgins explaining where she had gone to, and then she shut up the place and the two of them, she and this other woman, went away together in a car. I got back about ten minutes afterwards."

"Was it somebody you knew?"

Ruth shook her head. "I don't think so. Mrs. Higgins got the impression that she was a stranger—a new customer altogether."

"Well?"

"That's all I can tell you. I waited up till after midnight, but Sally never came home, and never even let me know where she was. When there was no message from her this morning I got more worried than ever. I wanted to ring up the police and ask them to make inquiries, but with this other affair hanging over our heads I was afraid it might lead to all sorts of trouble. At last I couldn't stand it any longer. I felt that something had to be done at once, so I decided to come to you and ask your advice." She drew in a quick breath. "What do you think? Ought I to go to the police or—"

"I'll get through to Greystoke; he's at the Yard. You wait here while I ring him up."

Before he had finished speaking Owen had wrenched open the door and was back again at the telephone. It is probable that Whitehall 1212 has never been dialled more rapidly.

"Scotland Yard," came a detached voice.

"This is Lieutenant-Commander Bradwell speaking. I have a very urgent message for Captain Greystoke. I believe he is with the Chief Inspector."

"Mind repeating your name?"

Owen swore inwardly. "Bradwell. BRADWE double L. Kindly put me on to him as soon as possible."

"Hold the line, please."

There were two or three spasmodic clicks, followed by an interminable pause.

"Hullo!" A crisp, familiar voice suddenly broke the silence.

"Sorry to disturb you, sir, but something has happened that looks pretty serious. Miss Barlow is here, and she tells me that Miss Deane has disappeared. It seems that a woman called at their place yesterday afternoon and persuaded her to go away in a car. She was only supposed to be going as far as Hampstead, but she has never come back, and nothing has been heard of her since."

"Any idea who this woman was?"

"No, sir. Miss Barlow was away at the time, and the only person there was a charwoman."

"Hm! May perhaps be a false alarm, but I don't like the sound of it."

"Exactly my feeling, sir."

"A bit too suggestive of our friend Craig's methods. Hold on a moment while I have a word with Elliot."

For another maddening interval Owen stood tense and motionless, the receiver glued to his ear.

"Are you there?"

"Yes, sir.'

"We should like to have a talk with Miss Barlow as soon as possible. Put her in a taxi and send her down here straight away. You stay where you are for the present. Got that?"

"Yes, sir."

"Carry on, then."

"What did he say?" Ruth had stepped out into the hall and was staring at him with wide-open, anxious eyes.

"He wants you to go to Scotland Yard immediately. I'll come down with you and find you a taxi."

"What about Sally? Does he think she's in danger?"

"She may be. It's possible she has been kidnapped. We are dealing with people who stick at nothing."

Ruth clenched her hands. "Can't you do something?" she demanded fiercely.

"My orders are to stay here, and I've got to obey them." A little thread of blood was trickling down Owen's lip. "There's one thing I can promise you, though," he added. "If anyone hurts her I'll strangle the swine with my own hands."

Ruth nodded. "I hope I'll be looking on," she said viciously.

Chapter XIII

"Thames Ferry, single."

James Wilson picked up his ticket, and thrusting the change into his pocket, passed out of the booking-office into the big, garishly lit station. The hands of the clock were pointing to nine-thirty, a relatively slack period in the crowded life of a London terminus. Unemployed porters stood around chatting to each other in small, confidential clusters, while a hiss of escaping steam, punctuated by the loud clatter of empty milk-cans, formed an inspiriting accompaniment to their exchange of views.

In his rather ill-fitting blue suit, with a soft hat drawn well down over his forehead, Wilson was not the sort of figure to arouse any particular interest. Disregarded as a possible source of gratuities, he pulled up in front of the large mechanical notice-board which directed passengers to their appropriate platforms. The train for Thames Ferry, 9.42, was booked in at number seven, and after a furtive glance round, which revealed no sign of any lurking danger, he summoned up his courage and strolled towards the barrier.

It was not, however, until he was safely ensconced in the corner of an empty carriage that he found himself able to breathe with comparative freedom. Now that the crucial stage of his enterprise was so close at hand, the mere possibility of being cheated of his vengeance at the last minute was sufficient to set every nerve in his body quivering with fear and anger. Only by a superhuman effort of will had he been able to present the appearance of casual unconcern which had carried him past the gate, and with the abrupt reaction that had followed upon the closing of the compartment door, it seemed as if a suffocating pressure had been suddenly removed from his stomach.

Tilting back his hat and wiping his forehead, he sat gazing out through the half-lowered window. He had selected a carriage almost at the far end of the train, and judging by the scarcity of passengers, it seemed more than probable that his solitude would remain undisturbed. Facing him on the opposite wall was a poster, a big, gaudy affair printed in yellow and black. It portrayed a harassed-looking gentleman gnawing feverishly at his finger-nails, while underneath, spaced out in bold, arresting type, ran the following explanatory letterpress:

Have you lost your self-confidence?
Are you restless and jittery?
Do you feel that you are threatened
By some imminent danger?

If so
you are suffering from
Nerve Strain

What you need is
LACTOGENE
The world's greatest Tonic Food

This information, though of obvious interest and value to a man in his condition, was unfortunately wasted upon Mr.

James Wilson. Before he had assimilated its full significance his attention was diverted elsewhere. Advancing slowly up the platform were a couple of elderly clergymen, both of whom were engrossed in what appeared to be some earnest and completely absorbing discussion. On they came, as though heading deliberately towards him, and with every step they took, the unpleasant foreboding that he was destined to share their company became more and more distressingly acute.

It was just as they had drawn level that the blow fell. A piercing whistle, enforced by a raucous bellow of "Take your seats, please," brought them to a sudden halt, and with the flustered air of one who has been rudely recalled to earth the shorter of the two grabbed hold of the compartment handle.

"Come along, Merrivale," he exclaimed. "We shall be missing the train if we don't hurry up."

In agitated haste they scrambled in, Wilson reluctantly drawing back his feet in order to make room for their entrance. As they brushed past him his hand went up instinctively to the brim of his hat. With a quick jerk he pulled it forward again over his forehead, and then, turning an inhospitable shoulder towards the rest of the carriage, resumed his former occupation of staring out of the window. Almost imperceptibly the train began to slide forward.

"Dear me, quite a close shave! It would have been too annoying if we had been careless enough to get left behind."

"A positive disaster! I can imagine what my wife would have to say. She is always scolding me for being absent-minded."

"I'm afraid it was chiefly my fault. I was so interested in the point you had just raised with regard to Blenkinsop's amendment—"

"Ah, yes, yes. A most untimely and ill-advised suggestion. I had a feeling that something of the sort might happen. An excellent fellow in his own way, no doubt, but…"

The voices went on and on, a monotonous flow of meaningless words, half drowned by the throb and rattle of the train. Outside, as the pace quickened, deserted-looking suburban stations flashed by with startling abruptness, and before very long the roofs and chimneys that obstructed the outlook had given place to a vague expanse of open country, dotted here and there with points of yellowish light. High up above a rather sickly half-moon peered out coldly through a rift in the clouds.

Sitting turned sideways in his corner, Wilson continued to gaze out unseeingly over the passing landscape. By now the presence of his fellow travellers had almost ceased to trouble him. They were obviously too occupied with their own affairs to devote any of their attention to a casual stranger, and in a little while the deep, smouldering hatred that obsessed his whole being was the only sensation of which he was actively conscious. It was that hatred which had given him the strength and cunning that had carried him so far upon his journey, and as the train rolled on, and the gathering dark deepened, the rumble of the wheels seemed to frame itself into a kind of triumphant refrain which sent the blood pulsing through his veins with a fierce and almost intolerable ecstasy. At times he had to dig his nails into the palm of his hand to stop himself from giving vent to his emotion.

Only during the last stage of all, the short run between Playford and Thames Ferry, did he succeed by a savage effort in regaining his self-control. As the sleepy-looking platform, with its closed book-stall and its solitary porter, glided into view, he shot a quick, surreptitious glance at his two half-forgotten companions. Their whole interest still appeared to be centred upon Mr. Blenkinsop and his troublesome activities. With a furtive twist he turned the handle, and slipping out as unobtrusively as possible, shut the door behind him.

Three other passengers had also alighted, a couple of bare-headed young men and a stout, shabbily dressed woman encumbered by an armful of packages. They were heading for an open gate in the white palings where the stationmaster had taken up his position. There was a shrill whistle, and, as though disclaiming any further responsibility, the train drifted off into the darkness.

◇◇◇

With his hands in his pockets Owen paced restlessly up and down the bare, distempered room. In his present state of mind he found it impossible to sit still. It was nearly nine hours now since he had received the news of Sally's disappearance, and during the whole of that long, dragging interval there had been no further communication either from Greystoke or Ruth. Until the time had arrived to set out for the Yard he had remained there imprisoned in the flat, listening feverishly for a ring at the phone. All the while a vision of Sally trapped and helpless in the power of a brute like Craig had been driving him nearer and nearer to the verge of distraction. For the first time the full strength and depth of his love for her had suddenly revealed itself. Brief as their acquaintance was, she seemed in some unaccountable way to have become the very centre and focus of his entire existence. The idea that she might be in danger of her life was grotesque—unthinkable! What the hell were the police doing, and why, at least, couldn't someone have had the decency to ring him up? If they kept him waiting in this damned dog kennel much longer—

"Sorry to have been so inhospitable." Marching into the room, accompanied by the Chief Inspector, Greystoke advanced briskly to where his visitor was standing. "I was having a final word with our friends at Playford, just to make certain that everything is in order." The shrewd eyes were scanning Owen's face with a questioning stare. "Feeling a little worried about that girl friend of yours, I suppose?"

"Not too happy, sir." Owen was surprised at the steadiness of his own voice. "Is there any news yet? Have you the slightest idea where they could have taken her to?"

Greystoke shook his head. "Nothing has turned up so far. It may at any moment, though. An all-station call was sent out immediately, and every man that can possibly be spared has been put on to make inquiries."

"We'll find her all right," broke in the Chief Inspector comfortingly. "Our job at the moment is to get down to Thames Ferry. It's a hundred to one that Craig is mixed up in it somehow or other, and if that's so you can leave it to us to squeeze the truth out of him." He turned to Greystoke. "Better be making a start, I think, sir. It's ten past now, and we shan't do it under three-quarters of an hour."

Outside in the courtyard, drawn up opposite the archway through which they emerged, stood a dark-green, powerful-looking Talbot. Beside the driver, who was in plain clothes, sat the sprucely dressed figure of Owen's old acquaintance, Detective-Sergeant Campbell. Without waste of time the three of them scrambled in, and nosing its way out on the Embankment between a couple of saluting constables, the car swung to the right and headed towards Parliament Square.

For a considerable while they drove in silence, but as they were approaching Kew and the first stretch of the Great West Road opened out in front of them, Greystoke roused himself from his apparent reverie and turned to the Inspector.

"By the way," he demanded, "did you remember to collect that gun for Bradwell?"

"Got it here, sir." Diving into one of his pockets, Elliot produced a small, short-handled automatic, which, after a brief examination, he handed across to Owen. "Not much to look at," he grunted, "but it will do its business all right, as long as it's handled properly."

"I think we can rely on that." Greystoke glanced at his watch. "Of course there mustn't be any Wild West stuff unless it's absolutely necessary. I want Craig alive, not riddled with bullet-holes; but in a business of this sort we don't know what we may be running up against. If he is in with von Manstein and he happens to be entertaining one or two of that bunch, I wouldn't put it past them to try to shoot their way out. Anyhow, as I remarked before, it's just as well to be on the safe side. I should strongly object to losing a promising recruit, especially at the present moment when we are so infernally short-handed."

There was a grim chuckle from Elliot, and in spite of his own private anxieties Owen was unable to repress a smile.

"Well, if it's like that, sir," he replied, "I'll do my best to remain alive."

Turning off the main road into a winding, hedge-bordered byway that led towards the river, the driver slowed down to a modest forty miles an hour. Once more silence descended on the party—a silence that remained unbroken until the blatantly "Tudor" front of a modern roadhouse loomed up suddenly in the glare of the headlights.

"That must be the joint Fothergill mentioned." Elliot jerked his head at the architectural abortion. "We swing right a little farther on, and the boat-house is just at the bottom of the lane. I've told Humphreys to pull up about twenty yards short of it."

Greystoke's only answer was a curt nod, and rounding a sharp, right-angled corner, the car purred its way forward between two lines of tall, overhanging elms. Then, with a somewhat abrupt jerk, it came to a standstill, and an instant later the lights were turned off.

Waiting until his companions had alighted, Owen scrambled out after them. A short distance ahead, on the right, rose the dark bulk of a large wooden structure, while beyond that the river, a broad, glimmering expanse of moonlit water, stretched away peacefully towards the opposite bank. Halfway across it, the clump of trees on the point of Otter's Holt stood out blackly against the night sky.

"You stay where you are, Humphreys." Elliot spoke in a gruff whisper. "I may want you to bring the car down to the bank later on, but if so I'll give you a shout." He turned to Greystoke. "Just a few moments ahead of time, sir," he added. "I expect Fothergill's inside playing around with his launch."

Leading the way forward until they were almost level with the boat-house, he unlatched an iron gate which opened on to a gravelled space dotted here and there with the mournful wrekage of worn-out punts and sailing craft. The sliding doors at the back of the building had been only partly closed, and framed in the gap stood the spare, angular figure of the Superintendent.

"Thought it must be you, sir," he announced, addressing himself to Greystoke. "We're all ready here, and what's more, I've got a bit of good news."

"Our friend is at home, eh?"

"That's right, sir. One of my chaps who was keeping an eye on the place spotted him looking out of a window. He hasn't been ashore; at least, not to my knowledge."

"When did he get down?"

"Must have been latish—some time in the middle of the night, I reckon." Switching on a torch which he was carrying in his hand, Fothergill conducted them through the opening. "He wasn't here yesterday, that's certain, and if he came back this morning it's odd that no one noticed him crossing over. You can see his punt tied up alongside the landing-stage."

By the fitful light of the wavering beam Owen was able to gather a hasty impression of his surroundings. It was a biggish place, between forty and fifty feet long, and apparently served the double purpose of a store and a repair shop. Down the centre ran a narrow strip of water, forming a kind of miniature dock. At the farther end, where it joined the river, a small arched bridge had been constructed across the top of the entrance, leaving just enough headroom to permit the passage of a fair-sized sailing-boat. The only craft availing itself of the accommodation was a smartly fitted electric launch painted a dull green. On the wooden staging beside it stood a curly-headed, stalwart-looking young man, clad in dark blue overalls.

"There she is, sir," continued the Superintendent proudly, "and this is Constable Plummer, who'll run you across. Lived around here all his life, Plummer has. Used to do odd jobs for the old General when he was a lad, so if there's anything you want to know about the place, he'll be the one to tell you."

"That may be very helpful. You have got a car of your own, I suppose?"

"Out at the back, sir."

"Excellent. I think the best plan will be to hand Craig over into your charge for the night, and we will make arrangements to collect him in the morning. We shall have plenty to do ourselves, going through the house."

"He'll be safe enough with us! I can promise you that." Fothergill paused. "I take it you want me to remain here sir?"

"If you don't mind, Superintendent. Sorry to leave you out of the fun, but we must have somebody on this side whom we can absolutely rely upon."

Motioning to the others to take their places, Greystoke stepped down after them into the launch. Seated behind the wheel, Constable Plummer bent forward over his controls. With a faint swish the propeller began to revolve, and in another second they were gliding silently under the narrow archway and heading out into the open stream.

Anything more calm and restful-looking than Otter's Holt it would have been difficult to imagine. Lying there in the moonlight, a nocturne in black and silver, it appeared to be the last spot on earth that could be associated with crime or violence. Somewhere between the trees a faint, friendly pencil of light flickered out across the water, while from the shadowy depths on the farther side of the island came the low, caressing murmur of the weir.

"Is there a back entrance to the place?"

"Yes, sir." The young constable glanced round over his shoulder. "Faces the opposite bank and leads out into the kitchen garden."

"That will be your job, Sergeant!" Greystoke nodded to Campbell. "Get round behind as soon as we land and rope in anyone who tries to leave the house that way. Plummer can go with you and keep an eye on the rest of the grounds."

"Very good, sir."

"What do you think, Elliot? Any improvement you can suggest?"

The Chief Inspector shook his head. "Seems about the best we can do. Don't see him dodging out of this, not unless he can make himself invisible."

With a broad white ripple trailing away astern, the launch sped on silently towards the deserted landing-stage. It was a solidly constructed affair, supported on thick wooden piles, with a stout iron mooring-ring at either end of the staging. Attached to the nearer of these lay a long, rakish-looking punt, and heading for the other a few feet farther on, Plummer switched off the motor and brought them neatly alongside. There was a sudden rustle of wings, and from an adjoining bush two or three startled shapes scurried away into the darkness.

As quietly as possible, the whole party scrambled out. From where they had stepped ashore a red-brick path led up to the front door, bordered on the right by what appeared to be a stretch of open lawn.

"Off you go, you two," whispered Greystoke. "I'll give you four minutes to get to your places."

As he spoke he took another glance at the illuminated dial of his watch, and fading away obediently, Campbell and Plummer disappeared amongst the shadows.

"Best leave Craig to me," murmured the Chief Inspector. "If we do happen to strike trouble that'll mean a free hand for you and Mr. Bradwell."

A brief nod was the only answer, and making no attempt at any further conversation, the three of them stood there with their eyes riveted upon the house. To Owen the time seemed interminable. With every moment that passed his anxiety about Sally became more and more desperate, and it was only by a superhuman effort that he forced himself to remain silent and inactive.

"That's about right. Now I think we can announce our arrival." Greystoke buttoned up his coat.

"I'll go first, if you've no objection, sir."

Stepping out in front, Elliot led the way up the path. In another second or so his hand was on the knocker, and a vigorous tattoo went echoing through the house. Somewhere in the far distance a dog barked protestingly.

A longish pause followed, and then, just as the summons was about to be repeated, a muffled tread of heavy boots could be heard approaching the door. Slowly and grudgingly it swung open.

"Who are you, and vot you doing here?"

A big, grotesquely hideous man who looked rather like a gorilla was peering out at them with an air of sullen hostility.

"I am a police officer from Scotland Yard. I have called to see Mr. Mark Craig."

"Dot is impossible. He does not see peoples midout an appointment."

"He'll see us all right."

With a sudden thrust Elliot sent the objector lurching sideways and, followed by the other two, shouldered his way past. They found themselves in a square, pleasantly furnished lounge-hall, from which a dimly lighted staircase led up to the landing above.

"Eet is an outrage you do." Recovering his balance, the big fellow took a step forward. Then he pulled up, clenching his fists and glaring at them malevolently.

"Where is he? Come along now; don't waste time."

"You haf no right to act zo, you—"

"I have a warrant entitling me to enter and search this house. If you don't answer my question—"

A sudden warning yell split the air, and from outside came the sound of running feet.

What the hell—

Greystoke and Owen, who were nearest, sprang forward simultaneously. Elliot was only a pace behind them, and after a brief, savage scuffle in the doorway all three stumbled out into the open. At the same instant a long-legged figure in overalls raced past, pointing towards the river.

"There he is, sir—shovin' off in the punt."

It was Craig right enough: one could tell that at a glance. Even now he was well clear of the landing-stage, and at each powerful thrust of the pole the gap steadily widened. A yard or so upstream, with its loosened painter trailing over the stern, drifted the long, green shape of the empty launch.

"Don't shoot—he can't get away."

Greystoke's voice rang out sharply above the uproar and letting go the automatic which he had been in the act of dragging from his pocket, Owen set off down the path in the wake of the fleet-footed Plummer.

That the latter was a man of action was swiftly and dramatically demonstrated. With a resounding splash that sent a shower of spray in all directions he dived headlong into the water, and before Owen himself had reached the edge of the wet planking he was already swimming furiously in pursuit of his escaping craft.

"Good man!" panted the Inspector as he and Greystoke ranged up alongside. "We'll catch the swine all right, sir: there's Fothergill coming along now!"

Wielding his pole with the smooth dexterity of an expert, Craig shot forward towards the opposite shore. He was making for a point slightly above the entrance to the backwater, and towards this, grim and relentless as an approaching Fate, raced the menacing form of the Superintendent.

Just as Plummer's arm was reaching up to grasp the launch the converging forces met. A yellow spurt of flame, accompanied by a venomous roar, lit up the adjacent bushes, and staggering backwards with a drunken lurch, Fothergill slumped down heavily upon his hands and knees.

"The murdering bastard!" Elliot shook his fist in impotent fury.

"Look, man, look! Who the devil's that?"

"Good God! It must be Humphreys."

From somewhere in the darkness beyond a third figure had suddenly hurled itself forward. Almost simultaneously another shot crashed out, and then, locked together in a frantic grapple, two writhing, struggling bodies reeled towards the bank. There was a harsh, agonised scream like the cry of a wounded animal, and plunging downwards in a tangled mass, they struck the water and disappeared beneath the surface.

"Quick, Bradwell," Greystoke nodded towards the house. "Slip back and see that ruffian doesn't destroy anything in the way of papers. I'll be with you as soon as I can."

By now the indomitable Plummer had already succeeded in scrambling into the launch. Owen caught a momentary glimpse of it swinging round in the direction of the landing-stage, and then, a trifle dazed at the catastrophic suddenness of the whole affair, he found himself sprinting desperately up the narrow path, with a vague glimmer from the open doorway shining out ahead of him. He was still several paces from his goal, when a breathless Sergeant Campbell came bursting hurriedly round the corner.

"What's happened? Anyone hurt?"

"Looks like it; but there's no time to explain now. Greystoke's sent me back to collar the beauty inside. Afraid he may be up to mischief."

"All right, sir. I'll give you a hand."

Together they strode through into the now deserted hall, where an overturned table, with a litter of books and other objects spread out around it, bore witness to the recent scuffle. Owen, who was leading the way, pulled up abruptly. Almost the first thing that had caught his eye was a small blue-silk handbag lying amongst the wreckage. He recognised it instantly as the one which Sally had been carrying on the day they had lunched at the Milan, and with a sudden oath stepped forward to pick it up. As he did so a partly open door opposite was pulled back, disclosing the repulsive figure of Craig's dishevelled-looking retainer.

Gun in hand, Owen wheeled round savagely.

"Where's Miss Deane?" he demanded. "You've got her here somewhere."

"I—I do not know vot you mean."

"Don't lie to me unless you want a bullet in your guts."

The man shrank back, his eyes fastened upon the weapon which was pointing straight at the pit of his stomach.

"She—she—is upstairs," he stammered. "In the liddle room mid the locked door. She is not hurt—no."

"If she is I'll smash your face in." Owen turned to Campbell. "Will you carry on while I go and look for her!"

"Right you are, sir." The sergeant whipped out a pair of handcuffs. "If you want any help," he added, "just give me a call."

Taking the stairs two at a time, Owen raced up to the landing above. Before him lay a broad passage, leading straight through to the back of the house. It was lighted by a shaded electric bulb suspended from the ceiling, and one revealing fact stood out at a glance. In the end room on the left the key was on the outside.

Hurrying towards it and twisting it round with a vicious jerk, he flung open the door. At first he could see nothing. Then, out of the darkness in front of him came a low, suffocated moan, and almost simultaneously his groping fingers encountered a switch. The next instant he was down on one knee, bending over the small, white-faced figure that lay stretched out on the bare floor.

"Sally! Sally darling!"

With feverish haste he began to unknot the thick coloured handkerchief that was fastened across her mouth. From above it two dazed blue eyes stared up at him through a tangle of red-gold hair.

"Owen!"

It was the merest whisper, so husky and faint that it barely reached his ears.

"Don't try to talk—not for a moment or two."

He had dragged out a knife from his pocket, and was sawing through the stout cords that imprisoned her wrists and ankles. As they fell away, exposing the chafed and bruised skin below, such a flame of rage swept through him that it seemed to leave him physically exhausted. Very gently he raised her up until her head was resting against his shoulder.

"It's all right: you're quite safe now, Sally."

She made a gallant but rather pitiful attempt to smile.

"How long have you been here?" he asked.

"I—I don't know. I just remember waking up and feeling horribly sick. Then—then a man came in, and began asking me questions about you. I wouldn't answer him, and that made him angry. He twisted my arm and it hurt, so I—I think I must have fainted." She gave a little shiver and her eyes closed. "Oh, gosh, I do feel so ill."

With an unsteady hand Owen smoothed back the soft, curling hair that had tumbled forward across her forehead.

"Don't worry, darling. You'll be out of this and comfortably in bed before you know where you are. We have only got to wait until Greystoke comes back with the launch. He won't be more than a few minutes at the outside. I'm going to take you downstairs, and you can lie on the sofa in the hall."

Another wan smile flickered momentarily across her lips.

"Don't drop me," she whispered, "or I'll probably be sick again."

Lifting her in his arms, he carried her to the end of the corridor, and very slowly and carefully made his way down the short, poorly lighted staircase. For the moment the ground floor appeared to be deserted, but as he reached the bottom step and turned towards the leather couch in the corner, the sergeant came in hastily through the open door opposite.

"So you've found her!" he exclaimed. "What's the trouble, sir?"

"Don't know exactly. Those devils have gagged her and tied her up like a trussed chicken."

Hurrying across and taking hold of Sally's arm, which was trailing down limply over the side, Campbell placed his fingers on her wrist. With an obvious effort she again opened her eyes.

"They—they've been doping me," she muttered. "I—I remember now. I tried to scream, and somebody jabbed a needle into my arm—" Her voice trailed off into silence.

"Isn't there a telephone in the damned place?" demanded Owen. "Couldn't we ring up a doctor and—"

There was a sound of steps on the path outside, and before he could finish the sentence Greystoke appeared in the doorway. He stood for an instant breathing quickly, his keen eyes taking in every detail of the scene in front of him.

"She *was* here, then: that's something to be thankful for." He strode forward to the couch. "How is she, and where did you find her?"

"Upstairs, locked in one of the bedrooms." It was Owen who answered. "She's half-drugged, and they've been knocking her about to try to make her talk."

The other gazed down on the small white face lying against the cushion. "Yes, she looks as though she had a rough time of it. The best plan will be for you to take her back to her own place and fetch in a doctor straight away. You can have the Yard car, and the driver will run you up there. We shall be having some more men along from Playford in a few minutes."

"What's happened to Craig, sir? Have you caught the swine?"

"I'm afraid not. All we seem likely to get hold of is his dead body."

"Who was the man who jumped out from the bushes? I thought—"

"We all thought the same, but it turns out that we were mistaken. Humphreys is over there now with Elliot and Fothergill."

"Then he wasn't killed—the Superintendent, I mean?"

Greystoke shook his head. "He's got a bullet in his shoulder, but I don't think he is in any serious danger. As for the other fellow, whoever he was he had nothing to do with our lot. He must have been hanging around on some business of his own and suddenly took it into his head to butt in. Unfortunately, it appears to have cost him his life. By the way, where is that damned German ruffian? You haven't let him get at any of Craig's papers, I hope?"

"He's quite safe, sir." The sergeant saluted briskly. "I shoved the bracelets on him and locked him up in the lavatory."

"A very suitable environment. He can stay there till we have time to attend to him. Now, Bradwell, if you'll carry Miss Deane down to the launch, I'll come along with you and give Plummer a message for Elliot. He'll fix things up for you about the car."

"Any instructions for to-morrow, sir?"

"I'll let you know in the morning. In the meantime your job is to take care of this charming and extremely plucky young lady." Greystoke leaned forward and very gently patted Sally's cheek. "She's the kind of lass we shall be wanting before long."

◇◇◇

"Almost there, angel. How are you feeling now?"

"Not too bad. Bit sleepy and stupid." The blue eyes opened for a moment and then closed again wearily. "Don't know how I'll explain it all to Ruth!"

"I'll look after that. You're going straight to bed directly we get in."

The little bow-fronted shop window slid into view on the right, and at the same moment the car came to a standstill. Descending quickly from the front seat, Humphreys presented himself at the window.

"Better stay where you are till I've rung the bell, sir. Then the young lady won't have to wait about."

He moved away across the pavement, and as he did so a glint of light shot out from between the drawn blinds. The next moment Ruth herself had opened the door and was pushing him unceremoniously to one side.

"Darling!" She ran forward eagerly. "It *is* you? Thank Heaven for that!"

"You—you must thank Owen, too. He helped quite a lot." Sally made a feeble effort to sit up, and then sank back again against the cushion.

"What's happened? What have they been doing to you? Why, you look as if—"

"She's not up to talking," broke in Owen. "We've got to get her to bed at once, and then rout out a doctor."

"I'll see to that, sir," volunteered their driver. "If you can manage all right, I'll slip round and fetch Doctor Burrows. He's the Chelsea Police Surgeon, and he only lives in the next road."

"Thanks: that'll save time. Now, angel, just shut your eyes and keep perfectly still. In about fifteen seconds you'll be upstairs in your own room. You go ahead, Ruth, and get that curtain out of the way."

Despite the conflicting emotions apparent in her face, Ruth obeyed his instructions. Waiting until he had helped Sally out of the car and picked her up in his arms, she led the way back into the shop and hurried on in front of them towards the foot of the stairs. Leaving Humphreys to shut the door, Owen followed her in.

Burdened as he was, the steep, narrow flight proved none too easy to negotiate. Judging by her slow, belaboured breathing, Sally had slipped off again into a kind of semi-stupor, and as he reached the top and set foot on the small landing he was suddenly overwhelmed by a fresh wave of anxiety.

"Bring her in here and put her down on the bed." Ruth had flung open a door and switched on the light. "Be careful you don't trip over that footstool."

Avoiding the article in question, and lowering Sally gently on to the embroidered Chinese coverlet, he drew in a long breath and straightened himself up. For the first time he was conscious of feeling desperately tired.

"Now tell me what's happened," demanded Ruth fiercely. "Where has she been all this time, and why is she looking so ill?"

"She was kidnapped and drugged. That damned woman must have been one of the crowd who murdered Sutton. I suppose they saw us coming out of the bungalow, and decided to get hold of her and make her talk. What they probably wanted was to find out how I came to be in the game."

"You!"

Owen nodded. "The real truth is that they're a gang of spies working for the Nazis. I was sent down there by the Naval Intelligence people to keep an eye on them, and like an infernal idiot, I let myself get knocked on the head. That's absolutely between ourselves, of course. You mustn't mention a word of it to anyone."

Ruth looked at him scornfully. "I thought the idea that women couldn't keep a secret was a bit out of date. You needn't worry, anyhow." With an angry scowl she stepped forward to the bed. "I'll take care of Sally and get her undressed. You go downstairs and wait for the doctor."

Accepting his dismissal meekly, Owen made his way back to the ground floor. For several minutes he paced restlessly up and down the shop, and then, unable to withstand the growing apprehension that made it impossible for him to rest or sit down, he opened the door with an impatient jerk, and looked out into the deserted street. A moment later there was a warning hoot, and the long green bonnet of the Talbot swung into view round an adjacent corner.

Before the first rush of relief had fully subsided, he found himself shaking hands with a short, round-faced man of about fifty who had bounced out of the car almost before it had come to a standstill.

"How d'ye do. Commander Bradwell, I take it? I'm Doctor Burrows."

"Very good of you to come round so quickly."

"Just happened to have got back from another case. Well, I've had a rough outline of your adventures from our friend the constable here, so I needn't waste time in asking you any unnecessary questions. I had better go up and see the patient at once."

"I'll show you the way."

Conducting his visitor inside, Owen piloted him as far as the bottom of the staircase. Then, surrendering him to the care of Ruth, who had already appeared in the lighted doorway above, he walked back to the shop entrance, where the stalwart figure of Constable Humphreys was standing patiently on the mat.

"Bit of luck catching him like that, sir," remarked the latter complacently. "I'll just run him home as soon as he's finished here, and then take you along to your place."

"Needn't trouble about me. I'll just get hold of a taxi."

"Chief Inspector's orders, sir. Said I was to drop you at your flat and then report back to the Yard."

With a stiff salute the speaker closed the door, and lighting a much-needed cigarette, Owen wandered across to the fireplace and seated himself on the high, padded guard in front of the electric stove. The only thing he could do now was to summon up his patience and wait for the medical verdict.

At last, after what seemed like a miniature eternity, there was a sudden murmur of voices on the landing above. It was followed by the brisk tread of footsteps, and then, bag in hand, with Ruth bringing up the rear, the little round-faced police surgeon came bustling down the stairs.

"Well, I'm happy to say things might be a heap worse." He produced a handkerchief and blew his nose vigorously. "She has been drugged right enough and pretty roughly handled, but she's a remarkably healthy young woman, and I don't think we need anticipate any serious ill effects."

"That's grand news." For a moment Owen felt like embracing him.

"I have left full directions with Miss Barlow, and I will look round again first thing in the morning. She will have to stop in bed for a day or two, of course, and she certainly mustn't be worried or excited!"

"I'll see to that," remarked Ruth grimly.

The doctor smiled. "In case it may be of any assistance I will ring up the Yard and give them my report. In the meantime just go on carrying out my instructions."

He picked up his bag which he had deposited on the table, and with a slight nod to each of them marched towards the door. The next moment it had closed behind him.

"I can't stay down here for more than a few seconds," announced Ruth. "I've got to make her some coffee." She shook back her hair and surveyed Owen with a disapproving frown. "I suppose it's no use asking you what really happened?"

"I can tell you one thing, anyhow. The swine who doped her and made those bruises on her arms is dead."

"Did you kill him?"

Owen shook his head. "Unfortunately someone else butted in first."

"Who was it?"

"I don't know yet. I didn't wait to find out. All that mattered then was to get her back home as quickly as possible!"

Ruth stared at him for an instant without speaking.

"You're in love with her, aren't you?" she demanded.

"Of course I am!"

"Yes, you'd be a fool if you weren't."

"You—you don't mean—"

"I mean that she says that she wants you to come and see her to-morrow, and if the doctor gives his permission I suppose I shall have to humour her. She's frightfully obstinate, you know."

Owen drew in a long breath. "Ruth," he exclaimed, "you're a brick!"

"Thank you." Her eyes twinkled. "If that's your idea of a compliment, you had better keep it for Sally!"

Chapter XIV

"Everything all right, Watkins?"

"Quite, sir."

At the sound of the familiar voice Owen uncrossed his legs and tossing aside the morning paper, hoisted himself off the sofa. He was barely on his legs before the door opened and Joe Anstey, with a bundle of letters in his hand, strode breezily into the room.

"Good Heavens! Why, you're up and dressed." He raised his eyebrows with an air of mock amazement. "What on earth's the meaning of this?"

"I told you I'd make a special effort in your honour."

"So you did, but I never imagined it would come off." An approving slap descended on Owen's shoulder. "Well, old son, how are you, and what's the latest news? Anything brewing in the way of a job?"

"Just a chance, apparently. I'm lunching with Greystoke at his club, so I may be able to tell you more about it to-night."

"Oh, they'll find something for you: I'm certain of that. Things are moving pretty swiftly, if you ask me. Judging by the way the Air people are hustling around, they've got the wind up good and proper."

"Not too soon either, I gather." Owen glanced at his watch.

"What time is this lunch of yours?" demanded Joe.

"One o'clock. Afraid I shall have to be pushing off in a few minutes."

"How about a drink first? I could do with one myself. You might fix up a couple while I'm having a look through this lot."

Leaving his host perched on the edge of the table slitting open his correspondence, Owen drifted across to the sideboard. He had just completed his task, and was about to return with the two tumblers, when a sudden startled "Hello" made him swing round with an inquiring jerk.

"What's the matter?" he demanded.

"Perhaps you can enlighten me." Joe looked up from the letter which he was holding in his hand. "It's from old Martin at Playford. Seems to be what you might call slightly agitated."

With an uncomfortable sensation of guilt Owen came forward and put down the glasses.

"I suppose it's about my clearing off and leaving my things in the punt? To tell the honest truth, I'd clean forgotten about it."

"That so?" Joe scratched his ear. "Well, well, we are all a little absent-minded at times." He paused. "Rather an odd coincidence that it should have been the same night that the bloke was bumped off in the bungalow. Appears to be worrying Martin quite a lot."

Owen reflected rapidly. "Do you mind my borrowing that letter? I feel I ought to show it to Greystoke."

"Indeed! So I wasn't altogether wrong? Beginning to think I must have a dash of second sight or something."

"Sorry to be so foully mysterious. If it rested with me I'd be delighted to cough up the whole story. Unfortunately I'm acting under orders."

"My dear ass, there's no need to apologise. I've the most profound faith in the British Navy, and I'm perfectly prepared to allow them a free hand." With a sudden grin Joe held out the sheet of paper. "There you are, then," he added. "Stuff it in your pocket and cut along to your luncheon party. By the way, are you coming back here afterwards?"

"Not for a little while. I've got to go down to Chelsea first. I've an appointment with an interior decorator."

"A *what*?"

"An interior decorator."

"Good Lord—don't tell me that you're thinking of setting up house?"

Owen gulped off his drink and strolled towards the door. "It had crossed my mind," he admitted casually.

◇ ◇ ◇

Getting up from a deserted corner in the big smoking-room, Greystoke walked forward to receive his visitor. His face looked tired and drawn.

"Ah, Bradwell, glad to see you. Come along over here and sit down." He led the way back to his former position, and made an inviting gesture towards a comfortably padded arm-chair. Now what is it to be—sherry or a dry Martini?"

"Sherry, I think, sir."

"You're a sound judge; we happen to have an especially good Isabelita."

Turning to a liveried attendant who was arranging some papers on a side table, the Captain gave his order. Then, with a half-stifled yawn, he took possession of an adjacent couch.

"Any fresh news about that young woman of yours? I have heard what the doctor had to say last night."

"She is going on quite well." Owen accepted a cigarette from the proffered case. "I rang up this morning and had a talk with Miss Barlow. I'm hoping to be allowed to see her this afternoon."

"Excellent! I have a little present for her which I will entrust to your charge."

"A present?"

"We will deal with that later. Hardwick, the First Lord, is coming along to lunch with us, and there's a considerable amount to straighten out before he turns up. Unfortunately I couldn't arrange to meet you earlier. I only left the Home Office about an hour ago, and since then I've been indulging in the luxury of a bath and a shave. Both badly needed, I can assure you."

"You mean to say you've been up all night, sir?"

"Yes, we have been having a fairly strenuous time of it; and what's more, there have been some highly remarkable developments. You understand, however, that what I am going to tell you now is entirely off the record. You will forget it as soon as you leave this room."

Owen nodded silently.

"Our friend Craig only made one serious mistake." Greystoke waited for a moment while the waiter presented them with their drinks. "In his hurry to get away he omitted to destroy a letter which he had been careless enough to leave in his desk. It was from a lady who lives in St. John's Wood—a lady who rejoices in the picturesque name of Miss Olga Brandon: at least, that is what she is calling herself at present. Ever heard of her?"

Owen shook his head.

"Well, I haven't time to enter into details just now, but it was such a suggestive document that Elliot took the responsibility of ringing the Yard and arranging for her to be detained at her own house until he could get up there and have a little heart-to-heart chat. There was still a good deal to do at Thames Ferry, and it was nearly eight o'clock before we had the pleasure of making her acquaintance. The police had been there since midnight, so she had had plenty of opportunity to think things over.

"It wasn't too easy a job, because, strictly speaking, we hadn't a leg to stand on. If she had kept her head and told us to go to hell we could have done nothing. Having a dash of the dago in her, however—we have discovered since that her mother was a Romanian dancer—she was already beginning to panic. As soon as I realised that, I knew how to handle her."

Owen ground out his half-smoked cigarette, "I suppose she was the damned woman who came to the shop?"

"I ventured to assume so. She denied it at first, of course; but when we succeeded in convincing her that Craig was dead and that the game was up, her one idea was obviously to save her own neck. I am not suggesting that she told us the whole truth. The impression she was anxious to put across was that she had been completely under Craig's influence, and that all she had ever done was to carry out his instructions."

"She owned up to having kidnapped Sally?"

"She did—after a certain amount of pressure. She declared that she had been forced into it by threats, and that she had been too frightened to refuse. Once we had dug that admission out of her things were a lot simpler. We were able to ram home the fact that she had laid herself open to a long term of imprisonment, and that her only chance of being let off easily was by turning King's evidence and assisting the police. She jumped at the notion almost indecently."

"How much is her statement worth?"

"Not a great deal, but enough to convince a coroner's jury that Craig had excellent reasons for wanting Mr. Granville Sutton out of the way. From the point of view of the Authorities, that will be distinctly helpful."

Owen paused. "I don't quite understand."

"Well, as I told you before, the chief thing that the Foreign Office are afraid of at the present moment is any sensational development which would put an additional strain on their relations with Berlin. In the first place, we are shockingly unprepared for a European war; and in the second, the Cabinet is still clutching at the hope that the whole situation will somehow or other iron itself out. I have been having discussions with the Ministers concerned this morning, and as far as any future action is concerned they are all of the same opinion. With three dead men to be accounted for a certain amount of publicity is obviously unavoidable, but the slightest suggestion that there might be more at the back of it than a sort of private vendetta amongst a gang of blackmailing crooks is to be ruled out at all costs. Their contention is that now that this particular spy ring has been successfully broken up, a public exposure of its activities would be of no practical advantage and might lead to the most disastrous results. In the circumstances, it is quite possible that they may be correct."

"How about von Manstein?"

"The Count is a gentleman of discernment. He must have tumbled to the fact that there was trouble in the offing, and in accordance with the best Hun traditions, he evidently decided to hand it over to his subordinates. He left Croydon for Paris yesterday afternoon. By now I should imagine he is probably well on his way to Berchtesgaden."

"So what it really amounts to is that we're in such a blue funk of Germany that the whole business has got to be hushed up."

"Precisely; and that is one of the main reasons why I was anxious to get hold of you as soon as possible. We have to consider the position of those two girls—"

"You mean Miss Deane and Miss Barlow?"

Greystoke nodded. "Unless we can rely upon their absolute discretion something or other is almost bound to leak out. The question is, can they be trusted to keep their mouths shut? It's asking a good deal of two young women who are naturally itching to talk about their experiences; but our only hope, as far as I can see, is to convince them of the vital importance of secrecy in the national interest. I am under the impression that you could accomplish that fact more successfully than anyone else."

A faint tinge of colour crept into Owen's face. "I will see what I can do, sir." He hesitated a second. "There is just one thing I would like to know, if I'm not being too inquisitive. Who was the chap who tackled Craig and went into the river with him?"

"In a way, that is the most extraordinary part of the whole affair. A few days ago, as you probably saw in the papers, a man named Wilson escaped from Dartmoor. The police have been hunting for him all over the South of England. When we got the bodies out of the water Elliott recognised the fellow at once."

"What on earth was he doing hanging about round Otter's Holt?"

"I fancy he went there on very much the same errand as ourselves. He wanted to square accounts with its owner, who, I gather, was largely responsible for getting him into trouble. I shouldn't be surprised, in fact, if that was his main object in breaking out of prison. What his actual plans were, and how he managed to get so far without being spotted, God alone knows. We can only assume that he was hiding amongst the bushes, and that when he saw his chance he stepped in and took it. As things are, we must regard him as a public benefactor."

"I suppose so." Owen smiled wryly. "I only wish I had been half as useful myself."

"Never underrate the value of your services: the people above you will see to that all right." Greystoke picked up his glass and finished off its contents. "And while we are on the subject," he continued, "there is another point which I should like to get settled before we are joined by our distinguished guest. Now you have had a taste of this sort of work, how do you feel about carrying on with it? We expect to be fairly busy in our branch of the Service during the next year or two, and for a man who has no objection to risking his life at a moderate salary the outlook is distinctly promising. I am disposed to believe that it would be more up your street than sitting at a desk at the Admiralty."

"It would indeed, sir." Owen's eyes brightened. "If I am not fit to go to sea any more, there is nothing I would like better."

"Well, I think it might be arranged. We can take it for granted that our friends in Berlin have plenty of other cards up their sleeves, and since it's my job to keep an eye on them as far as the Navy is concerned, I am allowed a fairly free hand in the matter of selecting my assistants. If I make an application for you to be transferred to my department, I have no doubt that the suggestion will be favourably received. Between ourselves, that was my idea in inviting Sir John to meet you. I felt that if you made a favourable impression on him—ah, here he is coming now! Pull yourself together, Bradwell, and we'll see what we can do about it."

◇◇◇

"Owen!"

Pulling a light silk wrap hastily round her shoulders, Sally sat up in bed.

"Angel!"

"Where have you been all this time? I thought you were never coming!"

"Terribly sorry. It was Greystoke's fault. I was lunching with him at his club and—"

"Never mind. You're here now, that's the great thing." She held out a welcoming hand. "Bring up a chair and give me a cigarette. You mustn't look at me too closely, because I've got practically nothing on."

"You're so beautiful like that it almost frightens me." Seating himself beside her, Owen leant forward and kissed the tip of her fingers. "How are you?" he demanded. "Nothing else really matters."

"I feel a bit empty, and my arm still hurts where that brute twisted it. Otherwise I'm going strong." She helped herself from the case which he had produced from his pocket. "Now go ahead, please, and tell me all about everything."

Owen glanced at his watch. "I have given my solemn oath to Ruth that I won't stop for more than ten minutes. She says the doctor's orders are that you're not to be tired or excited."

"Damn the doctor!" Sally puffed out a rebellious cloud of smoke. "I've got to know what's going on, or I shall just blow up like a rocket."

"The trouble is that there are one or two things I'm not allowed to talk about, even to you. What it actually amounts to, however, is this. For certain—what shall we call them— national and political reasons the Big Noises in Whitehall are desperately anxious to prevent the real facts from coming out in the newspapers. They want it to be regarded as a sort of private quarrel amongst a pack of gangsters, and if all the people concerned play the game and keep their months shut, they will probably be able to get away with it. Of course the two they are chiefly bothered about are you and Ruth."

"But how thrilling!" The blue eyes danced mischievously. "Makes me feel like the heroine in a spy story."

"That's exactly what you are—only it happens to be a true story. Between ourselves, you've butted into something that might very easily start a world war."

"Have I really!" Sally's expression suddenly sobered. "Well, if it's like that they needn't worry. You can tell them that, although we are merely a couple of females, Ruth and I are quite capable of holding our tongues."

"As a matter of fact, I have already gone bail for you to one of his Majesty's Cabinet Ministers. Greystoke asked him to lunch so that I should have the chance of making a favourable impression."

"Oh, I *do* hope he's going to do something for you."

"He has. He's arranged for me to be transferred to the Naval Intelligence branch."

"What does that mean?"

"Oh, just scouting around and keeping one's eyes open. I shall only be a sort of glorified policeman, but it's a bit better than being shoved on half-pay."

"And a bit more dangerous, I suppose?" Sally was surveying him with an air of disconcerting gravity.

"Shouldn't imagine so. I expect most of it will be as dull as ditchwater. According to Greystoke—Good Heavens, that reminds me! He sent you a present, and I've been talking so much I clean forgot about it."

"A present—for *me!*"

Sally took the rather crumpled envelope which he was offering to her, and slitting it open, pulled out its contents. At the sight of them a little startled gasp broke from her lips.

"Why, it's Sheila's letter—Sheila's letter to that beast Sutton!" She stared at it half incredulously. "Where on earth—"

"It was in the possession of that charming lady who tootled you out to St. John's Wood. She appears to have been rather a particular pal of Craig. He must have found it in the bungalow and handed it over to her for safe custody. I expect that when all this hullabaloo had died down they intended to follow in Sutton's footsteps and do a little spot of private blackmail."

"But this is too perfectly marvellous! I—I must ring up Sheila and let her know." Sally drew in a deep breath. "Of course it's all your doing, every little bit of it. I'll never be able to thank you enough—never as long as I live."

"I wouldn't say that." Owen took her hand. "If you like, you can have a shot at it right now."

"How do I start?"

"You just swallow twice, and say, 'Owen Bradwell, I promise to marry you as soon as I'm well enough to get up.'"

"But, darling, I wanted to, anyway—didn't you know that? Why, I've been throwing myself at you in the most shameless fashion. Ruth says—"

"Come along now! Time's up, you've had your ten minutes."

From somewhere below an imperative voice echoed up the staircase.

"Damn!" Owen glanced round ruefully. "Tell me, angel, do you think it would tire you if I gave you a kiss!"

Sally shook her head. "Not if it was a short one."

As he took her in his arms the shawl slid off her shoulders, and for a heavenly moment he could feel her lips pressed to his and the quick beat of her heart throbbing against his own. Then, flushed and breathless, she slipped out of his embrace, and with a long sigh sank back against the pillow.

"Just as well you're colour-blind, isn't it, darling?" she whispered.

"Why?" he demanded.

She laughed softly and drew up the bed-clothes.

"Because you can't see me blushing."

To receive a free catalog of Poisoned Pen Press titles, please provide your name and address in one of the following ways:

Phone: 1-800-421-3976
Facsimile: 1-480-949-1707
Email: info@poisonedpenpress.com
Website: www.poisonedpenpress.com

Poisoned Pen Press
6962 E. First Ave. Ste 103
Scottsdale, AZ 85251

CPSIA information can be obtained at www.ICGtesting.com
Printed in the USA
BVOW11s1336180915

418546BV00001B/1/P

9 781464 204937